The Energy Components Project

Book Two of *The Time Sphere Chronicles*

By Jennifer Thorpe-Moscon, Ph.D.

2

Table of Contents

Chapter One

"NO. Absolutely not."

I struggled against my bindings, but I knew it was pointless. He'd gotten good at tying me up.

Thomas' expression didn't change in the least. "When you enter into a battle, will there be people you wish not to destroy?"

"Of course, but…"

"Then what good is it to practice in hypotheticals forever?"

"It's not good, but what if I'm not ready? What if I kill it?" The puppy, a tiny beagle, yelped. It was on a pedestal about breast-high five feet or so in front of me, and it couldn't jump down.

We were in a warehouse in Greenpoint, one of the few that hadn't been converted into lofts or an "event space" or whatever rich kids were into these days. It was mostly abandoned with gray stone walls and cardboard boxes littered around containing who-knew-what. There was a forklift that seemed designed to move pallets of those boxes, but it didn't look like it had been used in a long time. Everything smelled musty, dust sprinkled heavily everywhere like a pasta-lover might sprinkle cheese.

"You won't," Thomas said.

I huffed. "You don't know that!"

He shrugged, his fitted pinstripe suit moving perfectly with every muscle, not even seeming to wrinkle, and walked closer to me, so close I could feel his breath. It smelled like chicken. "No, I don't." And then he stabbed me, right in the stomach, and dragged the blade across, up, around. I could feel my guts ripping and tearing. He had to make it bad. It had to be severe enough that my blood couldn't heal it all, so severe that it activated the *seeking*.

I reflexively healed some with blood, but then it stopped – it had done as much as it could. Blood was a slow healer – it could heal small amounts immediately, and large amounts gradually over time, but a lot of injury quickly was not its wheelhouse.

My stomach was still bulbous, my organs slipping out a bit at a time. It hurt like hell, and I felt the seeking start. It was a craving, but not the way blood was. Blood was hunger, thirst, desire, longing. This was like mind control, like someone's willful tentacles in the motor cortex of your brain. Like knowing full well you did *not* want to do it, but your body pushing you to do it anyway.

I couldn't redirect it at Thomas; he saw to that. Turns out, if you can do it, you can block it, so it was the puppy or nothing. It had to be nothing. I braced myself and clamped down on the compulsion to drain the puppy's soul energy, my willpower straining like a muscle lifting 500 pounds.

After what felt like forever, the seeking lessened, the metaphorical tentacles slipping out, and then finally stopped. I opened my eyes, which I'd squeezed shut in my efforts. The puppy was alive and looking inquisitively at me.

Thomas actually had the slightest of smiles. It was his nonverbal I-told-you-so.

He held his hand out toward me and let a thin blue stream pour into my wound. Was it part of his soul? Or had he stocked up on someone else's? I didn't want to think about it. After a moment, I was healed, the only evidence of what had happened my ripped dark-blue shirt stained with blood. The absence of pain was its own sort of pleasure, a relief at the gentle caress of nothingness. I let myself revel in it as Thomas pulled a set of keys out of his pocket and began the process of unbuckling me.

Once free, I shoved him. "Not cool."

He shrugged again. "You did not harm the dog. I don't see what the problem is."

I frowned. No, he didn't. I walked over to the puppy, who yipped, and I scratched its head. "You have become quite adept at preventing yourself from healing. I regarded you as having sufficient mastery of it, and I was right to do so." He paused, and I knew what he was about to say. "You should permit me to teach you how to heal deliberately."

I shook my head for probably the fiftieth time. "You know I won't. I don't want to do it. Ever."

"But you will." How many times had we had this same discussion? But here we were again. "You will do it, and if you do not know how to control how much you take, it will end badly."

"I *won't* do it." I scooped the puppy into my arms. He didn't understand. There wasn't an injury bad enough to make it okay to devour another person's – or puppy's – soul. I'd done it too much already, before I even knew what I was doing.

"There will always be a reason. Everyone can justify it. Even my kind, each of us has found times when logic and reason justified the use of this power. And you, and your emotions, will have a reason that is good enough too. Fear, particularly. It seems to motivate your kind more than anything. It is only a matter of time."

Your emotions. He said it with such disdain. But it wasn't personal. I'd gotten used to his prejudices. He tried to rein them in around me, but they came out every now and then. What would it take for him to see that emotions weren't bad, just different?

"You know, Thomas, you might not have hormones or emotions like we do, but you do have attitudes. Likes and dislikes. And that's similar."

His thin, manicured dark-brown eyebrows raised ever so slightly. "I evaluate my environment based on facts."

"You evaluate people, to decide if you like them or not."

"To decide if they are good in their intentions, yes."

"If you *like* them. Same thing." I smirked. I liked to make him mad, to see how far I could push him. I didn't really believe that he had no emotions at all, just that they were infinitely more subtle.

His lip twitched slightly. "It is not about liking. It is about objective fact."

I shook my head. "Then what objective facts explain why you like me?"

He might have smiled – just a touch around the corners of his mouth. "Why do you believe I like you?"

"You're here. Training me."

"I do that so that you are not a danger to the world."

"Okay. But if that's the only reason... you think I should learn how to use the power, how to actually do it on purpose. But I don't want to. And you haven't forced me." I paused, looking for a reaction, and got none. "You could force me, if you wanted to."

"How would I do that?"

I shrugged. "You're incomparably better at this than I am. I'm sure there's a way."

He said nothing, but then nodded, a slow nod. "I could. Perhaps I should." I waited silently. His light brown eyes never left mine. "Shall we do this again next week?"

I smiled. "Sure, buddy." He might have slightly pursed his lips. "But no more puppies. Or kittens, or bunnies, or anything. If I have to practice on a living thing, pick one of your people who can stop me if I screw up. Okay?"

He nodded. "And that dog?"

I looked at it, and when I met its eyes, it licked my face. "I'm keeping it."

*   *   *   *   *

I sat on my bed, placing the squirming puppy down on the carpet. It yelped excitedly and stared at me expectantly. Why had I taken it home? I didn't know the first thing about caring for a dog. But I didn't think Thomas would know either, considering his first instinct was to risk its life.

"Are you hungry?" I asked. It didn't answer, because it's a dog. I should have gotten food on the way home. I didn't have anything in the house, not even a scrap.

I felt the hair on my arms prickle, and I knew what that meant. I patted the bed and the puppy jumped up next to me as the Time Sphere appeared in what was now its usual location on the left side of my apartment. I'd had to rearrange my furniture so it would fit. The bed was now tucked into the right-hand rear corner facing the door, with the bedside table at a right angle to it, taking up the same width as my pillow. All of my cabinets and shelves got moved to the right-hand wall, pressed up against each other for the length of the room. I'd put a small circular wood table with two matching chairs just to the right of the door. That gave the Sphere the whole left-and-center of the room to materialize.

I hadn't realized how big it was until I saw it in my room. Or, I hadn't realized how small my apartment was. Maybe both.

The door to the Sphere opened and Quentin stepped out carrying a handheld recorder, tiny enough to rest in his palm. The dog barked at him and wagged its tail.

Quentin laughed. "I thought I was going to be the one with the surprise. A dog?"

"Thomas used it in our training, to give me something to drain if I screwed up."

Quentin's eyes bulged. "That's fucked up." I nodded. "But you didn't screw up, obviously."

"What did you bring?" I pointed at his recorder.

He smiled and flopped down on the bed next to me, sitting half on my black pillow and half on the bunched-up comforter. The puppy ran over to him and squeezed on his lap. He scratched its head. "Mozart's last concert. Thought we could listen to it tonight." He looked at the puppy. "Do you like Mozart? Yeah, everyone does."

I grinned at him and the puppy. It was pretty cute. The puppy was brown and white spotted with dark brown floppy ears and a thin white tail. The white hair was leaving a few strands on Quentin's dark gray pants. Now looking at his clothes, a dark gray jacket to match, I realized he'd probably recorded the concert *at the concert*.

"So what do we name…" he picked up the puppy, lifting its hind legs, "her?"

"I don't know," I smirked, "what do *we* name her?"

He put her down on his lap, but she quickly put her front paws on his chest, and now there were white hairs on his jacket too. He scratched her behind the ears. "Sheryl had a dog when I met her, a terrier named Azul."

"Blue?" His maker had a strange way of naming things.

He shrugged. "She liked blue things. The water, blue hair dye, violets. But she called the dog Zuley, which was funny when Ghostbusters came out."

I smiled. "So you're saying that a dog should be named after extradimensional demons, or a color, or just that it should end in – ee?"

Whatever her name, she'd settled on his lap. "I didn't really mean anything. Zuley was the only dog I ever lived with. My parents didn't think a dog should time travel. But her name should be something you like, or one that means something to you. And I guess –ee sounds are pretty cute."

I felt a surprising amount of anxiety about naming this dog. It was a terribly permanent decision, despite my ability to later cute-ify a nickname. "Well, I'm not going to name her after a color. Or a demon."

"No…" Quentin said, and then *his* face flickered anxiously. He'd thought of something that made him nervous, but what? I looked at him inquisitively. "Ah, um… it's up to you, whatever you want."

I peered at him harder. "It is, but you thought of something?"

He ran his right hand through his hair, undoing its concert-hall smoothness. "I thought, ah… well, a cute name, just one example of course, would be Cori."

My blood felt like it froze solid inside me. He said I should name the dog something I liked, something that meant something to me. He was suggesting that I name her after Coretta.

"I'm sorry," he stuttered, "I wasn't thinking…"

It had been, what, two years? Tracking dates and time was hard when you didn't travel through them linearly. I didn't think about it *all* the time… most of the time I just lived my life, but it would come back to me now and then in a moment that was like a punch to the gut. A more-or-less daily punch to the gut. And that punch didn't hurt one bit less with time.

I put my hand on his left one, which was resting on Cori's side. "No. I love it."

*   *   *   *   *

I'd had to tell Eva, Coretta's 2017 second-in-command, to execute Order M. It had taken me a day or two after we'd gotten back from the battle with Judah to do it, but I had to figure out how to get the words out of my mouth first. M stood for "morte" – Coretta, as per usual, wanted to be painfully blunt about it. Order Dead. *"One day I won't be here, Vivian,"* she'd say, *"and you are going to have to cope with it."* I had hoped she was wrong, just being vigilant… that if anything I would go first.

But she wasn't wrong. And… I don't know if what I was doing was coping. When Eva put the plan into action, Coretta's charity for homeless women and children, L'Espoir du Monde, passed its leadership to Eva, and the necessary cascading promotions ensued. That didn't require anything from me. But the other part of the plan, the inheritance of Coretta's assets, did. And one of the things I inherited was her massive house on the outskirts of Paris, full of… everything. Full of our lives. Pictures. Clothes. Memorabilia. Letters. And an attic full of things that the family who'd lived there before her left behind; those didn't belong to me. It was more than I could deal with. I kept Coretta's maid employed so the house wouldn't fall into disrepair, like some mausoleum covered in dust. But I hadn't visited, or begun to sort through any of the things she left behind. It was just too much.

So I wasn't exactly coping. More… distracting. Evading. And I was about to get the biggest distraction yet.

*   *   *   *   *

Ten pound bag of dog food? Check.

Several gallons of bottled water? Check.

Stacks of old newspaper, and some paper towels before the newspaper starts working? Check.

Anti-nausea pills you can roll up in some sliced ham? Check. Sliced ham? Also check.

Quentin got the pills from a vet's office, and we landed on ham after trying ham, bologna, and cheese, and realizing that ham was the winner. The irony of feeding a small dog the meat of a much larger mammal was not lost on me, but I was hardly one to argue with an animal's food needs. Would Cori be the world's first time traveling dog?

Thomas had said that I had mastered preventing myself from taking someone's soul, and I felt the truth in it. I felt ready, ready to really be in the world again for the first time since that battle nearly two years ago. And Quentin was dying to take me where I'd wanted to go since then.

It wasn't anywhere specific. I was hoping I could draw on Quentin's past travels and he would have a good suggestion. I wanted to go somewhere as different as possible from everything I knew. Where life looked completely alien, so much so that I wouldn't even recognize it as life. And Quentin had an idea almost immediately: a planet he called Dohain.

He wouldn't say any more about it than that; he wanted it to be a surprise. So I packed a bag – this time I would have some of my own things, including clothes and a hair brush – and we started off. Would I go back to being nauseated again? The first time I rode in the Time Sphere, I threw up, and it was the worst dizziness I'd ever felt. But it got easier as I traveled more.

And it turned out to stick. I let Quentin put the buckle still attached to the center area in the Sphere on me, just in case I became too sick to hold on, but I was able to stay standing and didn't feel terribly nauseated – just a bit woozy. And Cori did fine – Quentin held her steady as we moved, and the pills we got her didn't hurt either.

It was remarkable that all the furniture in the Sphere stayed put while we were traveling. Some of it was bolted down, like the twin bed just behind me to my left, the brown table to my front-left, and obviously the whole console itself, which took up the majority of the area to my front-right, but the chairs that went with the table were not bolted and yet still stayed put as though they were magnetized. Maybe they were; I had never asked.

When we landed, Quentin put Cori down and went to test the door while I unbuckled. As he put his hand on it, I heard it beep, so it was safe for us to go outside – no sun.

"Ready?" he asked.

"Ready," I said. He opened the door and I stepped outside.

I wanted to invent new words to describe it. The air sparkled as though there were thousands of fireflies flitting about everywhere. But the sparkles weren't insects, just disembodied light twinkling in the otherwise-black sky. The ground was covered in thick red sand that looked like a dry, fuzzy carpet.

I felt… tight. Compressed. Quentin stepped out of the Sphere too and stood to my side.

He inhaled noisily. "If you want to talk, you have to breathe harder. The air pressure is a little stronger here. Would be painful to a human, but we'll be okay." He smiled. "Do you like it?"

I grinned and sucked in air. "I love it. It's so beautiful. But… is it all like this? The whole planet? No life?"

Quentin smirked, that look I'd come to know on him when he knew something I didn't. His eyes twinkled with the lights. "The whole planet is like this, but there is life. Everywhere." I frowned and looked around. "Don't look. Feel. You can feel it."

It was some sort of soul energy. He recognized it from his studies, and I knew it from my power. When I tried to sense it, it was, as he'd said, everywhere. In the sky, in the lights. In the ground. Oh God, the "sand" I was standing on was *alive*. I stepped backward reflexively.

Quentin chuckled. "They don't feel pain like that. You can stand here. They won't mind."

I still wasn't sure I wanted to do that. I kneeled down, my feet and knees inside the Sphere, and ran my fingers through the sand. When I touched it, my fingers felt a little ticklish.

"Do they think?"

Quentin shrugged. "Not the way we do. Their language isn't words. It's… experience."

I looked up at him. "Experience?"

He kneeled down across from me and touched the sand. "They're all connected. If one has an experience, the others know it, feel it. So they don't need words. They share a common experience."

The sand beings were soft to the touch, despite looking dry. "Do they eat anything?"

"I don't think so."

As he said that, I knew something wasn't right. The tickling in my fingers became a soft burning, as though the sand beings were agitated. The lights started to flicker more rapidly.

Nothing exists forever. At some point, they had to be created. And something has to sustain them. Everything living needs an energy source to survive.

There was a story here.

But what was it? And how could I find out? Sand doesn't have lips.

Quentin said they communicate through experience… could I tap into that? The light burning started to travel up my hands, my arms. It began to hurt, just a little. As the burning ascended my shoulders I began to understand – the sand was trying to get my own cells as agitated as it was. To get my flesh to speak its language. But it hurt, more and more each second. The agitation was causing my cells to vibrate, faster and faster, the friction creating an ever-mounting heat. As it seared my brain, I bit my lip, and then the visions came.

I saw flashes of discontinuous images – stills of scenes like a picture book with most of the pages ripped out. There were images of beings that… well, I didn't know what they were. They weren't human. But they weren't sand either. They had coarse skin, some green, some gray. Tiny eyes, black dots that darted around. Long snouts, like aardvarks, and short arms with tiny hands. I thought that, if they'd been on Earth, they might have descended from dinosaurs.

There were towns here, once. Farmland, and huts, and forests. And these beings lived there. They used to graze together, and live together, and hunt together.

And then the images had beings far more humanoid. Only a few, and they had brought handheld machines, boxes with circular dials and switches like some odd combination of early computer technology and a basic radio. It was then I heard whispers, like ghosts on the wind – *your crops will grow; your harvests will be bountiful.*

But they weren't. The images became gruesome. Hundreds of these creatures lying dead on the grass; humans looking pensively but dispassionately at them. That had been bad, but it was nothing compared to what was next. The next set of images showed these beings in increasing states of mutilation. Their limbs were removed. Their organs were set out in jars. Their bodies were ground up into… oh God. Sand. Their bodies were ground into sand.

But the sand wasn't dead; somehow these humans had made the creatures into living dust. The images stopped then, but the sand grew moist, as though it were crying. How do you hug sand?

The lights' flickering slowed, and around my head thousands of them gathered into a tight ball that shone so brightly I reflexively winced. But they didn't burn me. The light grew brighter, and brighter, and as it did, I could feel pressure building in my head, but not like a headache, and not like I was going to cry. It was like the air itself was becoming tighter.

The light creatures dimmed and then separated, and the pressure spread out with them. They were showing me what was happening, and as I realized it, my hands still buried in the sand, I did begin to cry. Every creature needs sustenance. These beings had nothing but their own planet. They were devouring parts of their planet to survive because they had no other choice. They couldn't die, and they could never really live. All they could do was consume their planet until there was nothing left and they drifted out into space.

What sort of monster would do this? And to what end?

When I looked at Quentin, he was looking at the sand. I could hear soft sniffles.

"You saw it too?" He nodded, but didn't look up. "When you were here before," I asked, "did you notice any of this? Did you see any of the humans?"

Quentin shook his head, cleared his throat, and pulled his hands from the sand. "I was young when I came here – six, maybe seven. My parents didn't let me touch the sand. They told me it was alive, that everything here was alive and connected, but nothing more." He sighed heavily. "They must have sensed it. They must not have wanted me to see what happened."

I felt utterly useless. I shifted my hands in the sand, a terribly lame effort at stroking it. The humans that had been here, that had done this, were long gone. There were no buildings, no signs, nothing to mark their time here other than these memories. They had done a complete job of erasing their tracks.

The sand seemed to tickle my right hand at that thought. Was that not right? Was there some evidence they had left behind? The sand grew highly agitated at that, and deeper down, several inches below my hand, I could feel a strong heat radiating up. I put my fingers together and dug into the sand, following the heat. When I found the spot, I could feel something solid touch the tips of my fingers. I burrowed in a bit more, closed my hand around it, and pulled it out.

It was a button. A brown, ordinary button, to a suit or a jacket or something similar. I smiled.

"Thank you," I whispered.

Chapter Two

We went inside the Sphere with the button. Cori was asleep on the bed, quickly identifying the most comfortable spot and wholly uninterested in our discovery.

I sat down at the table and turned the button over in my hand. I could learn a lot from it – who had worn it, how it came off of the clothing item, where it had been most frequently worn. Would the clues be enough to locate the wearer? Maybe. I had to be prepared for the possibility that they would be enough. If they were, they would lead me down another rabbit hole, one whose end I couldn't see. Was I ready to do that? Was I ready to take on something of this magnitude?

A group of humans had massacred an entire planet. They would be powerful. They would be dangerous.

They would deserve justice. And the sand had asked me to help. If not me, who?

I closed my hand around the button and called my blood to reveal its secrets.

The first image was of the wearer, a man who looked to be in his 50s – though I knew perfectly well that could mean nothing. His appearance was… late 18th century. A brown double-breasted coat had borne the button and curved toward the back as it descended revealing narrow-cut tan breeches. White stockings ending in a black shoe with a large silver buckle evoked memories of Revolutionary-era America – he could have been from Europe, as well, but I had been living in the United States – or should I say, colonies – by then, so it was George Washington and his ilk that came to mind.

The man's hair was dusted gray, as was the style, and tied back into a ponytail. His narrow eyes hid their color. His nose was long and pointed, and his chin striking to match. A large creased forehead topped his face and made for a very stern visage.

The second image was of the man on Dohain, standing in front of a large brick building. I couldn't sense anything of the building's purpose – there was no signage or anything useful. He tucked a small notepad into the inner pocket of his coat and then fastened its buttons, and as he did, one that had been hanging on a loose thread came free and fell to the ground, which appeared at the time to have been made of dirt, not sand.

The third image was of an office, a room with wooden bookshelves lining the perimeter and a desk strewn with books and papers. The man sat at the desk flipping through a tiny book whose contents I could not see.

And then the visions ended. Was it enough? Enough to know the man if I saw him again, yes. Enough to know where he was from, or why he was involved with this cruelty? No. *When* he was from would not be specific enough.

After the visions subsided, I saw Quentin watching me. He held out his hand, and I passed him the button. He closed his eyes and took his turn.

When he opened his eyes again, he frowned. "Did you see him?"

I nodded. "Him, and the moment he lost the button, and what must be his office wherever he's from. But I couldn't tell where that was."

Quentin smiled. "But the button knows. And that's enough for the Sphere."

That's right! I smiled too. I forgot that the Sphere could trace the path of things through the time stream.

But his smile faded as fast as it had come. "Whoever did this… they had the ability to travel to a part of the universe normal space travel can't get to."

He was right – there were still more dangerous implications. This man could travel through space the same way the Sphere could.

Could he travel through time the same way as well? Every person who could travel through time was another risk to the timeline. "We don't know when the massacre happened. He might only have traveled in space."

"Maybe," Quentin said skeptically, "but the way the Sphere does it, it's the same whether you move through time or not. Same tech."

"He could have another method. We don't know."

Quentin went over to the console and pressed the button against the screen, on top of the part reading "Past".

"Ready to find out?" he asked.

I sighed. I stood, walked over to the bed, and picked up Cori and held her tight. "Ready."

*   *   *   *   *

When we opened the door, we were in the office from my vision, tucked in the corner behind and to the left of the desk. The man wasn't there; no one was. We stepped out of the Sphere and closed the door quickly to keep Cori in.

Okay, we were here. "Should we read the stuff on his desk?" I suggested.

Quentin nodded, but as he did, the door to the office, which was on the far wall directly opposite the desk, flew open. The man, wearing a similar suit as in the vision but in a much darker shade of brown, stood there looking completely frazzled. I caught a slight whiff of blood; was it on him? Or was it coming from outside the doorway behind him?

He reached under his suit jacket, pulled a pistol out of his belt, and pointed it at us, walking towards us until he stood in the corner opposite us behind the desk. "Qui êtes-vous?" he shouted, his eyes darting back and forth from us to the door to the room.

Okay, France, then, or French Canada? Or French Switzerland... Belgium... okay, the language wasn't actually super helpful. "J'allais te demander le même chose," I said, though I already guessed he wouldn't just tell me who he was.

He sneered at us. "Comment nous avez-vous trouvés?" he pressed. How did you find *us*? That was a start. We knew he wasn't working alone, but perhaps his allies were here as well.

I heard a commotion from whatever was outside the door – shouts, screams, some things breaking and slamming. What did we walk into? I glanced toward the door but didn't see anything, and I didn't want to take my eyes off of Button Man.

He smirked wickedly. "Vous ne pouvez pas nous arrêter. Si vous me tuer, nous allons continuer. Nous sommes partout."

You can't stop us. If you kill me, we will continue. We are everywhere.

We are everywhere.

Before I could process those words, a sudden boom like a crack of lightning made me jump, and then Button Man's eyes grew wide, staring at nothing. He slumped to the ground like a sack of rocks and blood pooled around his head. The smell was enticing, but when I looked to the source of the sound, the figure standing in the doorway, I wasn't hungry anymore.

She looked from me, to Quentin, to the Time Sphere, and then back to me, the pistol still smoking in her hand. "You wanted me to kill him, yes?"

I couldn't move. I couldn't think. My mouth hung open but no sound was going to come out. As she looked at me with her contemplative look, the one where she was quietly figuring everything out without saying a word, I felt myself begin to tremble.

She walked toward me, slowly, measuring every step. She looked at Quentin and cast her eyes up and down. "You are here." She studied his leg area; he was wearing dark blue jeans. "Wearing fabric known not to my world." She looked at the Time Sphere. "From the future, then." She returned her eyes to me. "And you... look like you've seen a ghost."

Whatever composure I was clinging to in that moment, I lost. In a smooth, rapid motion she came to me and held me up in her arms. I wept uncontrollably, and she squeezed me against her chest, my head resting on her shoulder.

And from over my shoulder, I heard her voice. "Mmm. So I've died then. Is that it?" I wept harder and she held me tighter. I clutched her to me so hard I was almost certainly hurting her, but she didn't fight me. Eventually she put her hands on my shoulders and moved me back so we could look at each other.

I thought I'd never see her again. She looked exactly as she always had, even with my blood tears now streaked down her bright blonde curls.

"I do not want to know my future," Coretta said. "I will learn it when it happens. But tell me one thing." She paused, and I nodded. "Was it worth it? That is, would I say that it was worth it?"

I felt my face ready to burst again, and as I nodded, I dissolved into tears.

"Ça suffit," she murmured into my hair. I inhaled deeply through my nose and forced back the waterfall threatening my eyes. The musky vanilla smell of her hair filled my nostrils. "Tell me then, who did I shoot?"

I wiped my eyes. "I don't know. We traced him here. From a planet that had been destroyed. He had something to do with it, but I don't know what…"

Coretta nodded pensively. "Destroyed in what sense?"

I felt myself near to bubbling again thinking about it. Coretta huffed softly and turned to Quentin.

"You, you tell me then." She frowned momentarily, and then smiled widely. "Ah, where are my manners? Hello." She walked over to him smoothly, her usual glide-like walk. "I'm called Coretta. But you knew that, I think?"

"Yes," he said, seeming overwhelmed by what was happening. "I'm Quentin."

Coretta raised her eyebrows. She'd known who he was for centuries.

"Um," he stammered, "Destroyed in that every living thing was destroyed. People who look like Earth humans mutilated an entire civilization until they became sentient sand that has to feed off its own planet to survive."

Coretta pressed her lips together. "I see. Perhaps I was hasty in killing him."

Quentin shrugged. "True. We could have questioned him."

Coretta snorted derisively. "I could have ground *him* into sand, one limb at a time."

"Doing your own dirty work?" I said, smirking at her.

She smiled. "For him? I could put in some effort." She sighed. "Quentin is correct. You need information. But we have it, no?"

Quentin and I looked at each other. We did?

"Why did he come here?" Coretta asked. "'Here' has something of importance to him."

Good point. "That said... where are we?" I wiped my full face with my palms, both now smeared with blood. Clarity was beginning to seep back into my brain. Despite everything, it was so easy to fall into our old patterns... the way we spoke to each other, the way we understood each other. It was reflexive. "And why are you here?"

Coretta sighed heavily and sat on the desk just behind her. "Paris, 1795. This man – if he is the leader here, I believe his name to be Geoffrey – this is his office. It is larger by far than this room." She lifted a brown satchel off of her shoulder – I hadn't even noticed it until then; the brown melded into the purple of her dress, and I had to strain to focus on anything besides her presence. She pulled out a stack of papers. "I gathered these from the other rooms." She paused. "Let me begin at the beginning of the puzzle. Near twenty women and children have disappeared. Their commonality is that they have no living relatives, besides one another in the mother-child pairs. My associates…" (she meant her ninjas, people she'd hired – and in some cases trained – to quietly… deal with… people who had escaped the justice system) "were able to find pieces of fabric left behind where the women had stayed. Small threads, but enough to offer a scent, and some with a bit of blood upon them. It took time to trace them, but one woman – working here, it became evident – was a bit sloppy and used a poor and hasty cloaking spell. Francine spotted her snatching a young lady and followed her here, and then connected this building to the smells and tastes." Coretta had always casually referred to her ninjas by their first names, as though I should know who they are. "I called a group together and we entered the building. There are many other rooms with many people, whom I can only assume are underlings, subordinates to this fellow. Well, *were* underlings. Francine and the others are tending to the mess. From the hall, I heard your voice. So, I came, and here we are."

I narrowed my eyes at her. "Why did you come at all? Why didn't you just send Francine's crew?"

She dangled her legs off the desk, swinging them idly. "This was something bigger. Ordinary men are easy to trace. These were more. Weak magic users mostly, but a coalition of even them, snatching women and children who are strangers to them, is noteworthy, wouldn't you say?"

I nodded. "Enough to warrant your direct involvement. Did you find the missing people?"

Coretta frowned. "I do not know. We found… biological residue. What appears to be ground-up bones in jars, blood in tubes."

I grimaced. "If these are the same people who destroyed that planet… why? What is their goal? Why do they grind everything up?"

Coretta shrugged, but Quentin spoke up. "Their goal, I don't know, but grinding things allows you to see something's constituent parts. And blood, there's a lot to learn about what something is made of there too."

"Right," I said. "DNA, genetics."

Quentin's eyes widened. "Lots of things *they don't know about yet.*"

Shit. "Oh, sorry…" I rubbed my face. My brain was sludge.

Coretta giggled. "I do not know what those things mean, so I believe you are safe."

Quentin looked at me sympathetically but sternly. "There may be people around who would understand enough to be dangerous, though. At any time. You have to be more careful. Last thing we need is a massive timeline violation."

I nodded. "I know. I'm sorry."

He shook his head. "It's fine, this time. Coretta, you say there were tubes? Test tubes? A lab?"

She nodded. "It appears to be a laboratory. Some notes in this stack are from that room." She held them out to Quentin, who took them and began flipping through them.

I looked over Geoffrey's desk. There were stacks of papers here too, and some sort of binder. I flipped it open, revealing a calendar. The first page read 'Janvier, 1795'. The appointments were mostly innocuous by appearance – "rencontre avec" a series of names I didn't know. But there were a few more telling entries – "rendez-vous en 1943" was one under June 23rd. So he could travel through time. I looked at Coretta. "What day is today?"

"Le treize juin," she replied, and her return to French made me realize that we had been speaking in English up until then, which was… odd, for 18th-century us. But everything about right now was pretty fucking odd. I looked back in the calendar and, lo and behold, under June 13th was "récupérer les résultats du Dohain". Retrieve the results from Dohain.

Quentin exhaled heavily, which made me look in his direction. "This is… I don't know what this is. The lab results are really rudimentary, but it looks like they're trying to do some sort of biological mapping… but with 18th century methods, the results are… silly, totally silly. This one," he waved one page, flapping it about, "is mapping the quantity of humours in these people's blood."

I kneeled down beside Geoffrey's increasingly-smelly body and fished around in his pockets. Tucked into the inner pocket of his suit jacket was, as I had seen in my vision, a tiny notepad. I pulled it out and read it in its original French.

"Virology tests in Dohain inconclusive. Initial longevity acquired but specimen experienced rapid decomposition of extremities. Despite biological signatures suggesting capability of upward of 150 years, specimen in isolation evidenced unexplainable organ failure. Specimen released into wild remained vulnerable to weapon injuries, locally-occurring pathology, and suicide."

Silence.

"They know about virology, but still research 'humours'?" Quentin mused.

More silence.

Coretta broke it with a huff. "What would he do with that knowledge next?"

Good question. I stood again and looked back at Geoffrey's calendar. "On the 23rd he's supposed to visit 1943."

Quentin's expression darkened. "That answers that. That's…" he let the sentence trail off. He didn't need to finish. That's very, very risky. What might Geoffrey have brought back from the future before? Was that why he understood virology? Putting that information into the 1700s could wreak havoc.

I inspected the calendar entry. "Doesn't say who he was supposed to meet or why. Crotona Park. Does that sound familiar?" It did to me, but I couldn't place it.

"Isn't that in the Bronx?" Quentin asked.

"Yes! I think so."

Quentin nodded. "Are you thinking what I'm thinking?"

"That we should attend his meeting for him?"

Quentin grinned conspiratorially, and Coretta clapped her hands together. "Delightful! 1943... will I have need of this..." she poked at Quentin's jeans with the tip of her shoe, which appeared to be made of fabric not unlike her dress, "attire?"

I stared at her. In my whole life, Coretta had rarely left Paris, nor her charity, which was by her own account a lot of work. "You can leave?"

She smirked at me and gestured toward the Sphere. "Is this not a time machine? What does it cost me to go if you can return me to this very date?"

"But... it's going to be dangerous. It's... it's not safe; we don't know what's..."

I stopped midsentence as her lips twisted into their impatient posture. "Are you truly attempting to tell me what to do?"

I closed my eyes and felt my voice catch in my throat. It came out scratchy and hollow. "I can't watch you die again. I can't."

I heard her huff. "If I am already dead, how can I die?"

I squeezed my eyes tight. "There are many worlds other than this. Everything that could be real is real somewhere. There's no way to be sure that the circumstances of your death couldn't change, making a new world where you died a new way..."

"But in *your* world, I am already dead. Does a world not require its own internal logic?" I remembered the worlds Judah had sent me to and shuddered. Not necessarily... "And even if not, it is *my* life, Vivian, and I will live it as I choose. Now, I shall go speak with Francine and tell her that I may be away for awhile – though perhaps not, from her view. We have collected all the evidence there is. Do not leave without me." I heard her slip off of the desk and leave the room.

I opened my eyes – Quentin was looking at me sympathetically. "Should we wait?"

The thought of seeing any harm come to her ever again filled me with sinking dread. But the thought of never seeing her again made me feel that as well, and nauseated too. And she was right. It was her life. She would never – had never – made my choices for me. She deserved as much from me.

I nodded. "We'll wait."

*   *   *   *   *

When we entered the Time Sphere, Coretta clapped her hands together and looked around excitedly. "Lovely! So many lights." The ceiling was lined with some sort of crystal that pulsed red, pink, lilac, and blue – not all the time; most of the time they were inactive, a static pearl. But sometimes they came on, or flashed, or twinkled. I didn't know if it meant anything; there didn't seem to be a pattern.

Quentin nodded, and I could see pride in his eyes. "She's even more beautiful in motion. You'll see."

Cori… oh God, did I have to tell her the dog's name?… yelped at seeing her and ran over to say hi. Coretta laughed. "You have a dog? How precious." She kneeled down and scooped Cori up, scratching her behind the ears. Cori licked her face. "Bonjour, ma petite!" she cooed. "Comment tu t'appelles?"

Could I lie? No. Not to her. I averted my eyes, staring instead at the floor. "Her name is Cori."

Silence… and then Coretta burst into laughter. I looked up at her. "Is this true?" she asked. "You've named the dog after me? That is adorable."

I shuffled my feet. "It was Quentin's idea."

Quentin pursed his lips at my attempted deflection. "An idea *you* said you *loved*." He smiled, and Coretta was also smiling, and everything felt surreal.

But we had things to do, so I walked over to the console, ignorantly displaying "Past" and "Future" as though the whole world hadn't just inverted itself. No, just my world. The Sphere had larger concerns.

A thought from my own past flitted into my mind. "If we're going to 1943 New York… should we get the others?"

"Others?" Coretta asked.

"You mean Gerard?" Quentin asked. "I guess his magic could be helpful. We don't know what we're up against." He looked at Coretta. "Gerard is a friend of ours from our last journey… about two years ago now. He can manipulate the powers of darkness to do pretty powerful stuff. But he uses it for good things."

Coretta cocked her head to the side. "Good things. For you? So far. Working with darkness must be… precarious."

Quentin nodded. "He knows the risks. He hasn't fallen victim yet."

Coretta slowly nodded.

"And Adelita, and Scott," I added. "They're mortals, just people, but they're smart. Adelita is tough; you'd like her. And Scott has been studying with Gerard. They all have; they've been studying together, or they said they would. At least we can see what they've learned."

"I see," Coretta said. "I think collecting any allies you have is a fine idea."

I turned back to the console. "Okay. Let's do this. Lock down." I put my hand on 'Future', imagined Gerard's house and focused on 1943, and felt the whirring begin under my feet.

About a minute later, we landed with a thud. I released the edge of the console, which had left deep indents in my left palm. I lifted my right hand off of the screen and turned around.

The guard chain was fastened around Coretta's waist and she was still holding Cori, gazing up at the ceiling and softly smiling. Quentin had his arms protectively on either side of her waist and was looking at her… oddly. He seemed perplexed by something, but when I caught his gaze, his eyes brightened and he smiled.

While he unfastened her, I went over to the door and placed my hand on the handle. The door clicked approvingly, and I opened it.

Gerard straightened the collar of his black suit jacket as he sat down along Adelita's dining table to Scott's immediate right. Darkness Manifestations in Historical Lore, he was reading, his brow furrowed behind his black-rimmed glasses. Gerard was glad to see Scott reading that section, as it was one of his favorites, and, he thought, one of the most insightful tomes into the essence of the darkness. To see how it lived and breathed and thrived throughout history told its tale – and it revealed that the darkness had played a role in near every important occurrence throughout time. And not all for the bad! He thought that darkness was very much like the myths that the Norsemen told about Loki – dangerous and chaotic, but important, and powerful, and responsible for much good as well as ill. Its practitioners only had to approach it with respect and caution.

Adelita was to his far right, in the tiny foyer at the front of her house that held the door to the outside. She was pacing, holding a book in her left hand and gesticulating with her right, reciting something to herself. It was how she rehearsed, studied, finding the motion of her lips and hands to somehow lock the knowledge into her brain tighter. And she had acquired so much knowledge. He felt a swell of pride watching her. Indeed, he felt that the three of them had become a little family, and he cared for them both.

Yet he knew that it was likely they would not agree with that feeling. Scott struggled with much of the material, his training and education prior to meeting Gerard not preparing him well for this type of study. He was smart, and well-spoken, but not especially oriented to book learning. Gerard wished that he had other opportunities to offer him, and had for a long time encouraged him to continue with the police force, but Scott was unwilling to leave his side, and noted that with the hours Gerard kept at his City Hall job, should he work his usual police job, they would never see each other. Gerard found that a suspicious excuse. The police worked all hours and Scott could have pressed for a nighttime job if he had wished.

He worried that it had more to do with Adelita. Her proficiency at their study had made Scott envious, and it strained their relationship. Gerard had assured Scott that he valued the important work of law enforcement as much as their work understanding magic and the darkness, but Scott still seemed to feel that he had to attach himself to Gerard's work. Perhaps his encounter with Judah had made him believe that magic was essential to understand to defeat future villains. Of course, that was untrue, but it must have been a traumatic experience to have one's soul stripped from one's body, so he could not fault him.

Gerard leaned close to Scott. "Do you have any questions I might answer for you?"

Scott's shoulders sunk, his tan suit jacket sagging and crumpling near the top of his arms, and he turned to look at Gerard. "None right now. It's interesting, yet I cannot say what it means."

Gerard smiled. "Perhaps you and I could discuss it once you have read it all. Like the philosophical coffee houses of old."

Scott smiled faintly. "I'd like that, though I hope you won't expect great insights from me."

Gerard shook his head softly. "I expect only your ideas, and they will be of great interest to me whatever they are."

Scott blushed and quickly turned his face back to the book, his blond hair falling across his cheek. "I'd like more such time generally. Yet you spend much of it with Adelita."

There it was again. "I aid her in her studies as well, that is true. But I do not spend more time with her than you. I do the best that I can to help the both of you."

"But she doesn't need your help," Scott protested, his body becoming agitated but his voice becoming hushed.

"Scott, you are each at your own place, and each strive to advance... it is not a competition."

Scott scowled in one of his rare displays of anger. "That isn't my meaning. I mean that there is no purpose to her advancing. To what end? She cannot be fulfilled with work such as this. She ought to focus her time on more appropriate pursuits."

Scott had come from a career surrounded by men. He was not accustomed to working alongside women, nor spending time with women who desired career pursuits at all. Or, perhaps more aptly, who expressed and pursued those desires.

"She does enjoy this study, Scott. It is you I worry are not fulfilled in it."

Scott's face softened. "I don't know what fulfillment means for me. I... seek it, but it feels unattainable." He swallowed hard.

Gerard's heart sunk. He put his left hand on Scott's shoulder. "If there is anything I can do to help you attain it, please do inform me."

Scott closed his eyes and nodded wordlessly.

Chapter Three

We had landed in the street in front of Adelita's yard. Not Gerard's, so the Sphere had made an executive decision there. Her house looked a lot nicer than the last time we'd seen it… that felt like yesterday, and yet so long ago. Now, the exterior was freshly re-shingled, clean light blue covering the front face. The stairs leading to the door were recently-laid concrete, and the door a strong wood unlike the flimsy thing that had been there before. I approached, knowing Coretta and Quentin were following behind me.

I climbed the stairs, hesitated, and then knocked.

Within ten seconds the door opened revealing Adelita. She didn't look terribly different from when I'd last seen her. She had some fine lines around her eyes, in their corners and underneath them. Some more fine lines appeared at the sides of her mouth when she grinned. She was clutching a book in her left hand and sporting a brown knee-length dress with a beige belt and buckle.

"Vivian!" she exclaimed, the 'v's in my name feather-soft on her tongue. She hugged me so fast I stumbled back. "You've come to visit! But… why?"

When I'd seen her last, she, Gerard, and Scott had agreed to continue working together. Judah was gone, but Adelita couldn't just go back to an average life. She wanted to learn about the darkness and fight the wicked. And Scott now knew about magic too – though only that it exists; I didn't think he knew much beyond that, including what we were – and refused to return to his home time. He stayed with them, though what they'd done since – well, I guessed I'd find out.

"We need you. All three of you. If you're still together?"

"We are!" She stepped back to let us pass, and as I stepped forward, the blood drained from Adelita's face. She was looking just past me, eyes unblinking. "You're… you're dead."

Coretta had been standing on the step behind me. Adelita had seen her die too.

Coretta smiled. "Not yet."

Adelita looked at me helplessly. She hadn't acquired an appreciation for Coretta's blunt humor. "Adelita, I'd like you to meet Coretta. I stole her from 1795."

Coretta shook her head. "You cannot steal me if I am the one who insists upon my coming. Adelita, is it?" Adelita weakly nodded. "I will say to you what I said to her. I do not wish to know about my future. I know that I die, but that is hardly news. We all die. And I get the luxury of knowing that it was for a worthy reason. But do not tell me any more than that."

Adelita nodded but started to look misty-eyed. She was holding it together much better than I had. "I am sorry," she mumbled.

Coretta frowned. "None of that, either," she said flippantly. "Guilt is useful only insofar as it improves your behavior in the future. So improve. Unless you do, the words have no meaning. Now, if you must weep, might you do so inside? It is beginning to rain."

Adelita stared open-mouthed at Coretta for only a moment before stepping back and letting us pass.

We walked in to find a continuation of the outside. The floor! You could see the floor. The place seemed so much larger cleaned up as it was. There was brand-new furniture, or at least it was pretty new. In the room just past the entranceway, they had installed a huge bookshelf and work desk, both dark brown and covered in their respective paper products. A single-person couch-like chair was tucked into the near corner, adorned with brown flowers. There was also a long flat table starting about halfway into the room and stretching the rest of its length, past the tiny table on which the infamous jar had sat, unadorned with anything except loose papers and Gerard and Scott seated close together. They looked up at us simultaneously.

Gerard stood, smiling, his hand coming to rest on Scott's shoulder. Scott took off thick black-framed spectacles – had he needed reading glasses when I'd met him last? – put down the book he was holding, and frowned.

"It is pleasant to see you," Gerard said.

"You can't have come for a good reason," Scott said. His forehead wrinkled and I noticed creases were forming across it.

Coretta laughed. "I like you," she said, nodding in Scott's direction. "You must be Scott. And you, Gerard."

"And you are?" Gerard asked, taking a step toward her with his hand extended.

"Coretta," she said, and as she took his hand, his body jerked. "Oh, apologies," and she looked over her shoulder at me. "Did he know of my death too?" I nodded, and she turned back. Gerard smiled again, much more faintly. "It is in my future. As is yours."

Gerard smirked, and then laughed. "Indeed."

Scott looked nervously from one person to the next. "Is this… more travel through time? Are you from the past?"

Coretta smiled at him. "Whose past?"

I groaned and stepped up alongside her. "What she means is, yes, she is from the chronological past." I looked at her. "Could you give just one simple answer, maybe?"

She shrugged. "Seems to me they like it complicated. Or else when you'd described them, you'd have mentioned that they were romantically entangled. As they're not, it suggests they insist on making things harder than they need be."

Dead silence.

Coretta shrugged again. "Lots of people seem to prefer complication. It is not particular to you."

Gerard was staring dumbfounded at Coretta. Scott looked down at the table.

"It is my fault," Scott said. "Gerard, I am sorry. Truly. She says these words because she can sense my affection for you. I know it is not… correct behavior. I will understand if you wish for me to leave."

Gerard turned to face Scott. "Affection for me?"

Coretta rolled her eyes. *Blind to what was before him,* she thought to me, smirking.

Scott did not look up. "Yes. I am sorry. I will leave…" and he began to stand up.

Gerard stepped toward him and grabbed his shoulders. Scott finally met his eyes.

"No. Do not leave." Gerard's eyes softened. "Stay." He let his hands drop. "I… also… feel affection for you."

Coretta yawned, pulled a rolled cigarette out of her purse, and lit it.

"If you would like it," Gerard continued, "I would like to be… *'romantically entangled'* with you."

Scott's eyes widened, and then rapid-fire darted over the rest of us, seeking our judgment most likely. He didn't find it.

"I would like that," Scott said, grinning.

"Oh," Adelita exhaled. *"Finally."* She smiled at Coretta. "I wish I had found your words years prior."

Coretta inhaled from her cigarette and shrugged yet again. "Words have their time and their place."

Gerard cleared his throat. "Ah, uh, Vivian. You have not said why you have come, and brought your interesting friend."

"Scott was right. It isn't good news. Quentin and I were visiting a planet whose entire civilization was destroyed by humanoid creatures doing bizarre experiments on them. We followed one person back to 1795, where he had an office and a laboratory where they were kidnapping women and children and doing experiments on them, too."

Gerard's eyes narrowed. "What manner of experiments?"

"In the lab," Quentin said, "it looked like they were trying to map the genome, but couldn't get past bodily humours. They were mapping the 'constituency' of bile, etcetera."

"And the notes he had from that planet were about 'virology' and 'longevity' experiments," I added.

Gerard looked at us in confusion. "So the experimenter was a time traveler?"

"I don't know if he took part in the experiments on that planet. But he did travel there and back, and was going to travel here, to this time. I don't know how."

"And he had knowledge of science from the future, but his own laboratory relied on theorems from the past?" I nodded. "Perplexing," Gerard decided. "And to solve this conundrum, you have come to us, and brought a witness from the past?"

I eyeballed Coretta. I'd let her reply for herself.

"I am here," she began, "because this gathering of deplorables has stolen women and children who were to be in my care. When those in my employ went to retrieve them, to bring them to shelter, they were missing."

"The women and children in the 'humours' experiments," Gerard said sympathetically, more of a statement than a question.

"Yes," Coretta confirmed. "I cannot help them now, but I may be able to prevent further abduction, further harm."

Gerard firmly nodded. "I will assist as best I can. What is our plan?"

"The man," I began, "the experimenter, he was supposed to meet someone here, in the Bronx, in... what day is it?"

"The nineteenth of June."

"Okay, so in four days. We decided to attend the meeting in his place."

Gerard raised his eyebrows. "And the man, he is..."

"Dead," Coretta piped up. "I shot him in the head."

Scott was agape, and uttered his first sentence in several minutes: "I hope you are certain that he is your villain?"

"Quite," Coretta said. "My associates traced the kidnappings to his premises."

"And I saw him, in a vision, on the planet before it had been massacred, impassively gathering notes on their torture," I added. Scott had come to terms with us being... magical. He just didn't know how.

"We only know that he's meeting someone in Crotona Park," Quentin added.

I moved to Scott's far side and sat next to him. "We were hoping that you three could help us learn more and prepare."

Scott reached over to a pad of paper, tore off a blank piece, and slid it over to me. "Let us assemble what we know."

I nodded. "Do you have a pen?" He nodded and retrieved one, a black fountain pen, from under one of the books on the table and passed it to me. I smoothed out the sheet of paper and wrote the first line: *Where: Crotona Park. When: June 23, 1943.*

Adelita leaned over my shoulder. "Who was he going to meet?"

I shook my head. "I don't know."

"You said they are to meet in a park? A public park?"

Now that she mentioned it, it did seem odd. "That was what he had written in his calendar." But they wouldn't meet where everyone could see, would they?

Gerard frowned. "They might implement a cloaking spell. But to what end? Why would they not meet indoors?"

"But they might," Scott added. "There is a bath house built in the park."

Gerard's face lit up. "Indeed! I had forgotten. A bath house that some reserve for private gatherings. Perhaps I might consult the city calendar and see who has reserved it that day."

Day. Ugh, I hadn't thought of that. I groaned. "The meeting is probably in the daytime. These are mages, and maybe humans."

There was a moment of silence while I stared at the paper in front of me, and then I realized I was really stupid. Maybe I was still in shock.

"Sooo…" I continued, as though I'd not meant to stop, "Gerard will be working, I guess, and, uh…"

"I will attend," Adelita piped up, saving me. "If you are all… indisposed… I will attend the meeting. Perhaps Scott can join me, seeing as he is not employed."

Scott scowled. "How could I be, when there're magical villains to fight?" He shook his head. "Though I am not a magic user. I want to fight but know not what I can contribute."

"I am not a magic user either," Adelita huffed, "but science is not magic, and what we learn can help Gerard to wield the darkness to our advantage." She paused, and then smirked. "And you know not what the future might bring, Scott. *I* suspect you will have magical ability." She looked deliberately at Coretta, who met her gaze in the mutual-understanding look that she usually reserved for me. "One day."

Coretta audibly snickered. "Do you think so?"

Adelita nodded. "Once Gerard decides not to be so needlessly *complicated*."

Coretta nudged me. "You were right; I do like her."

Gerard looked like he would be breaking a sweat if that were something he could do. He cleared his throat forcefully. "We must stay on *point*, do you not think so, Vivian?" And he looked at me pitiably.

I twirled the pen. "You'll check the city calendar and see who has the bath house reserved and at what time. We'll then determine who'll go. Now, depending on whom he was supposed to meet, we might understand more about the topic of the meeting. Scott, when Gerard finds out who it is, maybe you can help him research that person, or people, or organization – what they do, what they own, who they know, that sort of thing. Okay?"

Scott nodded, though side-eyed Gerard, the prior conversation not having fully left his thoughts yet. "I will do what I can."

I put the pen down on the sheet of paper. The details would have to wait until we knew more.

Gerard moved to the front of the house and then returned wearing a long black jacket made of perhaps cotton. Wasn't it June? Ah, but to go out without a jacket would be improper for a gentleman of the 40s. Not that it mattered; he wouldn't sweat. "I shall make haste."

Scott shook his head. "He always works such odd hours. It is a wonder you are able to enter City Hall at this time."

Gerard smiled. "Mayor La Guardia is always at work. He is typically pleased to have the company."

I narrowed my eyes at Gerard and put the thought in his head: *If you're going to be in a relationship with him, you have to tell him.*

Gerard winced, looked at me somberly, and nodded ever so slightly before waving goodbye and heading out.

*　　*　　*　　*　　*

While Gerard was away, I decided to retrieve Cori from the Sphere. I couldn't leave the poor puppy alone in there, and a house was a better place anyway. Adelita did not seem to mind.

"Oh, how cute!" she squealed, a more excited sound than I was used to hearing from her. She kneeled down on the floor and Cori, craving attention, ran into her arms. Adelita cradled and pet her. "Why do you have a dog?"

Did I want to explain the training, and Thomas? Not especially. "I sort of rescued her, and then she was just… there. I couldn't leave her behind when we left, so, here she is."

"Do you have any sense of where you are?" Adelita asked Cori, who answered by licking her face. "No, no you do not." She looked up at me. "What do you call her?"

This again. "Ah…" I bit my lip, "Cori."

Adelita's eyes widened just slightly in understanding and glanced at Coretta, so I did too. She'd taken comfort in the recliner tucked into the corner of the room nearest the door, her legs splayed over one arm and her back against the other. Her dress, which I finally processed, draped its long purple silk trimmed in lighter-purple lace onto the floor. One of her arms was propped up on the back of the chair.

I loved the juxtaposition; I always had. She wore such gorgeous, elegant clothes, but her demeanor was something entirely different. She saw us looking at her and grinned smugly.

After playing with Cori to her heart's content, and wearing Cori out in the process, Adelita made some dinner for her and Scott, and of course the rest of us "had already eaten", except that we *hadn't* and this night had drained my willpower to zero, so I found myself irritably pacing the room. When Gerard returned four hours later, he came bearing "wine", and I had to resist kissing his cheeks.

As Gerard poured, I picked up the pen again. Scott watched and sighed.

"I wish we could find a wine we both enjoy," he lamented. "I cannot develop a taste for what you buy."

Coretta snorted. "Have you tried to on many occasions?"

"Twice," he said. "Gerard warned me that I would not like it, but I wanted so much to…"

"Oh," now Coretta was lamenting, putting her head in her hands, "this is unbearable. Gerard, please, I cannot stand it."

Gerard tensed up visibly. "Is now truly the moment? We have a great need…"

"That is four days from now," she continued. "And if I'm to be effective, I can hardly tolerate this continual idiocy. Look at the boy, how you've left him to this pathetic state. He wants to like what you like, and you've flummoxed him."

Gerard exhaled heavily and put the "wine" bottle down. "How does one begin? I've no sense for what to say."

I snickered. "You can't possibly reveal yourself in a worse way than I did, so just jump in." Coretta had found me draining a man in an alleyway. I would probably have told her eventually, but in a more gentle way.

Coretta laughed. "Did you think that was bad? I thought it was perfect. No illusions, my love, not as to what you are, nor as to what I would be."

Quentin had been silent until then, having taken a seat opposite me at the table and coping with his own hunger by pressing his lips tight, but now took a big gulp from his glass and shook his head. "V, I don't know what *you* did, but I think I win this contest." He looked so sad as he said it. I reached across the table and squeezed his arm. God, that was a lifetime ago. Several, in fact.

Adelita chuckled darkly. "Are we comparing notes on misdeeds? I have a few of my own. My mortality has not spared me that."

Well, we had certainly backed Gerard into a corner. Scott was staring at all of us, the poor guy, totally in the dark. "Mortality?" he squeaked out.

Gerard sighed and kneeled down in front of him. "I've not been honest with you. You believe that I am a magic user... a mage. Yet, that is not accurate. My powers come from another source. I..." he hesitated, staring down at the floor... "there are many names for what I've become, but whatever you may call me, these are the truths: I work during the night because I must, because I cannot be exposed to the sun without burning. I drink this 'wine', but it is not wine; it is blood. Blood is the source of my magic and how I live on. I can die, but will not unless I am killed. I will not age, not physically."

As he spoke, Scott's eyes grew wide, but he didn't seem afraid, just surprised. When Gerard was done, Scott looked up at the rest of us. "You as well?"

"Not me," Adelita said. "But them, yes."

Scott twisted his hands together nervously. "Ah, um... I see... then, I suppose... thank you. For not eating me."

We lost it – all of us burst into laughter. Even Gerard laughed and finally made eye contact with Scott, who was awkwardly smiling.

Coretta regained her composure first. "Do you see, Gerard? All is well. Now, who has the bath house reserved on the 23rd?"

Gerard rubbed his face and stood up. "Yes, of course... a gentleman by the name of Phillip Drefford. What was notable about the reservation was that it is for 9:30 p.m., which is far later than we usually allow such bookings. Do you think it implies that some at the meeting will be..." he looked at Scott hesitantly, "as we are?"

I nodded. "Maybe," and I wrote my next note on the paper: '9:30 p.m., bath house, Phillip Drefford.' "What else did you learn about him?"

"I was not able to discover much. He is the President of the New York Regional Office of an organization called SFL, and I uncovered an address, but it is a large office building in the city and it would be closed at this hour."

"I could go there in the morning," Scott suggested. "Though, I know not what I would seek."

"It is not what they will tell you that we want to know," Adelita said, "but what they will not tell you. At the least, we can uncover their public face. And then the others can learn the rest from Phillip at the meeting."

It was a good plan, but I wanted as much information as possible before showing up on Phillip's terms. "Can you find out more about him personally? His life, his background?"

Adelita nodded, and Gerard did too. "Tomorrow I can begin to investigate more deeply… through legal and other routes," he added.

Very well. "Then there isn't much else we can do tonight," I said, and turned to my glass, finally taking a very satisfying sip.

"And it grows late," Gerard added. What time *was* it? I looked at the clock – 3 a.m. Not run-to-bed late, but the sun did rise early this time of year. "I ought to return home."

"May I come with you?" Scott asked, and then instantly blushed a bright crimson. "What I mean to say is… if I am to know the truth of you, I would like to see how you live. Where you sleep, and the like…" he blushed harder, his ears and neck turning red too… "I do not… I only mean that…"

Gerard smiled softly. "You would like to see my coffin, then?"

Did he actually sleep in a coffin? In 1943, it was possible. Some modern vampires, especially the younger ones, had embraced technology – roll-down windows, electronically-secured doors and the like – but in 1943 you had either a coffin, an underground bunker, or some really well boarded up windows. Or a house with no windows, but I'd seen Gerard's house and it definitely had those.

Either way, Scott nodded. "I can return home while you sleep."

Gerard scratched his neck. "You need not, if you are tired. You may sleep on my couch, if you wish."

Coretta frowned. "You don't have a bed at all? Then where do you…" She stopped mid-sentence. "Never mind." After that, I wasn't sure Scott's face would ever recover.

1650 Broadway, off of West 51ˢᵗ Street. The car ride had seemed to take an eternity, though Adelita had to acknowledge the improvement over the horses and buggies that rode these streets previously. She would have to learn to drive. Scott had seemed bothered by her desire to learn, and asked what need there was in it. Adelita pressed her lips tight. The same need as you have in it, *she thought.*

After a time he found parking and they approached the 12-story brick building, which in most other neighborhoods would have been tall, but here it was dwarfed by so many others. Humans had never needed magic to create wondrous things, and nor would she.

They entered the lobby of the building – a large room with light gray walls and a fancy chandelier hanging in the center – to find a long silver desk at the far end with a man behind it dressed all in black save for a gray bowtie. Adelita looked around hoping to find… there it was. A directory, a large plaque on the far left wall listing company names and floors. They had to uncover something of 'SFL' before they could hope to walk in past the black waist-high gates next to the security desk.

Nothing was named 'SFL' exactly, but one company was called 'Society for Longevity'. 11ᵗʰ floor. "That must be the correct name," Adelita mused.

Scott nodded. "Vivian remarked that they had conducted longevity research. How shall we approach them?" he asked, more to himself than to her.

Longevity was the solution to death. What if one of them was critically ill? "Perhaps we say that one of us is near to death. That we saw their name in the directory and came in our desperation?"

Scott silently stared at the directory. He stroked his chin, which was an odd gesture from a beardless man. "I've an idea – you are gravely ill with a cancer, and I've brought you here as my wife to try to cure you."

Adelita had to breathe a few deep breaths before responding. "A marvelous idea."

It would be a kindness to have other women around the house, especially women of Vivian and Coretta's sort. Gerard and Scott were intelligent, kind men, to be sure. She would always be indebted to Gerard for repairing and restoring her home. But... when they were together, they were the picture of gentlemanliness, perhaps attempting to impress one another. But apart... Scott could be dismissive of her ideas, and Gerard, though he did value her intelligence, seemed to treat her as his clever daughter, not as a woman of equal worth. Adelita wondered if either man would dare to treat Coretta in such a way. She seemed the sort of woman who'd put them in their place rather quickly. They might have more luck with Vivian, who would despise the treatment but seemed perhaps to adapt more to her surroundings. Coretta struck Adelita as a woman who bucked the trends. A woman outside of her time, metaphorically as well as literally.

"Good morning," Scott addressed the guard. "We wish to visit the office of the Society for Longevity. We have urgent need of their services." He sniffled thickly, but his eyes were clear, so he seemed more to have caught an illness than to be mourning hers.

The guard looked back at him curiously, his round eyes narrowing. "Sir, the Society for Longevity does not receive visitors. Do you have a pass?"

Scott stammered, "No, but... please, the need is quite urgent... my wife is gravely ill."

The security guard shook his head. "There are no exceptions, sir."

Adelita leaned forward across the desk toward the guard. "Not for those seeking to meet Mister Drefford?"

The guard's eyes widened. "A moment." He lifted a receiver from the desk and dialed only the numbers 413. Adelita had rarely seen a telephone in use and found the concept fascinating – speaking to another person you could not see! More human ingenuity, no magic necessary. "A man and woman to see Mister Drefford, sir." Silence. "No sir. Yes, of course." He returned the receiver to its resting place. "Someone will be down to see you momentarily."

"Thank you," Scott said, and they walked away from the desk, out of earshot. "They are very secretive."

Adelita nodded. "Drefford's name evoked a response. As though his identity were not commonly known." Odd indeed for a President to aspire to secrecy.

After ten minutes and a handful of people passed them by, a man came from the elevator shafts and marched through the black gates straight toward them. He was extremely tall and wiry, his dark hair thinning all over his head, and wore the thickest eyepiece Adelita had ever seen.

"Are you Mister Drefford?" Scott asked, extending his hand.

The man looked at it warily. "No. What business do you have with him?"

Scott eyed Adelita uncertainly. "My wife… Annabelle… is gravely ill. We came to learn of your organization and are desperate for your help."

"What do you know of our organization?" The man's voice did not shift in tonality at all. He was inspecting Scott as though he were a bug under a magnifying glass.

"Only that you have the means to increase the lifespan," Scott said, a bit more than was true.

"How do you know Mister Drefford?" the man asked flatly.

Scott did not have a prepared answer for that question. He floundered as he spat out "Ah… I've not met the man… I… uh… apologies, I did not get your name?"

"Nor will you. How do you know of Mister Drefford, then?"

"He… is a public figure; at least I thought so… I saw his name on some… documents…"

Adelita looked urgently at Scott. Do not link this inquiry to Gerard, Scott, *she thought desperately, but alas, humans had not science-d that ability out yet.*

"What manner of document?" the man pressed, his eyes taking on a much more alarmed appearance.

"Only a… lease… that he'd rented this office. I… I am employed with the City, you see."

Adelita had to fight not to roll her eyes. This would trace back to Gerard somehow.

"And from this lease you inferred that you could come here, utilizing his name to gain entry, access to our office." Again, his voice was flat. Scott nodded. "What afflicts your wife?"

"She has a cancer… of the feminine parts."

Adelita internally rolled her eyes hard.

The man looked her over. "The doctor can find no remedy?" Adelita shook her head. And then, for the first time, he smiled. "Would you be interested in an… alternative… therapy?"

Chapter Four

Adelita slammed a baggie of pills down on the table. *"Alternative therapy"*, she railed. "That is what they called it. What are these pills? They would not say."

"Okay," I said. "Slow down. Tell me what happened after you agreed to try the therapy."

"He took us up to their office. There was naught mysterious about it. An ordinary medical office. I could see nothing that warranted the secrecy they've cloaked it in. They poked and prodded me as doctors do. When they run my blood test they may see that I am not sick. They handed me these pills, instructed me to take two per day, one in the morning and one in the evening. They watched until I took one in their presence, and then shuffled us out as fast as they could. Eyes were fixed upon us the entire time we were there."

"And you never saw Phillip." Adelita shook her head. I picked up the baggie and turned it over in my hand. We would need to find an independent lab to analyze the contents of the pills. I hoped Adelita would not experience any effects from just the one. "So we know they are continuing the pattern… experiments on longevity… but… there must be legitimate agencies conducting work like this. Their secrecy suggests that they're doing something… illegitimate."

"Like grinding people up?" Quentin said sardonically. He swirled an empty glass in his right hand – we'd had some breakfast before Adelita got back. He was sitting across from me and dressed in the fashion of the time, a gray pinstripe pair of pants with matching suspenders over a white button-down shirt. A gray tie with black polka dots hung loosely off of his neck, and the jacket to his suit hung on the side of his chair.

Adelita frowned and shuddered. "Perhaps I'd not have a cancer if I lacked the cancerous body part. I'll not be trying any more to test that theory."

"Who did you meet? Anyone you could identify?" I asked.

Scott shrugged. "No one would say what he was called."

I sighed. So we knew they were some form of medical facility, but that was it. Not who Phillip was, nor how they'd come to trade secrets across time, nor what their relationship was to the "experiments" on Dohain.

"Then it is to me to uncover details of Phillip, as I have promised," Gerard, who was standing to my right, mused. Today he was wearing a tan suit with an olive-green tie that poked out above his buttoned-up jacket. "The difficulty, of course, will be my career. I am glad to connect us with those who have the information we need, but our inquiry into private citizens' personal information cannot be linked back to me."

I nodded. "Why do you have to do it? Tell me who to talk to, and I'll find out what we need to know."

"I can help too," Quentin volunteered, "if you need me."

"Who will we need to talk to?" I asked Gerard, "and will persuasion be necessary?"

"I would prefer if you'd not use our abilities on this man," Gerard requested. "He is clever and would wonder on his surprising dereliction of duty. Not that his mind would turn immediately to magic, he is too rational, but he would likely turn to investigating you. I know not if that is a risk you would be keen to take."

I tapped my fingers on the table. "If he investigated me, he would eventually find me." I paused and frowned. "1943 me. The me living in Manhattan who has no idea about any of this. So it's more than a personal risk."

Gerard nodded. "Yet persuasion can take other forms. I understand he is not averse to green paper."

Adelita crossed her arms. "You mean to say there is a second of you in this city? All this time?"

I nodded. "The me that lived through this time normally. 80-plus years ago, for... me-me," I patted my own chest. "Long before time travel... before I knew it was even possible."

"Her involvement in any sense would be a massive timeline violation," Quentin said. "We can work with money."

I felt myself sulk. "*You* can work with money."

Quentin heard what I meant in that sentence and frowned. "More easily. Yeah. You *could*, though... maybe... I don't know what the man would do..."

I rolled my eyes. "No, you don't know, which is why having you do it is the safer play."

Coretta, who had been leaning against the wall several feet to my rear, came up and put her arms around me from behind. She was still wearing her purple dress from the 1790s, but it didn't matter as she hadn't left the house. "Should it suit you better, I could do it?"

I laughed. "No. No, okay, let's stick with Quentin."

Coretta leaned in to my right ear. "Are you certain? I'm *very* persuasive."

I rubbed my face. "I know. Let's start with money though, okay?"

She unwrapped her arms from me and I could feel her shrug and smirk even though she stood behind me. "As you like."

"Tell me about this guy, Gerard," Quentin pressed.

Gerard pulled out the chair to my right and sat down. "His name is Robert Jenkins. Brown hair, wears gray suits most often. Keeps a blue kerchief in his jacket pocket. He maintains the City's Census records, among other data. He would at least be able to uncover Phillip Drefford's age, birthplace, residence, color. Perhaps other information as well."

"He works at City Hall?"

"No," Gerard said. "Nearby, in the municipal building. But he will not be there at night. You will need to seek him at home… or perhaps better, at his preferred bar on Chambers Street. Money and alcohol make for loose lips."

When we had last ventured to a bar with Gerard, it was one he knew – I hadn't asked how; perhaps his government contacts, or even Jimmy Walker's associates – but… the front door didn't hang open, let's say that. But now, the place on Chambers would be wide open to all, to an enthusiastic populace that had never been educated on how to drink properly but were eager to do so regardless.

Quentin reached in his pocket, but then pulled his hand out empty. "I'll need money from you, Gerard. I don't have the right bills."

I tried to remember what they'd looked like. "Were they so different?" I'd seen so many bills, so many permutations of monetary design, it was hard to keep track.

Quentin shrugged. "Not really, but the year of printing would have to be before now, and it's easier to take Gerard's money than to scrutinize every bill."

That was an interesting thought experiment. Putting a bill printed in, say, 1960, into the hands of someone natively living in 1943 would definitely be a timeline violation, but what would be the consequence? They'd have to notice the wrong year. And even if they did, most would assume it was a misprint. They'd have to take the bill to the mint and run the serial number to see that it had never actually been printed. Would anyone go to that length? And if they did, what would they do next? Probably nothing.

But, mint visit or not, there were conspiracy theorists out there. I thought back to life in the early 21st Century, life with access to all the world's knowledge on tiny handheld devices, and even then, there were people who believed that the Earth was flat. It was lunacy. Even when I was a child in the 1430s, most people didn't think the Earth was flat – despite what had come to be a commonly-held belief in the 21st Century, everyone in the 15th Century knew the Earth was a sphere. How would anyone have navigated boats if they thought otherwise? Putting a bill from 1960 in 1943 could give fuel to the loonies of the time… and that was the last thing anyone needed. Anti-intellectual forces had been pressing for power throughout time and had quite enough of it as it was.

Gerard fished in his own pockets and pulled out a disorganized wad of cash. He sifted through it and identified a slightly ragged $50 bill. "You may give him this upfront. If he asks for more," he sifted again, "here is more." He removed two $20 bills and a $10.

It was a *lot* of money for the time. The equivalent of at least a thousand in the 21st Century. "He could get in a lot of trouble if it's discovered he offered us this information," I said.

Gerard nodded. "Trouble with the city. Trouble with the organization. We do not know."

Quentin took the money, stood up, grabbed the jacket from his chair, and swung it on. He stuffed the money in the jacket pocket. "I'll bear that in mind." I expected he would turn to the door and head out, but he started collecting the empty glasses from the table and brought them into the kitchen.

It was 15… 1581? Fifteen-eighty-something. Coretta had begun soliciting seed funding for her charity. I was still living with her then, so I sometimes came along – not out of interest in fundraising, but because she insisted. She thought it would be good for me to learn some business sense. In reality, what I learned was that schmoozing rich men was not in my blood. That night we were at the lavish home of a prospect, and it seemed that Coretta would make the deal. And that I would be on my own getting home. The man – François Cravatte – I don't know why I remember his name – had stripped off his jacket and laid it lazily across the side of the long, dark blood-red tabletop. He was writing a promissory note, and Coretta had her right arm dangling over his left shoulder as he did.

She'd secured his business before flirting with him. It was important to her that the two interests stay separate – her work was her work and had to be pure in action as well as intent, and her sex life was something else. But if a business associate was *also* someone she considered attractive, well, why waste the opportunity?

Cravatte handed her the note, which she tucked in her small purple handbag. "Monsieur Cravatte," she said, "you will not regret your investment. And now that our business is adjourned… should you wish us to leave, we will, but if you are… available? I have nowhere else to be."

I started collecting glasses off the table – Cravatte's empty wine glass, and Coretta and my full ones. I brought them to his kitchen and began looking to see if there was any water around. I found a water pump over a steel basin and dumped the wine out of the glasses into the basin. I began pumping some water with my right hand while picking up the washing brush in my left.

I heard impossibly-soft footsteps behind me, and before I could turn around, Coretta was at my side.

"I'll head home," I said. "Will you be home tonight?"

Coretta raised her eyebrows, and I knew suddenly that she hadn't come to discuss tonight's plans. "Yes. What are you doing?" Her eyes darted over the glasses.

"Washing the glasses?"

She rolled her eyes. "For a man you do not know, in his house. You're his guest."

I shrugged. "True, but – it needs doing."

She scoffed at me. "Do you imagine he would wash the glasses in our house?"

I pushed the water pump back to its resting position. "No."

"So?"

I exhaled heavily. "That men wouldn't do something doesn't mean I shouldn't. We're nicer than they are." I believed that then, too, in a much more absolute way. Women were better people than men – plain and simple. Time taught me to generalize less, to see the good in some men. But it took a long time.

"Being nice ought to be reserved for those who would be nice in return."

I gestured back to the room I assumed Cravatte was still in. "He's giving you money."

She rolled her eyes again. "From which he'll receive money back. It is an investment, Vivian, not a gift." She sighed, and looked at me with one of her *looks* – this one was both soft and deep, her eyes gentle but seeing right through every fiber of me in a way that would make me extremely uncomfortable if it were anyone but her. "Be nice, but do not be gullible."

"It's just habit," I protested.

"*Habit*," she said derisively, flinging her hand out toward the sink, "is another word for *training*."

I clenched my hand into a fist around the horsehair brush. The hard hairs poked into my skin, drawing blood.

Coretta put her hand on my shoulder. "Be nice. Be the good person you are. But reserve it for those who deserve it. And most men do not."

I nodded. "I know." I stared down at the wet glasses.

I blinked, and I was back in New York. Coretta would change in her thinking over the years too. She did nice things for people, including men, as a daily part of her charity work. Once she launched it – it had been intended to help homeless and poor women and children, and mostly did, but as the years wore on, she met more and more men who cared for children as poor fathers and also needed help, men who brought her money not as investments but as gifts, men who wanted to help, who loathed the way women were treated. We learned together, in a lot of ways.

But to that very day, I had never seen a man clean up a house he didn't live in.

I got up and followed Quentin into the kitchen. The sink was opposite the entrance to the room, a silver metal basin and faucet installed atop a marble cabinet. I could hear the running water. Such an amazing development.

I walked up to his right side. "Want me to dry?" I asked.

He glanced quickly at me and smiled. "Sure," he said, and passed me a clean, rinsed glass.

I grabbed a dishtowel and started drying. "Why are you doing this?"

"What do you mean?" he asked absentmindedly.

"The glasses. Why are you washing them?"

He narrowed his eyes as though I'd asked why the glasses he held under the water were wet. "Because they're dirty?"

"But they're not yours, and this isn't your house."

He continued to look at me as though I was saying something very bizarre. "I thought it would be nice?"

I laughed and shook my head. Maybe it was bizarre. The world Coretta and I had been *trained* in, that world was bizarre. "It is."

Quentin continued to eye me oddly as he passed me the next glass. He didn't get why I was asking, and I really liked that he didn't. It wasn't odd at all to him to do this. In his world, it was completely ordinary for men to spontaneously do domestic chores in other people's houses, even with women around, as a nice thing to do. I envied him that world. I hoped I lived in it now. I didn't think that I did, day in and day out. But I'd enjoy this temporary view.

The Financial District was one of the last parts of Manhattan to be built up, an extension added to the island the way rich people might add rooms to a house. Mostly city officials had lived here, but over the years more and more buildings, taller and taller, were added and it was, for a time, a playground for the city's businesspeople. Though which businesspeople, and what that looked like, would change dramatically over time. Quentin had no particular attachment to the district, nor any time period in it, but did find human migration patterns extremely interesting. And it saddened him any time he saw another place become uninhabitable for average people.

Nonetheless, it was 1943, and he had to focus on that. His plan was to hopefully identify Robert on sight, and if not then to inquire with the bartender. He would sit across from Robert and get right to the point, making him the offer. Gerard had asked him not to use supernatural persuasion – not to compel him to accept the offer forcibly, shifting his thoughts directly like Obi-Wan stopping the Death Stick dealer. Though Quentin did not run the risk that Vivian did – there was no alternate version of himself living here to endure any consequences, and it would be difficult to identify him as he largely had no tracks in societal records except his birth and schooling – he didn't think it would be necessary anyway. Gerard hadn't asked him not to compel Robert to accept the offer in more subtle ways, and that would help the monetary offer go down more smoothly.

The exterior of the bar made it obvious on sight that it had been a speakeasy, and not one of the nicer ones run by the mafia. Dark brown, chipping wood; no windows; the door bearing some sort of metal bolt near the handle that now served no purpose. No, this had been a guy with a bathtub, and the alcohol was probably part actual-poison. If that guy still owned the place, that meant that the drinks were dirt cheap, which was certainly the draw.

The inside was no different. The place looked as though it had been hastily patched together in the aftermath of Prohibition to look legitimate in ways it had not needed to before. The bar, which had three sides and took up most of the small, dark room, had a new stone slab laid across the top, but underneath the stone, where people's knees would rest and scrape, it looked as run down as the exterior had. The stools had new fabric laid for people's sitting pleasure, but the legs of the stools looked as though they would not support larger men, and probably not average-sized men in another month.

On the third turn of the bar, the side farthest from the door, sat a man in a gray suit with a blue handkerchief. Quentin walked to the corner of that side and sat down, leaving one empty stool between himself and Robert.

The bartender, an Irish man with frizzy, short red hair and a moustache to match, approached him. Quentin realized he'd only brought the $100 Gerard gave him and not any smaller bills or change. Yet it would look odd to sit at a bar without a drink. Well, Gerard hadn't said anything about using persuasion on the bartender.

The bartender didn't speak but looked at Quentin expectantly. He struggled for a moment to remember what drinks had been popular at this time, in this place. "A gin rickey, please," he arrived at. The bartender nodded and turned to his bottles, so it was an acceptable choice.

Quentin tried to study Robert through the side of his eye. Gerard had said he worked for the City Census, but that didn't tell him anything about level, rank, reputation, wealth. That he liked money said nothing about those things either. Gray suit and blue handkerchief... the handkerchief slightly shone when the bar's lights hit it, suggesting a smooth, silky fabric, maybe silk itself. He glanced downward... shiny shoes too, probably leather, freshly shined. He inhaled slowly... through the smells of the bar, alcohol, stickiness, and dirt, he could smell cologne... something musky. Robert's hair was neat and cut into a fashionable style. All the physical indicators were that he had money...

But he could have just been presenting himself that way, to earn his peers' respect. He was sitting in a run-down bar, not a fancy one, and nowadays there was a choice. He got his drinks cheap, and he got them alone, no coworkers to be found. Would they *be seen in such a place? Would he want them to know he came here?*

The bartender placed the gin rickey in front of Quentin and finally spoke: "Cash or tab?"

Quentin placed his hand on the drink and met the bartender's eyes. "You want to encourage first-timers to return. This drink is on the house."

The bartender blinked. "Yeah. I got this one."

As the bartender turned away, Quentin turned his thoughts back to Robert. Something his father said to him a long time ago, one bright morning they had found themselves on a planet that had been completely overrun by the rich, echoed in his mind. "Men present themselves how they wish to be seen, how they wish you to think of them. If you want to persuade them, they need to see that image of themselves in your eyes." That visit was when Quentin had decided that the pursuit of money would never be important to him. He saw there what it turned people into. That planet... had it been called Carnith?... had once been much like Earth in its diversity of people, but, through a century of political manipulation and war, the rich had created such a remarkable divide of wealth that the poor mostly starved to death or died from treatable diseases, and that meant that only the members of Carnith's socially-dominant race and religion survived. And yet they still were not content; when Quentin was there, the survivors were aligned against one another in a sort of wealthy tribal warfare... even though everyone had plenty, everyone seemed to believe that anyone else's gain was their loss.

Quentin shook his head. Whatever Robert's social status, he wanted to be seen as prosperous, so prosperous he would be. "You're Robert Jenkins," he said matter-of-factly.

Robert's head snapped to the side to look at him. "Who's asking?"

Quentin smiled and turned on all the charm he could muster. "Your reputation precedes you. There are rumblings that you have a bright future in the City government. That one day you could even be Mayor."

Robert stared at Quentin for a long moment, and then his face swelled with pride. "You've heard that? From whom?"

Quentin shrugged. "Oh, many people. It's understood. Many are envious."

Robert bit his lower lip. "I've not seen you around."

Quentin nodded. "I work in City Hall, not the municipal building." Robert seemed satisfied by that. "I was hoping to find you here. I understand that you have access to the City's Census records... all the more proof of your influence, that you could have access to such personal data. I am... in need of aid, and willing to compensate you." He reached in his pocket and pulled out the $50. He laid it on the bar between himself and Robert.

Robert eyed the bill eagerly, but reined himself in. "What aid do you seek?"

"Information on a man. Phillip Drefford. I know he is the president of a company called Society for Longevity, but nothing beyond that, and I have to know more. Though I can't say anything about why."

Robert frowned. "That information is secure. I can find it easily but if I gave it to you..."

"You would get in a lot of trouble if anyone found out. I know. That is why I offer you a significant sum. But... here, for your trouble." Quentin reached into his pocket again and placed one of the $20 bills on top of the $50.

Robert reached out and fingered the bills. "If you are willing to give this, you'd be willing to give... $100?"

Quentin nodded and pulled out the rest of the money. He was relieved that Robert had stopped at that amount. Not that he couldn't have promised the delivery of more at a later date, or upon receipt of Phillip's information.

Robert took the wad of money. "Phillip Drefford, you say?" Quentin nodded. "I'll look him up tomorrow. Meet me back here tomorrow night and I'll have what I can find. If you can bring another... $50, say... I might be able to find a lot."

Quentin smiled. "That seems reasonable."

Chapter Five

"Another $50?" Gerard had grumbled. "That is more than what would be reasonable for the task."

Yet he'd given it, and the next night, the 22nd, Quentin returned to the bar to get the information. He met us back at Adelita's house at midnight, when it was just turning to the 23rd, the day of the deed.

He flopped down on Adelita's recliner and immediately loosened the tie he was wearing, one with a gray background and dark blue swirls. "Phillip Drefford is a 'Caucasian' man born in 1891, which puts him around 52. He was naturalized, born in Germany."

I appreciated the way he said *Caucasian*… not many people knew that it was a garbage, racist term that had nothing to do with actual ethnicity. "But Drefford doesn't sound particularly German," I noted.

Adelita shrugged. "People often change their names when they arrive here. Who may know what he was called before?"

Quentin nodded. "The records don't say. They do say that he lives in an apartment in the very same building the Society's office was in, and there's some evidence that the apartment is paid for *by* them."

"He had to do some extra digging for that bit," I observed. The Census didn't track leases.

Quentin smirked and shrugged. "I guess the extra $50 was *reasonable* for something." Gerard raised his eyebrows at that but said nothing.

"So we know he's highly placed in the company, but we knew that already," I mused. "But what we learned is that his life is completely entangled with the company. He lives near its office, on its dime."

"Living under their eye," Adelita added, "he's not likely to be a vampire. Would seem he permits himself to be supervised far too much."

I nodded. "So the meeting being at night is not due to him in that way. Maybe he has a colleague?"

"Or," Coretta piped up – she had been lounging idly on the work desk's chair that turned out to have a leg rest – "perhaps his days are full of other tasks. Research, meetings, all manner of things. And we know not who requested this meeting. Perhaps it was arranged by Geoffrey. Perhaps there is something… illicit… about it. Even for the Society."

That was an interesting possibility. "That would explain why things don't line up. Why they could have notes on virology while researching humours. Something is being done that's… unauthorized."

Adelita coughed, a slightly mucous-filled sound. "I believe the actions of the Society for Longevity are quite enough trouble without other intervention."

I looked her over. She didn't appear any different… no signs of sickness like becoming pale, having a red nose, or exuding heat. "How do you feel?" I asked.

She shrugged. I heard her heart begin to race. "I feel fine," she said, and it wasn't a lie, but she was still clearly anxious.

I narrowed my eyes at her. She'd not-lied to me before.

"As of now," she said, and her voice became as nervous as her heart. "But I am afraid. Am I wrong to be?"

I shook my head. "No. You'd be crazy not to be."

I glanced over at Scott, sitting at the table, mostly ignoring the rest of us while reading. He was munching on a sandwich that he'd asked Adelita to make him. Did he realize that this was partly on him? Adelita had told me how things had gone at the Society –

that he claimed her idea of being sick, that he volunteered her to be the sick one, that he suggested her *feminine parts*. They should have… I don't know, flipped a coin or something. And certainly Adelita should have gotten to choose which part of herself was diseased.

Quentin stood up from the recliner. "There's one last thing we can try before the meeting. Now that I have a name, and a company, and a bit of information, I can try to track them, or him, through the vortex. See where else they've been. Or where they came from."

It was a good idea. "I'll come with you." I held up Geoffrey's notepad. "This might help, too."

The two of us retreated to the Time Sphere. "Do you want to try the notebook first?" Quentin asked.

I shrugged. "The button worked to track Geoffrey. Does it respond to physical objects more than thoughts?"

Quentin shook his head. "Not especially. The Sphere doesn't care about the form of the thing. It's all energy and matter."

It was worth a try. I walked over to the console and pressed the notepad to the screen.

Nothing happened.

I stepped back and put the notebook down on the side of the console. "Geoffrey is dead; we've been to Dohain. It could have sent us to when Geoffrey wrote his note…"

"Paradox," Quentin observed. "He'd see us before the first time he saw us."

I shrugged again. "Wouldn't have to… we could go to Dohain earlier, see what they were doing…"

Quentin walked up alongside me. "We did see what they were doing. And we more or less know why. Longevity." He sighed. "What we need to know is how, and who."

"So the book doesn't give any clues to the Society, its origins or structure. Does that mean Geoffrey didn't know either?"

Quentin shook his head. "But Phillip probably does." He leaned forward toward the console and put his hand on the screen. "Show us what Phillip knows about the Society. Where… when… did the Society begin?"

Nothing happened.

Quentin frowned. "Where is the Society's leader?"

Nothing.

"Where does the Society keep its findings?"

Nothing.

"Where is the Society's main office?"

Silence.

Quentin's shoulders slumped. "Am I asking bad questions?"

I frowned. "Maybe Phillip doesn't know either?"

Quentin huffed. "Forget Phillip. Show me the Society's headquarters."

Still nothing.

"Show me something of importance to the Society. *Anything.*"

Did the Sphere have a battery that needed charging? It had never been so… quiet… before. Quentin took his hand off the console and sulked.

"Has it ever done this before?" I asked. "Not responded to you?"

He shook his head. "Never. It's acting as though there… *aren't*… answers to my questions. How could that be?"

I put my hand on his arm. "There must be. But maybe we don't know enough yet to ask them correctly? To ask about the right things? We'll learn more from Phillip, and then try again."

Quentin nodded silently, but didn't seem satisfied by my resolution. I hoped I was right… Phillip was now our best, and for now only, path to learning anything more.

She pushed the newspaper aside, not looking at its headline. Newspapers were dangerous. She turned to the book Gerard had given her chronicling his studies on the nature of darkness. It was supposed to "bring her up to speed", an English colloquialism she had to infer meant to get her to the same place, knowledge-wise, as the rest of them. She chuckled to herself and pushed it aside too.

Coretta had retreated to a tiny office/library on the second floor of Adelita's house. The room was lined with bookcases and books of all sorts, and had at its center a round table, which is where she sat. There was no place for her at the moment in what they were doing. The meeting would be soon, and it was fruitless until then. Vivian and Quentin were trying to track the group through the time vortex, but Coretta knew they would fail. Right now, she had nothing to do but wait.

Less time than she thought. She heard the door creak open and saw in her peripheral vision Quentin walking in. "Nothing, then?"

He shook his head. "Whoever they are, they're great at covering their tracks. The Sphere was acting like they didn't exist. Like the questions I was asking about them were nonsense, or had no answers."

Coretta nodded. "Sophisticated magic."

Quentin sat noisily in the chair to her left. "It's not any kind of magic I've ever seen." He sighed and ran his hand through his hair. "Nothing makes any sense."

Coretta nodded again and shrugged. "You will come to it in time. I have faith."

Quentin leaned in toward her. "We will, will we? Is that a fact?" Coretta raised her eyebrows at him and he sat back in his chair again. "I get it. You're perceptive. You notice the details that tell you more about people and events than most others realize. But this isn't that. When you saw Gerard and Scott that very first night... yeah, maybe I should have picked up on the cues. And maybe you could have in much less time, five minutes even. But you were standing in front of them for five seconds. That's not perceptive.

That's... you know more than you're saying. And your English is really... late. 20th or 21st Century English. There's no reason you should know that unless you've been exposed to it before. And, you didn't seem sick at all in the Sphere. Like you'd traveled in it before already, and gotten used to it."

Coretta tapped her fingers on the table. "And?"

Quentin shook his head and then shrugged. "And... I don't know. How much more do you know?"

Coretta smirked. "On what scale?"

Quentin sighed heavily. "I know better than to ask you what's going to happen to us. But... can't you say anything? There must be something we could do better."

Coretta felt herself reflexively frown. "Is there? Yes, there are bad things. That is life. And there are..." she sighed, "very bad things. But if I undo those, if their undoing is possible, what else do I undo? How much good? And what right do I have either way?" She leaned her arms on the table. "Every choice you make leads to good and it leads to bad. If you made other choices, they would lead to good and they would lead to bad. Maybe more of one and less of the other. But I could never know in advance. The outcomes of your choices are yours... yours to choose, and yours to live with."

Quentin frowned. "Your choice of words is interesting. 'Yours to live with.'"

Coretta nodded slowly. "And every bit intentional."

"Does Vivian know?"

Coretta laughed. "Which part? That I know more than I let on? That has always been true, even without time travel. So yes, she knows that aspect. Does she know that I have seen parts of her future, in the flesh, not only in my mental inferences and extrapolations?" She paused. "I do not think so. She senses something is amiss, but I do not think she knows the extent. But she will. Eventually."

Quentin bit his lip. "You won't tell her? Knowing that I know?"

Coretta shook her head. "No. She'll come to it another way when the time is right."

Quentin stood up slowly. "Do you know why I can't track this group through the vortex?"

Coretta smirked. "Yes. But knowing why won't help you find them."

His shoulders sagged. He started walking toward the door, but paused just in front of it. "They're really horrible, aren't they? Dangerous, immoral... evil."

Coretta didn't look at him. She didn't want him to see what was in her eyes. "Evil is in the eye of the beholder."

There was a long moment of silence. "You should tell her," Quentin said. "You shouldn't have to bear the burden on your own." And then the door clicked shut.

Coretta reached in her bag and fumbled out her stash of rolled tobacco. "No need," she mumbled under her breath, "you're going to tell her for me."

*   *   *   *   *

Scott sat on the deep purple couch, loosened his tie, and then leaned back on his hands, his fingers brushing the fabric, tracing lighter lines in their path. The light from the chandelier sparkled in his blond hair, making it seem silvery.

"You seem upset, Gerard," Scott said. "Is something the matter?"

Gerard shook his head. "It is nothing." But that wasn't true. Worry plagued his mind, worry about Adelita. He didn't want to tell Scott, who already envied Gerard's attention to the girl. But she seemed ill, and he was certain it was to do with that pill.

That pill that she took on an errand for Vivian.

Yes, Adelita had volunteered to go. But that was her way, a kind heart looking to help. Gerard didn't think that Vivian had meant harm to come to her, but she also didn't think through the *possible harm either. He wondered if Vivian remembered how vulnerable human women were.*

"Are you tired?" Scott asked, shaking Gerard from his thoughts.

Gerard smiled and shook his head. "No. There remains an hour until sunrise." He sat down next to Scott. "Are you? You keep odd hours to stay awake with me."

"Not at all," Scott breathed, and Gerard felt his blood quicken. It had been a very long time since he had been in a relationship. He had a... friend... whom he would call on sometimes, and who would write him scandalous notes to tease him into calling, but that had ended when the fellow moved for work. It was the closest thing, yet it was not close at all.

"Good," Gerard said, and leaned in toward Scott. "Scott... promise me something. You will take care when dealing with the Society? I would prefer you stay away from them altogether, if possible."

Scott tilted his head sweetly. "I will be cautious, as I hope you will be?"

Gerard nodded and leaned in still closer, his face just an inch from Scott's lips. "Always."

Scott lowered his eyes sheepishly, and then raised them to meet Gerard's. He leaned in and kissed him, softly but firmly, and Gerard was happy Scott had taken the initiative. He cupped his right hand on the back of Scott's head, feeling his silky hair between his fingers. As their kissing became deeper, more insistent, Gerard could feel a different desire rising in himself. He pulled away a few inches and turned his head down.

"Have I done something wrong?" Scott asked, his voice quiet and tight.

Gerard shook his head but didn't look up. "No, not at all. It is only that... I do not wish to hurt you."

Scott was silent for a long moment, but then put two fingers under Gerard's chin and lifted his head. Gerard sighed as Scott stroked his cheek, and saw Scott's eyes dart from his eyes to his mouth and back again.

"Gerard," Scott began, "I trust you." He inclined his head to Gerard's right and leaned forward.

Gerard clenched his teeth. "Are you certain?" he murmured through mostly-closed lips.

Scott nodded. "I am."

The invitation was itself arousing, and it would have been so easy to seize Scott and lose himself in the moment. But he wanted it to be gentle, a good experience for Scott too. He leaned in and kissed under Scott's ear, just under that, and then another kiss or two down until he was nestled in the perfect spot where the blood pulsed and throbbed. Then, with as much tenderness as he could muster, he bit. He heard Scott gasp, but softly, and his breath quickened.

It was always good… always a sort of rapture… but with the physical attraction and care he felt for Scott, it was nothing sort of ecstasy. But he kept his mind with him, not only to control himself, but also so that he could put his right hand on Scott's knee. And as Scott's breath quickened more, he moved it up his leg, just a bit at a time. Scott never stopped him, and finally there was no further to go. Scott took the cue and returned the favor.

It didn't take long for the ecstasy to reach crescendo, and it was good timing as Scott couldn't afford more blood loss anyway. Gerard looked at Scott's face, which was pale but happy.

Scott kissed him, and then smiled. "I knew I could trust you."

Gerard smiled too. "I will never hurt you. And I will always protect you. Against anything." Or anyone, he thought.

*   *   *   *   *

Adelita rubbed her eyes as she walked toward the bathroom. It was the morning of the meeting with Drefford and she could no longer sleep. She was not tired. She had not felt tired in two days.

Adelita removed her nightgown and turned to step in her new, beautiful shower – she remarked again the power of human ingenuity, and thought how incredible access to the stream of hot water was – and as she did, something caught her eye in the mirror. She turned her head and saw that there was a dark red rash wrapping from her pubic area to her right hip. She touched it gingerly. It did not hurt... it was oddly smooth compared to the rest of her skin. She pressed lightly on the part of the rash on her lower belly, and underneath felt... hard. Not a lump, but a flat mass, as though under the rash were a strip of metal.

She had only taken the one pill. What would taking more have done to her? What was the end goal of this biological transformation? Would it heal on its own?

... or would she need help? She was friends with vampires. Their blood could heal, couldn't it? Vivian's blood, in small annual doses, was keeping her alive and youthful longer than was natural to her. Would more be able to heal this rash?

Adelita felt her heart sink. If the Society for Longevity found out that they were vampires... what would they do with that knowledge? She looked again at her wound. Her friends were at risk; did they realize it?

Adelita turned to the shower and stepped in. She would let the rash do what it would for the time. If the Society located her, being unexpectedly well would be a red flag for them. It was a risk she could not take.

Chapter Six

I had bought a new dress for the meeting, a red one that came to mid-calf. It had slightly padded shoulders and puffed short sleeves, a faux belt at the waist, and a large bow at the inflection point of the V-neck. With it came a matching red hat that was like a thickly-textured beret, and I added a similarly-matching red handbag with a short gold-plated chain. I also bought a pair of brown shoes with a small heel and interlaced bows across the tops. Gerard was getting a little bit annoyed with financing our various expenses, but still mostly stayed quiet about it. Under his generally-calm demeanor, I could see something simmering, like ocean waves before a storm. But he never exploded, nor broke stride. What was making him boil that way?

Our plan for meeting Phillip was… bad. It was all we could do, but it wasn't much of a plan at all. We'd approach invisibly to scope out the area, to see whether he'd brought allies, to try to get a sense of their abilities. Then we would retreat and approach normally with the knowledge of what we were getting into. But we didn't know what we would say to him, mostly because we didn't know what he would say to us. We only knew that we had Geoffrey's findings, both from 1795 and from Dohain, as discrepant as they were. And we knew we wanted to know more about the Society for Longevity. And we'd get that information with whatever means necessary.

Gerard had made Scott stay back, but Adelita insisted on coming, which created an awkward tension between them that I hadn't noticed before… but at the same time it was clear to me that this tension wasn't new. It wasn't that Scott wanted to come, but he was deeply peeved that Adelita would come while he would not. And Adelita seemed to take pleasure in his frustration, which made me wonder what he had done to earn that. Scott had never done anything overtly sexist, not to me anyway… but I could trivially overpower him if needed, whereas Adelita could not.

Men's relative physical power had always seemed to make them feel that they were also more… personally powerful… that they were essentially better, stronger, not just in their muscles but in their very being. And since they had that power, they had to use it, and often to hurt, to establish dominance. If I was reading this right… Scott seemed flustered by Adelita's assertion of power, that she would do something Scott wasn't being "allowed" to do (though there was nothing exactly stopping him from saying no to Gerard). Was he flustered by my power too, but smart enough not to show it? Or had he decided that I was… something else. Not really a woman, so not someone he had to be stronger than to prove himself?

Not-really-a-woman was a variant on not-really-a-person. Unfortunately, only-a-woman was also a variant on not-really-a-person. I was familiar with both kinds, and neither was particularly good. I'd have to confirm all this with Adelita, but if Scott was indeed being hostile to her for being her badass self, someone was going to have to talk to him about it.

Coretta, strangely, volunteered to stay behind with Scott. She had come to 1943 to learn about the Society and stop them from harming others, but she didn't want to come to the very meeting where we could learn most about them? She claimed that Scott shouldn't be left "unattended with danger afoot", but that was even more odd. It wasn't like her to value protecting a mortal man she barely knew. I made a mental note to ask her later, in private, what was going on. Did she see more of what was going on with him and Adelita than I did? It wouldn't be surprising; she saw more of everything.

So it would be me, Quentin, Gerard, and Adelita meeting Phillip and who knew who else. I brought Geoffrey's notepad, tucked away in my matching red bag, and we began our journey. After the lengthy drive, we left Gerard's car a few blocks away on Fulton Avenue and walked the rest of the way. About a block back from the entrance to the bath house, Gerard summoned what shadows he could to cloak himself, and I took Quentin and Adelita's hands and made us all invisible.

As we approached the concrete staircase that rose to meet the main entrance archway, red brick with towers on either side of the arch, I could feel the hair on my arms and neck stand up on end.

It didn't matter that we were invisible – the spell our presence set off hit us all just the same. Over the course of several seconds, my muscles felt as though they were being frozen from the inside out. My limbs locked in place, and I felt the same happening to the others, Quentin and Adelita's hands becoming tense and firm in mine. The freezing locked my blood, too, and I couldn't hold the invisibility anymore. We appeared, and Gerard emerged from shadows a moment later. When I saw Adelita, I panicked, though more in my mind than my body – my blood was having trouble throbbing its way through my veins. The rest of us could survive sub-zero freezing. Could she?

Two men and one woman stepped out from under the arch onto the stairs that we had not yet begun to ascend. They had been invisible too and their opacity came on slowly, as though they were cloud creatures slowly solidifying. One man fit the vague description of Phillip – tall, White, German features, a broad nose and shoulders – and the others I did not know. Despite the silliness of it, I was a little disappointed none of them were wearing lab coats. Phillip wore a light blue button-down shirt and navy slacks, while the other man had chosen a maroon shirt and black trousers. The woman wore a tan long-sleeved blouse and a long brown skirt that almost looked tweed.

They were smart to set off a spell like this – we could hardly attack them in this state. But nor could we move our jaws to speak. Fortunately, I didn't need that. It was harder than usual because getting my blood to do *anything* was a challenge, but this wasn't zero degrees Kelvin, so I had some energy to work with. I focused every ounce of willpower on getting out two sentences:

Unfreeze Adelita, or you'll kill her. And then when I unfreeze, and I will, I will kill you.

I went for Phillip's mind, figuring he was the one in charge. His eyes widened a bit – he didn't know I had such a power – but after studying me carefully for a minute walked over to Adelita. He looked her over too, and then touched her gently on the top of her head. Slowly she began to defrost.

And the moment her jaw came unlocked, she used it. "Bastard!" she shouted, rubbing her arms forcefully, and then she began to cough.

"Sit," Phillip said, his voice coming out with a slight accent I wasn't expecting. It was similar to German but… there was something else too. "I am sorry; I had thought you were all immortals. You will recover but you must take it slowly." The more he spoke, the more I thought his accent might be Yiddish.

Adelita didn't grow any less angry at his words and attempted to punch him, but her knuckles cracked loudly when she folded them into a fist and she hissed in pain. Resigned, she sat on the stair.

"A colleague of mine, whose name shall remain unsaid, informed me that you were seeking information about me," he said, and when he said 'you', he cast his eyes toward Quentin. "Geoffrey is not with you, nor, I gather, did he tell you of me." And then Phillip did the last thing I expected – he too sat down on the steps, and he sighed, his face transforming from confidence to a sorrowful relief. "Thank goodness. It is too much."

His male companion, who was a Black man likely around 40 years old with soft eyes, the kind of broad lips Coretta would call "kissable", and deep brown hair, walked down the stairs to stand at his side. "Phillip, the knowledge would be good. They'd have centuries to work with it. Think what we could learn."

Phillip scowled. "At what cost, Nicky? At what cost…"

Nicky kneeled in front of him. "Shh, don't say such things. We have a bigger purpose; don't forget that." The remaining companion said nothing but gazed at Phillip in annoyance.

They stopped talking, and I couldn't learn more like this. *If you unfreeze us, I promise we won't eat you. Scout's honor.*

Phillip looked at me, his face still pained. "I do not know what you will do. Why are you here? For whom do you work? Not..." and then his voice turned hushed, "*her*, or you'd have known who I am with no aid. Not Geoffrey. Then who?"

I didn't know who "her" was, and I didn't know what answer would sway this scientist-mage, but I did know that he was a man who seemed to care about the *how* of what he did, not just the *why.*

I work for the women and children Geoffrey killed to learn about bodily humours. I work for the people who were ground into bits for experiments. I don't care what you've done before. I want to help you do the right thing now.

Phillip stared at me again, this time his nose and cheeks scrunching. I had hit a nerve. He stood, walked over to me, and touched my head. I felt warmth passing through me, filling one fiber at a time, flowing through my limbs to the tips of my toes. I instantly called my blood to heal me, and it did, sending the warmth through me even faster.

I cleared my throat and shook the last ice pieces free. "Better," I said, trying not to scowl at Phillip; that would get us nowhere. "Now, while you unfreeze my friends, why don't you tell me what good it does you to learn about bodily humours from a man from 1795?"

"None," Phillip said as he began executing on my request. "It was all pretense. We have to maintain the time stream."

Nicky stood up abruptly. "You should not tell them these things, Phillip. What if *she* finds out?"

"No one can hear anything we say here, not with their ears and not with their minds," I said. "My friend you are unfreezing now can describe it better, but suffice it to say that mages are not the only ones who can put up wards," I snarked, hoping they had survived the freezing because they weren't precisely attached to Gerard.

Phillip glanced around and nodded. "Darkness wards. Very effective. Very dangerous. You risk your immortal souls toying with this."

I frowned. "I believe all of us here have done things to risk that." I had read him right; Phillip's face sunk at that.

"Horrors I cannot speak," he nonetheless choked out as Gerard came to life again and he moved on to Quentin. "Geoffrey believed that he was to share data on humours with us, as you say. And we would have pretended to be interested, and given him our own data… data we would say was equal in quality, but was far more advanced than his, yet redacted and rephrased to be understood in his time, by his scientists."

Even though Quentin was still half frozen, I could see he was fighting to speak. I knew what he would say. "You play a dangerous game messing with the time stream that way. Redacted or not."

Phillip nodded. "Yet it is how we can learn what can enhance and lengthen life far more quickly. Geoffrey would use our knowledge to build on his own, and when I would return to my office from our meeting, there would be a new book, containing centuries of new data, extraordinary work, taking us so much further than we had been before."

I thought about what I knew of Geoffrey's work. Besides the 'humours' research, he had that report from Dohain, which was from *Phillip's* future. That wasn't redacted at all.

Quentin must have had the same thought, because as he unfroze, he squeaked out "not everyone is such a *professional* at redacting! He had raw data from the future! That could be catastrophic!"

Phillip frowned, and the woman with him, a very slight, very short brunette with wiry glasses and short curls that came just below her ears, scoffed. "We oughtn't be surprised. Geoffrey did not care for our ethics. He wanted to be 'the one', the man who would solve the puzzle of immortality. Say what you will of *her*; she ought never have placed him as manager of Region 248.4. That he would have stolen unauthorized data from the future would be no shock."

Phillip nodded somberly. "Have these stolen data penetrated his time period?"

I shook my head. "We recovered them once he returned from the future. But… whatever system you have in place of exchanging data across time is very, very dangerous if there can be slipups like this."

"Few have as high authorization as Geoffrey did, though it is worrisome that someone of his sort could gain access," Phillip mused. "If he had provided us with data from our futures… even if we were to balk at the timeline violation, it would be in our minds permanently, and we could not help but use it."

"Perhaps it is the access that led to his corruption," Gerard speculated. "Power breeds nefarious deeds, and if he could travel through time with impunity…"

I was traveling through time with impunity, but I appreciated Gerard's point. "So we understand why Geoffrey was meeting you here, and what he hoped to gain. And what you hoped to gain. So, there remains one question – why *are* you telling me this? And why have you become remorseful now?"

Phillip returned to the stairs and sat again next to Nicky. "I lost my wife seven years ago. It was not long after that *she* came to me. She promised that my knowledge could help us understand how to create the perfect immortality – a way to never die, not by disease, not by injury, not by any means. So that no one would have to lose their beloved again. Initially the project seemed innocent enough. We studied the patterns and habits of those who lived into their 100s. We studied medicines and therapies. We studied spells, yet it was mages who died the fastest no matter what longevity spells we tried." Ah, Gerard had explained this to me… mages' power was drawn from the soul. The more spells they cast, and the more powerful spells they cast, the more life it sucked from them until they had nothing left. "And then… then she directed us to use *their* research. She said that they were pushing the boundaries of experimentation. That their ideas and methods could inform our work." Phillip took in a heavy breath. "And it was all horror. What they do to people…" he sniffled thickly, and Nicky patted his arm.

"I tried to justify to myself that we could save infinite lives with this work, that those who suffered would not have done so in vain. And yet with each day I cannot look upon myself in the mirror. I cannot think upon myself without disgust. We endeavor to save lives and yet I do so by destroying my own soul. I wish to escape but I fear what she will do to me to keep me from leaving with this knowledge, with knowledge of her and what they do."

"Phillip," Nicky chimed in, "you are not conducting their research. If you choose not to use it to further your own knowledge, it will not make their deeds cease. It will go on, and yet do no good for humanity at all."

Their...

Oh God. It was 1943.

The Nazis.

I wanted to say… something. *It will only go on as long as no one stops it.* Something. But I had to be a better time traveler than they were. My mouth opened, and then shut. I looked at Quentin helplessly. He seemed lost in thought.

"It will go on," Phillip asserted, his voice straining through mucus. "Nicky, they have only begun. You know as I do…" his voice trailed off.

People in the early 21st century were sometimes taught about the Holocaust and World War II, but only as a very brief note, and there were things the history books didn't capture. Children were taught that the world was a chaos of war until the heroic United States stepped in. And that was… partly true. But when you asked why the United States waited so long to get involved, the response was something to the effect of, we didn't know about the camps, or we didn't know the Japanese would come for *us*. The first was a bald-faced lie; Americans knew perfectly well about the camps. The second was glossed over but cut to the core of the issue. We didn't get involved because we knew, but it wasn't *us*, so we didn't care. There were protesters for years before the US entered the war saying that we shouldn't, that we should be isolationist, that we should mind our business. We turned away refugees. We closed the door to refugee children, and everyone knew. Every American who could read a newspaper knew what was happening but we didn't go to war until it was at our doorstep.

But these people weren't military; they were scientists, and they were working for… well, I didn't know, but not Hitler, and I didn't think the Nazis in general either. So who?

"And… *she*… won't do anything to stop the Nazis? She'll just use their data and let them be?"

Nicky pursed his lips. "She hates the Nazis. But if we can use their research to help others…"

The short brunette with glasses scoffed. "You have no sense of what she thinks. You've not met her, nor have I."

I frowned. "Have any of you met her?" They shook their heads. "What's her name?"

Phillip laughed. "We do not know. No one knows."

"Only those with the highest clearance know her personally," Nicky added. "But I have to imagine she hates the Nazis. I… I have to."

Glasses-lady seemed increasingly outraged. "Why do you tell them this? You jeopardize our mission with each word. They are not authorized to know any of it!"

"Helen," Phillip said, and then he paused, his face falling. "I am tired. You… you have the heart for this mission. You can overlook the 'how' and focus on the good, the 'why'. I cannot. Not any longer. Perhaps I am too old."

Or perhaps he's *Jewish*? Did they not know? I tried to remember. Many Jews came to New York after World War II, but there had been many here before then too. But there was a lot of prejudice. Most of what people "knew" was lies, things made up to demonize the Jewish people. It was a perplexing but longstanding form of bigotry… I could remember hatred toward the Jews going back centuries. So if Phillip was hiding his ethnic origins or his faith, it was easy to understand.

He needed an out, but Helen had an in.

"It's longevity research, then," I prodded. "Geoffrey's notes from the future suggested as much. You won't be surprised to find that we," I gestured at my friends, "have a keen interest in longevity. Was Geoffrey to bring one of our kind here? This meeting is oddly late."

Phillip nodded. "He had a colleague who is as you are. One who would be better positioned to interpret the science he found. For his time, in any case."

Probably dead, with all of those Coretta's ninjas killed.

"Though you were only expecting science about humours. Geoffrey had science that was much better than that. From the future. That I read."

Helen's eyes perked up, which was what I was hoping for.

"And it's not a timeline violation because I *am* from the future. I'm from *your* future, in fact, so I can do even more with that science. So... is that something *she* would be interested in?"

Helen let a smile slip out. "I am certain of it. Do you have the training necessary?"

I wasn't trying to pretend I did. "No... but she would? Or, she would know who would. Who she could assign the work to?" Gerard remained silent, not offering his skills. Perhaps he wanted to see how this played out.

Helen nodded, but then frowned. "I know not how to reach her to ask. She sends us orders and information requests. We do not have direct contact."

"Do you store your information somewhere in particular? That she would know about?"

"Our offices," Helen shrugged. "It's simply that she has better things to do with her time than hunt down the data herself. We study it, compile it, share it. She receives the end product, any important revelations only."

Important revelations… I looked at Quentin, who was looking at me as though he was having the same thought. Early-21st-century science *would* seem like quite the revelation for the 1940s… and if we offered anything good enough to get her attention, we could call her out.

But it would have to be something that wouldn't disrupt the timeline if found. Their security was obviously not what it needed to be.

And… would it be enough to cut off the head? Or could this whole operation continue without *her*, whoever she was?

We needed to know so much more. How many units were there? How far was their reach? It sounded massive, from the very-particular coding system. If they're assigning decimal points to regional code numbers, they're being precise, and were those regions time-based as well as spatial? Did region leaders communicate? How? What were the systems in place? To what extent was this effort centralized or not? And who *did* get to know who *she* was? How did she maintain her relative anonymity?

Too many questions. We had to work with what we knew.

And I knew I would have to tread gently.

"I'm surprised you haven't met her, Helen. You seem to know a lot, and to be the most committed to this mission of anyone here."

Helen swelled at that. "That much is true. Sadly commitment does not translate to rank."

"No?" I prodded. "Surely *she* would help you advance, to better serve her."

Helen scowled. "She would need to know me first. To *see* me. Yet, so much goes on, it is a challenge to get her attention. I would need an opportunity of great magnitude, and I've been working under Phillip for five years without one arising."

I nodded slowly. "Perhaps we can all have what we want today. Phillip… you seem so tired. Have you considered retiring, and turning your role over to Helen? Then she could have the visibility she craves."

Phillip seemed alarmed at my suggestion, which answered my question – was he staying in his role to keep Helen from doing harm? While formally retiring might keep his family safe from the consequences of outright defection, it would grant Helen power.

I looked him in the eyes. *She will lead us to her. And we will take them down. They must be stopped. Retire and be safe with your family.*

Phillip quickly looked at his hands and sighed. With his head still down, he said, "I haven't. But I should. I *am* tired." He looked up at me, his eyes pleading to me. I nodded.

"You should," I said, and turned to Helen. "And as your first project in your new role…" I took Geoffrey's notebook from my purse, "the future." Helen smiled broadly, and I smiled too. She started to move toward me, hands obviously outstretched for the notebook, but I quickly returned it to my bag. "It's not redacted. We still must follow her ethics, right?" Helen stopped in her tracks and frowned, but reluctantly nodded. "But if *I* know it, and use it in a way that furthers science *now*, but doesn't reveal anything timeline-violating, we're safe. Right?" Helen's eyes widened, and she nodded again, this time eagerly.

I did not actually think we were safe.

Phillip looked at me nervously. "If you mean to work with Helen, with our lab, you must know… Helen and Nicky's unit… we hold ourselves to high ethical standards there. But… there are other units that do not… another laboratory that does not. Should you encounter them… you should know what you will face."

This was getting to the meat of it, to the darkest parts of the work. I felt certain he meant the lab Adelita had gone to. "I'm sure they only do what's necessary for the larger mission, saving everyone's life in the long-term," I said, trying to string Helen along, "but yes, it would be good to be prepared."

Phillip turned his eyes from me and looked at the ground. "There are many studies that they conduct. Varying in…" he paused and shook his head. "But the worst, the most horrific of all, is the Energy Components Project."

Helen rolled her eyes. "I've not heard such awful things, Phillip. Its goal is noble."

Phillip scowled, the first anger I'd seen in him all night. "You have not seen the project in action. I have. I spared your unit working with them intentionally." He sighed. "The goal of the project is to determine what combination of energies, of power sources, is ideal for resisting different forms of damage or decay. It has had many iterations to date. I have only seen some. I saw a girl infected with leukemia, and then exposed to the energy combination being tested at the moment."

"What was it?" Gerard asked, the scientist in him piqued despite the topic. I was curious how they'd figured out how to *infect* someone with leukemia, but figured that was missing the point right now.

"I do not know. They did not either. It was double-blind. It didn't matter. The girl died. I saw a man have his limbs surgically removed and then made to consume a drink, again of unknown ingredient. His limbs grew back, mostly, missing a few fingers and toes… but they pushed it further, removing his eyes, and they grew back, but blinded. Now they keep him imprisoned under the pretense of observation. They…" he swallowed hard, "skinned a little boy. I heard it happening. I heard his wails." Phillip's voice was thick and moist. "They exposed him to another treatment, and his skin grew back, but the cells grew too much and with too many mutations, and he now has boils, cancerous lesions, all over his body. They keep him connected to an IV, continuously administering morphine, to dull the pain. But he will die too, and the rest of his life will be suffering. There is an old woman whom they did not harm initially, seeking to undo her aging. They had her take a daily pill. At first her wrinkles seemed to smooth and her strength returned to her… but then something went awry and her bones began to grow, so much they thrust through her skin. They keep her tied to a bed because she refused to continue, but they wish to see it through, forcing her to swallow her daily pill, and regularly cauterizing her wounds so she will not die. Once her treatment is complete, she will likely be euthanized. There are other such cases. Women, men, and children seized from the streets, from among the homeless and orphaned. People who will not be missed. Whose lives will pass from this earth unvalued and unloved."

I felt sick. This was no better than the "experiments" the Nazis were doing.

Even Helen seemed distressed. "I'd no idea of these experiments. We do not conduct work such as that. I do not."

"No," Phillip assented, "and please never do. Let the horrors stay apart from you." Helen nodded.

"Did... *she*... order this project?" I asked.

Phillip shrugged. "I do not know. Only the project lead knows. My leadership of that lab is administrative; I do not oversee the research there. I could not. Had that been part of my role, I would have refused."

"But... *she* must know about it? She is allowing it?"

Phillip nodded. "She must know, yes."

I didn't know much, but I knew we had to uncover who was responsible. There were two possible routes, as I saw it... through Helen, if working with her could get us the attention of *her*, or by maneuvering our way into the other lab. But at the moment we had no useful contacts there, and Phillip might know some, but I didn't want to involve him further. Helen was the low-hanging fruit.

"We won't do things the way they do," I assured Phillip. "Right, Helen?" She nodded. "We'll do the research right. And then *she'll* see that our methods produce results."

Helen grinned at that. As long as we would strive toward visibility to the top, Helen was game. I didn't know how exactly it would work, but we had to do something. The Energy Components Project, and the doctors who'd treated Adelita – the whole lab – had to go down.

Chapter Seven

We agreed to meet Helen as soon as possible after sunset at her lab – which was *not* the same location as the one Adelita had visited, but rather a few blocks north of Columbus Circle – the next night. Not the same night, though she'd offered for us to go back with her immediately. We set the meeting up suggesting that Helen needed time to gather her most sophisticated lab equipment for us. It was a half-truth; we *did* need that equipment, but more importantly, we needed a game plan.

Gerard flopped an enormous stack of books down on the table in Adelita's living room. "We know what a virus is," he started, and thrust the top book at me: *Filterable Viruses* by Thomas Milton Rivers. "We know that viruses are the cause of likely many illnesses for which bacterial causes could not be found. Further, we know that some viruses may be able to destroy bacteria."

That was an idea that had lost steam, and humanity would suffer for it. When penicillin was discovered, people (in "western" countries, anyway) flocked to antibiotics and many forgot about bacteriophages, the viruses that could kill bacteria. Science in the 21st Century would look to the idea of weaponizing viruses against disease again… using the HIV virus to kill cancer was one crazy idea that sometimes actually worked. But if we began to look for a new cure for bacteria, it was only once the old one stopped working and people had already started dying.

I read Geoffrey's note again:

Virology tests in Dohain inconclusive. Initial longevity acquired but specimen experienced rapid decomposition of extremities. Despite biological signatures suggesting capability of upward of 150 years, specimen in isolation evidenced unexplainable organ failure. Specimen released into wild remained vulnerable to weapon injuries, locally-occurring pathology, and suicide.

So maybe the note wasn't as much of a timeline violation as I'd thought... for 1943, anyway. But Helen didn't need to know that.

Building on my thought, Quentin, who was standing behind my chair and reading the note again too, said, "What if we make something up? Helen doesn't know anything about future virology. She'd believe anything as long as it's consistent with scientific theory."

"But would *she*?" I pondered. "What does *she* know?"

Quentin pulled out the chair to my left and slumped on it. "Where is she from? Where has she been?"

I shrugged. "I'm beginning to think no one knows the answer to that. Not even the Sphere."

Quentin sulked. "It means she's been too many places to know where to begin. That her timeline is too twisted to follow."

I frowned. "But she can't have been *everywhere*. That's impossible. So we need to invent something that's foolproof. So realistic that she thinks it's something she doesn't know yet, but real. That would draw her out. It has to."

Quentin's eyes lit up, and I turned toward him. "If she really has been through huge parts of time... she has to have some kind of immortality."

I nodded, urging on his thoughts. "So she's an unscrupulous mage, like Judah, or a vampire."

"More likely a mage. Her officials seem to be mostly mages. Like likes like."

"So if we give her something futuristic that seems like something vampires would know... that we might keep to ourselves, keep secret..."

Quentin nodded excitedly. "And we could make it sound real. Gerard could help, with all he knows. In fact... what Gerard actually knows, now, could be enough. And not a timeline violation at all."

"But… obviously that wouldn't have come from Dohain."

Gerard piped up then. "It could be something I… interpreted… from the Dohain findings. The findings expanded on my own knowledge, perhaps."

It was a good idea. "But *what?*"

Gerard smiled, a little wickedly, his cheeks crinkling. "Perhaps… perhaps the viruses studied in Dohain included ones infected into vampire blood to eliminate its weaknesses. Just as viruses can destroy bacteria, perhaps they have found a virus that destroyed… our blood's allergy to the sun. Longevity without needing to suffer that consequence."

Boy, that would be something if true. "But it was imperfect, and had side effects." *Decomposition of extremities.* I shuddered. "But whereas they, not being vampires themselves, couldn't really suss out why…"

Gerard nodded. "We could. And it might be a longevity in which she would be particularly interested. If she is a mage worth her power, worth her status, she will know that soul energy powers her. And if she has found a manner of immortality, she has had to rely on sources beyond her own soul."

I thought about my own soul power. "Can mages do what the fae can?"

Gerard shook his head. "Not to the extent. They can harness the power of souls to drive their magic, and that may include healing magic. But it is an indirect process. The fae, it seems, use the soul energy directly, no intermediate spells needed. How do I put it… for mages, the soul *powers* the spell. For the fae, the soul *is* the spell. The direct process suggests that the fae could do much more with souls than a mage ever could, though whether that includes anything beyond healing, I cannot say. As you know, they guard their magic fiercely."

For good reason. "Okay, so we have an initial science-y thing to try. A virus that eliminates the whole sun thing, but with 'side effects'."

Quentin ran his right hand through his hair. "And if that's not enough… it sounds like you've got a backup, V."

I knew what he meant but I didn't like it. "I don't want her, or anyone else, to know about that. That could put me in a position where I had to heal with souls to prove that I could, and I'm not going to do that." I stared at the table. "Plus, it's not related to Dohain or virology or anything like that. Gerard's idea is better."

"But how do we use it in front of Helen, in the lab?" Quentin asked.

I pondered that. We had enough for an initial 'note' to *her*, but we had promised Helen to use it to run our own experiments. And if it was on vampire blood…

"Do you think they have samples of viruses in the lab?" I asked.

Adelita had been sitting quietly on her recliner, the one Coretta had before lounged across. But Adelita was not lounging. She sat forward, hunched with her elbows on her knees. "They do," she noted. "Or at least, the other lab did." Her voice sounded strained.

"Are you okay?" I asked.

She smiled, but it wasn't right; she was definitely forcing it. "Yes, only tired. You keep hours that are challenging for me."

I nodded. "You should get some rest." But what I really wanted was for her to go to her room so that I could find her there alone later and ask her what was really going on. Because *that*, 'only tired', was a baldfaced lie.

Adelita slowly nodded and stood. As she walked to the stairs next to the kitchen entrance, she leaned more on her left leg – just slightly, but enough that it was noticeable. Once she was upstairs, I returned to the conversation with the others. "So we can examine the viruses they have to see if we can identify which might have a similar effect on our blood. In test tubes, of course."

Gerard nodded. "She could subject them to light on our behalf and observe what happens."

I shrugged, only half-paying-attention now. "It won't work. It doesn't matter if it does or not. We'll get the note to *her*, and hopefully draw her out, and maybe learn more in the lab too." I stood up. "You two can figure out any science-y stuff we need to be sure to say to sound like we know what we mean." I wasn't looking at them anymore, and went upstairs without another word.

A few steps down the brown-carpeted hall and I was there. I knocked on Adelita's door. "It's me," I said.

Shuffling and floorboard creaks emanated from the room. She opened the door wearing a light blue nightgown. "Hi," she said, but she saw my eyes, and I knew that she knew I knew. She stepped back and let me in.

"What is it doing to you?" I asked.

She lifted her nightgown in response, and… it was bad. There was a brick-red rash all over her stomach, spreading down past her underwear to cover her thighs. It was on both sides but looked angrier and was larger on the right side.

I shook my head. "Why didn't you tell me?"

Adelita sighed heavily. "I was afraid that if I healed too much they would know we had unnatural healing powers and target us. Though now they know that anyway."

"Has it healed at all? Or only gotten worse?"

She sighed again, and this time there was definite fear in her voice. "The rash has become worse. The redness has spread. It does not hurt… what hurts is what is growing underneath." She took my hand and put my fingers to her belly. It was hard underneath, hard and flat. "Whatever it is, it puts pressure on my hips. It is harder to walk. I feel as though I am becoming a machine. And not only because of this thing like metal inside me. Because I cannot sleep. I am never tired, not at all. Yet without sleep I am beginning to see visions. Lights, images, dashing in the corners of my eyes. And there is no rest from it."

I felt my blood racing through me. "All this from one pill. What was the end goal?"

Adelita shook her head. "I cannot guess. Had I taken the others, would this transformation become faster? Will it ever heal?"

I lifted my arm and bit my wrist open. "Drink."

She looked at it. "They will know."

"They already know. Drink. And then we will find you a real doctor."

Adelita paused with my wrist just a centimeter from her lips. "What would I say to him? How this has come to pass?"

I smirked wistfully. "The doctor doesn't need to know that."

Chapter Eight

"I don't need to know that," Dr. Harrison mimed, and then turned back to Adelita.

For anyone else, dragging a doctor out of bed at 2 a.m. would be a tricky proposition, but for us, it was easy.

"But this… I have never seen anything like this," the scruffy doctor continued. "I will need to run tests." He was wearing a white lab coat over his white nightclothes, which seemed redundant. His… six-o'clock shadow? Five? I forgot the saying. His mini-beard emerging from his face looked rough and dark against his washed-out skin.

Dr. Harrison's office was… sterile. Adelita laid upon a white metal chair that looked more like something into which one would be strapped. The floor was white and black checkered tiles, and the walls a grass-green.

What tests would he run? I watched him draw blood, and he instructed Adelita to pee in a cup. But what would those tests pick up? He gave her a prescription to get an x-ray at a radiology office downtown, which she could do the next day, though if what was inside her *was* metal, or metallic, the x-ray would at best not work. But it couldn't actually be metal, could it?

Adelita was quiet whenever not asked a question, and remained so the whole way home. At dawn I had to sleep, but she stayed up, arguing that her x-ray would be soon anyway, but I suspected that she couldn't sleep. Because of what the pill had done to her? Or because of worry?

I had done this to her. Not directly, but I brought this problem to her doorstep. And she couldn't have done nothing; it wasn't in her to sit by. I knew that. Just as I brought Judah upon

Coretta. Would I leave a wake of destruction in my path? How many people would get hurt because I had to "save the day"?

My sleep was restless and unsatisfying. I dreamed… something, but when I woke, it only tickled the corners of my mind, fragments of a story I couldn't rebuild. *I'm sorry too*, a muffled, fuzzy voice said. A sword swung somewhere, and a male voice I didn't recognize screamed, an agonized, high-pitched scream that ripped at my insides, and I felt…

I couldn't even name it. It was… too much… like so many feelings at once that my brain couldn't process it.

I woke up shaking. I didn't know what the dream was, or who had screamed or why, but I knew I never wanted to feel like that again.

I stood up and shook myself off. Adelita's results would come later on. In the meantime, we had a note to write and science-y things to try.

Adelita stayed home with Scott and Coretta to tend to her. I wondered at the dynamic of the three of them together. Truthfully, I didn't know much about Scott. But I knew Coretta as well as myself, and she would be an excellent listener and confidant, but a horrific nursemaid. I remembered the burnt, charcoal smell when she would try to make coffee for any guests she entertained. I would playfully mock her, little rich girl who couldn't even boil water. But the things she could do, the things she *did* do, were life-changing for so many.

Did I tell her that? Did I say it often enough?

I blinked and focused. We had work to do.

Gerard drove us to the address Helen had provided in his blue Cadillac V-16. I had been familiar with the car; it was known for its powerful engine at the time, but I had never ridden in one. It was a very smooth ride for the time.

We arrived in about an hour and a half. The building wasn't very tall, dwarfed by its surroundings, but sat stoutly on 7th Avenue near 62nd street and next to a bodega. Had it been called a bodega then?

The entrance was a revolving glass door centered on the building, beyond which was a large bleach-scented lobby and, at the far side, a long silver desk with a boy no more than 16 behind it, dressed as though he were a man. And he was, for much of history. What constituted adulthood at any given time had always been nonsensical. Was he a man when his voice deepened? When his schooling ended at some arbitrarily-chosen age? When he married? When he could plow the farm? And let's not even go into women's perceived adulthood status, which for all of recorded history had absolutely nothing to do with anything about *her* and instead only related to what she could be used for.

Focus. I squeezed my eyes as Quentin told the desk clerk our names and he let us pass.

We moved to the left toward a bank of elevator lifts. Another boy – did this place hire at the local school? – operated one for us, bringing us to the third floor. When the doors opened, we saw a short tan hallway with a steel door at its end. Nothing else.

As we reached the end of the hall, we saw that the door had a number pad, but Helen hadn't given the number. Gerard knocked. A minute passed. No one came, so he knocked again.

Gerard shrugged. "Shall I continue knocking?"

"No," I said. I'd met Helen, so I could handle it. *Want to let us in?* I put in her head.

A few moments passed and then the rushed clopping of dress shoes came toward us. The heavy-looking door swung inward.

"My deepest apologies," a slightly-sweaty Helen gasped. Her brown hair was matted and stuck to her forehead. "I had thought our Office Manager would be here. He must have retired for the evening. Please, come in!"

Inside the door was a reception area. Directly before us was a pitch-black desk with a small stack of papers on top, and to the right were brown couches that made an elbow in the corner of the room. The right side of the room ended there except for a door next to the couches marked with the image of a toilet. The room extended out only on the left side to an open hallway and another steel door.

Helen was wearing a pleated blue skirt that swayed below her knees as she moved. "The administrative offices are down the hall," she told us, "but my lab is this way." She walked over to the steel door, which twinkled in the glare of the ceiling light, and punched in a code. The door again swung open inward. "Please, follow me."

We proceeded down a light-green hall past a plain wood door on the left with a small placard marked "Dr. Li". After about thirty feet, we reached a split in the hall – forward was just the wall, but there were hallways going left and right. Helen directed us to the left. At the end of that shorter hall was another plain wood door, this one with the name "Dr. Smythe" on it. It did not have a lock; Helen opened it and let us in.

Immediately to the left upon entering was the tidiest desk I'd ever seen. Resting on its chestnut wood surface was a small notepad and a fountain pen laid diagonally across it. A square calendar sat in the upper right corner – and that was it.

The rest of the office was equally neat. Bookshelves on the left wall with every book upright, nothing leaning. I glanced over their titles… chemistry and physics topics of all sorts, but they weren't arranged by topic; they were alphabetical by author. I turned away from the books; across the room Helen was standing in front of a silvery-metal table with assorted science equipment – test tubes, petri dishes, a microscope, all sparkling clean and arranged in an orderly line. A clipboard hung from the side of the table with a single sheet of paper held snug.

Gerard handed Helen the note he'd drafted for *her*, and Helen eagerly read it aloud.

"Research from the planet Dohain suggests the identification of a virus that we have long sought and struggled to find – one that eliminates sunlight allergenic response in vampires. Yet Dohain was unable to apply the virus without significant and lethal side effects.

We begin a line of research designed to isolate what eliminates the allergy and determine how it can be administered without side effect. Request additional funding and resources toward that end."

Gerard nodded. "You ought to copy it in your own hand and sign your name. Then you may leave it where she may find it, and perhaps she will come to our aid." And he smiled conspiratorially at Helen.

Helen grinned, not attempting to hide her glee. "This is remarkable. Are you a scientist, then?"

Gerard shrugged. "I have no formal training. Yet I read, and I learn, and I have practiced much. I certainly have the most scientific credentials among our group."

Helen nodded. "I too have learned through reading and practice, alongside Phillip, and my father before him. Though I read much more than that, as well. And you?" she looked to me and Quentin.

Quentin also shrugged. "My knowledge is very specific. I also don't have formal training, but I was informally taught a lot of physics."

Helen's eyes twinkled, the light in the lab reflecting off of her glasses and adding to the effect. "You mean to say, time travel? You," she glanced at me, "said you are from the future. So you must have arrived in some manner…"

Quentin nodded. "Yes. Time travel."

Helen bit her lip. "Indeed… I have read much on it myself. A fascinating area of scientific inquiry. We have many books here that are more advanced than the common science of the time. Tell me, do lay scientists, in your time, know of quantum entanglement?"

Quentin's eyes widened. I didn't need to read his mind to know what he was thinking. That was *really* advanced for the 40s. Had that knowledge been acquired lawfully, through their passback-of-redacted-knowledge strategy? Or was that a violation? "They do," he said hesitantly.

"Oh *good*," Helen intoned. "It is truly *awful* keeping secrets from other scientists. We all seek to expand knowledge!" She turned to me. "And you, finally?"

"I… don't have deep knowledge in anything, really. Just a surface-level knowledge of a lot of things. Through reading, also. Seems we've all got that in common."

"Not much advanced schooling opportunity for us, is there?" Helen observed.

"No, never was," I agreed.

"In any case," Gerard spoke up, "perhaps we begin our experiments? Helen, might you show us what viral samples are available for our use, so we might identify the one closest to what was used on Dohain?"

Helen wagged her head eagerly. "Of course." She moved behind the silver table and began opening some drawers on its other side.

Quentin and I let Gerard view the samples – he was the only one who could even look like he knew what he was doing. After some label-reading and dropping some stuff in other stuff and watching what happened, Gerard selected one dish labeled "Lentivirus …" something after that, a string of letters and numbers I couldn't make sense of. "This," he began, "is likely to be the nearest approximation. Shall we attempt an initial experiment, using it in its raw form?"

Helen nodded. "I will need two tubes of your blood. One of you; I care not which."

Not mine, I thought to Quentin and Gerard, *who knows what the fae blood might do? I don't want it in their hands.*

"I suppose mine will do," Gerard offered, pulling off his olive suit jacket and rolling up the sleeve of his white undershirt. "A true scientist appreciates participating in experiments as well as conducting them." It was the best choice, I thought. Who knew what time travel did to the blood? Gerard was native to this year and so the least risky.

Helen retrieved two test tubes and a narrow clear plastic tube that was hooked up to a thin needle. She inserted the needle into Gerard's left arm, the vein rather prominent in that elbow, and then pushed the first test tube into a little cap that sat at the other end of the plastic tube. The whole system seemed airtight as the test tube filled up. Once full, she removed that one and popped in the other one. It all took maybe two minutes and it was done. She pulled out the needle and attempted to put some gauze on the wound, but it closed up immediately, rendering the gauze useless.

Helen held the tubes out to Gerard. "Do what you must to insert the virus into one of these tubes. Then we may observe the changes."

Gerard nodded and took the tubes. "Should the receiving blood… *survive*… the virus, you will need to observe them under sunlight in the morning and report your findings to us."

"It will be my pleasure," she said.

Gerard extracted some of the virus from the dish with a syringe and injected it into one tube of blood. I peered at it – of course the project wouldn't work for the sunlight part, but this part was still somewhat interesting, despite not knowing what a lentivirus is.

Nothing happened.

Gerard nodded sagely. "It is not a surprise that there is no visible change. Indeed, the virus may not kill what is already dead."

What he said felt like a dramatic oversimplification of our blood, but I took his point. A vampire couldn't die of any virus I knew of, not pneumonia or the flu or anything. It wasn't a stretch to think that something capable of destroying our sensitivity to sunlight, though, could destroy other things in us, too. Fortunately that wasn't a risk we were really taking.

Helen took the test tubes and put them in a wooden rack. She looked at them, a thin smile on her face. "Then in the morning we will see."

Chapter Nine

After leaving Helen's lab, I returned to Dr. Harrison's office. Adelita met me there, again at an unusual hour for a doctor but exactly when I'd suggested. Two round-backed gray chairs were on our side of his rectangular wood desk, the surface's color obscured by stacks of folders and papers a foot high. On his side, he sat in a large black chair looking extremely somber.

"Miss..." he looked at the paper in his right hand... "Delgado", but he pronounced it *Degade-o*, "I have your test results." I'd suggested to him that he... prioritize... this test. One day was already too long to wait. "The mass inside you is not true metal. Not completely. But neither is it a proper womb. It appears to be some manner of alloy. It is a material we could not identify without a biopsy to get a sample of the tissue, but... I am not confident we would then, either. Certainly, chemically, we could understand its form, but..." he looked up at us, a mix of frustration and sympathy on his face, "it would do you no good. It is not toxic, so far as we can tell, but it will never be able to grow a child."

Adelita's face remained unmoved. I rubbed my own. "Not toxic, so won't hurt her," I said, "but it is hurting her; she can't walk properly."

Dr. Harrison nodded. "Yes, nonetheless we will need to remove it. We can schedule her surgery a week from now." His eyes shifted to Adelita. "We will need to know your medical history to grasp how this may have grown. And if you would like, we can study it and attempt to determine... how this may have developed... after removal. I would be most curious as I have never seen anything like it in all my years of medicine."

I looked at Adelita, who said nothing. "Is that what you want?" I asked.

She nodded. "Yes. Remove it and then learn what you can."

Dr. Harrison nodded and then put the paper down, folding his hands in front of him. "Miss Delgado, I want to be sure that you understand the implications of what has happened to you. You will never bear children. I am sorry."

She nodded, her eyes blank and steady. "Yes, I understand."

He frowned, his face a cross of sympathetic and patronizing. "You do not seem to. It means you will never be a mother…"

Something inside me became wildly, irrationally angry. I stood up in a blur, knocking half the papers off his desk, and leaned in toward him. His face told me how I looked. *"She knows what it means,"* I snarled. Dr. Harrison jumped to his feet and took a few steps back, stumbling a bit on the leg of his chair. Was it that he was infantilizing her, as though she wouldn't know what a hysterectomy meant? Was it that he seemed to care more for her fertility than that she would live? I didn't know. Probably both.

Adelita stood alongside me and put her hand on my arm.

I took a few deep, deliberate breaths. "Schedule her surgery."

He nodded quickly. "Sunday. 8 a.m. I don't usually do surgeries on Sunday but… I'll make sure it happens. Beekman Hospital."

"That will be fine," Adelita said, and tugged on my arm lightly.

I stood up straight, slightly calmer. "I can't come with you."

"I know," Adelita said, "I would rather have it done alone all the same."

I nodded and rubbed my face again. "Okay."

Adelita thanked the startled doctor, and we left the office. Neither of us said a word until we were in the cab on our way home.

"I'm sorry," I said.

Adelita shrugged. "I understand why you were angry. He irked me as well."

"No… I mean, yes, but… that's not what I mean. I… I'm sorry…" I felt my throat close up.

Adelita sighed, her eyes dimming a bit. "You did not do this to me. They did. I did… I volunteered to go, to put myself in that position. But even so… they did this. To me, and to others too, I would guess." She exhaled heavily and turned away from me, looking out the window. "I do not know what I would have wanted. I suppose… I imagined I would bear a child, but that is what we are told from when we're young, yes? That is what women do. It is the only thing society seems to value us for doing."

I nodded. "And in theory more than in practice. Maternal care, ensuring the health of children… society has never much cared for those things."

Adelita looked back at me and nodded too. "There is part of me that will mourn the loss of the chance to be a mother. But there is also part of me that wonders if perhaps I was always set on another path." She tilted her head and her eyes became inquisitive. "You… cannot bear children either, or…"

I shook my head. "No, I can't. My body is only really designed for one thing."

She smirked at that. "I think you do many things. But I take your meaning. Did you ever… mourn that? Or, did you have children… before?"

I leaned back in my seat. The only other person who knew the full truth of this was Coretta. "Never mourned it. And I had no children. And thank goodness for that." I paused, and Adelita said nothing, sensing I would continue. "I think I was pregnant once. I was 16. I had felt nauseated on and off for several days… I thought it might be something I ate, or maybe I was dying, who knew. Then one day in the middle of my shift… I was a waitress; I worked at a restaurant… I felt… a lot of pain. In my lower stomach. I felt something starting to drip… I hadn't had my time of the month in probably two years, and now I know that was because I was too skinny, too underfed… but I suppose something had still been working in there. In any case, I went to the outhouse, and… the next thing I knew, I had woken up on the floor, scrunched up against the wall, covered in my own blood. And I felt so incredibly weak. I don't know how I survived it. And I didn't fully grasp what had happened then, but years later as I came to learn more, learn to read, read books, I understood. I had miscarried. And I was horrified, but grateful."

"Grateful... to have lived?"

I laughed. "Oh, no. I suppose now I am. But then, I think I wished I'd died. No... grateful because... I probably would have never known whose baby it was, but it didn't matter because there was no good answer. And I'd likely have died in childbirth, and if the baby had lived..." I felt my whole face and neck tighten then, as though the blood there were thickening around my sinuses, "I'd have cursed it to living out my life, or worse. Almost certainly worse."

Adelita nodded slowly. "Is that why you did not mourn the loss of your fertility?"

I shook my head. "No. I didn't mourn it because... for me, it would have been a prison. My whole life, my childhood, everything until the night I became this, was like living in a jail where the guards had full reign to torture me. And maybe some people could love the role of a mother, see a child as a way to start anew, but... for me, it would be another prison. And I wanted to be free."

Adelita took my hand. "We are all in our own forms of prison... but we should not add to that feeling where we need not."

I squeezed her hand. "If you need me, while you mourn, I'm here. Just because I didn't... I know how it is for others."

Adelita nodded. "Coretta." I nodded too. "She has seen much suffering, hasn't she?"

I sighed. "Beyond compare."

*　　*　　*　　*　　*

If there is one thing that is true of all people, and has been true for all time, it is the assumption of permanence. People go to bed assuming the loved one beside them will be there the next day.

They assume that the democracy they live in will stand for all time, or at least for their lifespan. They assume that buildings will stand in perpetuity, monuments to the time of their creation and the life that flows within them.

And yet nothing could be more wrong. People die. Governments crumble. Buildings fall. I'd seen them all happen... and yet reliably made the same mistake, over and over, the one thing our minds won't let us learn. Nothing is forever. Nothing is permanent.

That fact did not console me. That nothing is permanent was not an excuse for me being responsible for death coming faster.

"What's going on?"

I looked up from the table at Quentin, staring at me. He was fully ready for bed, wearing a black pair of shorts and a Dead Kennedys tee-shirt that was torn at the bottom, the collar, the sleeves.

I laughed involuntarily. "You'll wear that until it's threads, won't you?"

He looked down at himself, ran his right hand through his hair, and then looked up at me with a grin. "I like this shirt. But that's not an answer to my question."

I adjusted the bottom of my own nightwear, a long white cotton nightgown that had crumpled unevenly underneath me on the chair. "Oh, nothing. I just kill everyone I touch."

Quentin raised his eyebrows. "A *bit* of an overstatement?"

I sighed. "Is it? Coretta. Now Adelita's fertility... yeah, she's not dead, and yeah, she's making her peace with it. But I took that from her. I took that choice from her, and that's not who I want to be. Taking away someone's choices... it's putting another person in a kind of slavery."

Quentin frowned and moved next to the table. "You didn't do that to her. She chose to be involved. To go investigate. To take the pill."

I rubbed my face. "But I did. I did all of this. She wouldn't have done any of that if I hadn't brought this problem to her doorstep."

"But she still *chose* it."

"*Did she?*" I shouted, louder than I'd intended, my voice cracking. "Quentin, she drinks my blood. I gave it to her to drink so she would live long enough to give me the note that starts all of this. And before you say she *chose* to drink it, she took it and drank that first sip out of guilt. Because of that thing with her sister, and Judah. And I *knew* that; I knew she was doing it out of guilt and to make amends. In that moment I probably could have asked her to do *anything*. And so she drank, and you know what that means. She won't *just* live longer, Quentin, she... *likes* me. More than she would on her own. Which means she's more likely to want to help me, even at cost to herself." I stopped and put my head in my hands. "I made her do this."

I heard Quentin pull the other chair out, and as he sat in it, I looked up at him. "I think you're being unfair to her. Okay... she drinks your blood. But she's still her own woman. With her own mind. Don't go so far down this hole that you forget that, that you think you're her master or something. She has her own mind and can make her own choices." He leaned back in the chair and shrugged. "Maybe she likes you more than she should. What does that mean? Coretta *definitely* likes you more than she should." He smirked at that.

I stared at him in disbelief. "Bad example? She *died* for me."

He leaned in toward me, more assertively than I'd expected. "And would you dare tell her that it wasn't her choice? That she didn't know her own mind because she has some feelings?"

I had no response to that. He was right.

He leaned back again, returning to a calm posture. "Mhmm," he murmured confidently. But almost as soon as he said that, his face darkened, his eyes telling me he'd thought of something bad. "You didn't choose, though."

What?

He shook his head, more to himself than anything else. "You didn't choose," he repeated, "and I did that to you."

My mind clicked on and I understood. "No. Don't do that," I said.

He looked at me. "What do you mean?"

"Don't do that. Yeah, I didn't choose, to die, to become this, to lose my fertility, whatever it is exactly you're thinking of right now. But I hadn't chosen *anything*. At that moment, I might not have made a real, meaningful choice in my whole life, because I couldn't, and yeah, you didn't give me a choice in that exact moment, but you gave me all of my future choices. You gave me the ability to choose everything I chose after that. So don't, okay?"

He didn't seem to know what to say to that. His mouth hung a bit open. I really had laid it on him there, hadn't I?

But he recovered. "Okay," he said, nodding. "Okay. I just... one thing, okay?" I didn't say anything. "Did I do anything that you regret?"

I shook my head. "No. Well..." I laughed, breaking the moment, "that whole disappearing-after thing. Wasn't a fan of that."

He pursed his lips. "*I* didn't do that."

"Suuuuure you didn't," I teased, and he shook his head, smirking.

Chapter Ten

Helen had suggested we return to her lab first thing the next night, and when we arrived, she threw open the door, looking like she was going to jump out of her skin.

"Come in, come in!" she screeched, so we did. We were only barely inside when she yelped out, "It worked!"

… what?

Gerard seemed just as flummoxed despite knowing what the virus was. "It… was successful?"

Helen nodded vigorously and led us deeper inside the office, back to her lab where we'd given her Gerard's blood. She gestured wildly at the table the vials had been on, so I looked.

One vial of perfectly ordinary-looking blood stood in the rack that both had been in the night before. The other was shattered, its pieces burnt black in a tidy pile on the table.

Nothing we said or did was supposed to work. It was supposed to be a suggestion to get a rise out of *her*. How could it have worked?

I stepped forward and gingerly touched the remaining vial, closing my eyes. I could see her, Helen, outside in the sunlight. I reflexively winced, but the image couldn't hurt me. She held her arms out in front of her, and something sat flat on her palms, covered in a dark black cloth. Carefully, she reached under with her right hand and pulled out… well, I couldn't see it in full because as soon as it hit the sun it burst apart, leaving bloody gashes in her palm. The blood from the tube charred on the glass shards. As much as it must have hurt, and she grimaced, she didn't drop what must have been the tray, and was undeterred. She carefully took the tray in her injured right hand, gritting her teeth, and reached under the cloth again with her left hand this time. But when this test tube emerged... nothing happened.

NOTHING. FUCKING. HAPPENED.

I released the tube and... that was it. I had nothing else.

"Did you see?" she squealed. "Did you see it in your mind?"

I nodded. I don't think I was blinking. I tried to find my voice, and I sort-of croak-whispered out: "It worked."

Helen was literally jumping. "I must tell her! This, this she will want to know! Oh, we have done it! We have found something remarkable!"

I turned around quickly to face the others. It *was* remarkable.

"This..." Gerard murmured, "may alter all we do. Our entire way of life."

Quentin was gazing at the tube skeptically. "Not so fast. Even if it did work in a tube, that's no guarantee it would work in a body."

I thought about the xkcd where guns kill cancer cells in a petri dish. "You're right. We need more experiments. But... this is promising. You have to admit that."

He nodded slowly. "Promising. Maybe."

Either way, that hadn't been our original purpose. "Helen, you write her that note, and then let's do some more science." Helen eagerly nodded and ran away into an adjacent room through a door in the back right corner.

With her momentarily gone, I turned to Gerard and Quentin and shook my hands in the air, wordlessly conveying my shock.

Gerard shook his head. "This is profound."

"Did you know?" I whispered urgently. "That the lentivirus stood a chance of actually working?"

Gerard looked flummoxed, his eyes wide. "I knew I could make some scientific justification as to why I'd recommended its attempt. Beyond that… this is stunning to me as much as anyone."

"So what now?" I pressed, desperate for some plan of action before Helen returned.

"Quentin's suggestion was apt," Gerard said. "We must test the lentivirus in a living host."

"But who?" I said, my voice coming out scratchy, as the thought of testing anything with unknown consequences on another person made my throat clench.

Quentin frowned, something in his eyes turning dark. "Why not let them decide?"

"What do you mean?" I asked.

"This could be a chance to meet other scientists. See how they work. See who *they* test on. A lab needs a source of subjects, right? So what's theirs? We could use that, and learn what we need to learn, and not need to volunteer anyone else we know."

I'd seen something of this in him before. When he refused to take Devin with us in the Time Sphere, it wasn't just that it was a timeline violation, or we didn't know him well enough, or anything like that. It was a punishment. It didn't matter if taking him with us had been a good idea or a bad one, or if he could have helped us save lives. We were, then as now, trying to do something that could help many more people than ourselves, but there in his eyes was something selfish, something protective of those close to him at the expense of anyone else.

I liked it.

Gerard seemed to sense it too, and felt a little differently about it. His eyes narrowed. "We ought not harm further innocents in our mission."

"What's the alternative?" Quentin pressed. "Learning nothing? Then what was this for? Or risking another one of us? Haven't we paid enough?"

Gerard didn't know what Adelita was going through, not the extent of it, but that wasn't mine to tell. He seemed to take Quentin's point, but wasn't satisfied. "Be wary of who you are willing to harm in the name of good."

Quentin's eyes narrowed further. "Would you volunteer Scott for this experiment, if he were one of us?"

Gerard had no response. When Helen walked back into the room, his mouth was hanging open silently.

She looked at us with a bit of suspicion but cast it off. "The note is written and left. With luck, she will respond." Helen clapped her hands together. "But if she does, or does not, as you said, Vivian – we must continue to study this! And if our initial note does not catch her eye, perhaps further findings will."

Quentin nodded. "Do you have experts here to help us? I think now we'll need those who've formally studied... whatever's needed."

Helen nodded. "We do. Come, let me introduce you."

Helen brought us down the hallway that had led to her office, but instead of turning right back toward the front door, kept going straight toward the other end of the same hallway. More light-green walls with no adornments at all. These were not my first encounters with scientists; I was pretty sure in general they were not averse to color or pictures. Maybe no one had the time to decorate?

But the room we entered at the end of that hallway, through a door labeled "Dr. Moreno", was another world. I didn't recognize most of the equipment scattered throughout and along the walls – huge bulking white and gray machines that did who-knew-what – but this room was covered in paintings. Most were framed in some shade of brown wood, and all depicted cityscapes. Yet I wasn't sure I'd ever seen a real city that colorful – buildings in bright pastels and bold hues against rows of stunning flowers and lush grass. And the skies – I'd seen innumerable pictures and movies with the daylight sky, but these were painted so starkly they seemed surreal. Blues and yellows seemed to leap from the canvas, beckoning. The room carried the slight aroma of burning wood.

And there in the room was a woman, roughly my height, her form shrouded in a lavender jacket with buttons down the front that I supposed was her lab coat. Her hair was a bold, definitely-dyed blue and pin-straight. She was kicking one of the tall white machines with pointed black shoes. When she turned to us, ripping goggles off of her face and throwing them to the floor, she was breathing heavily. She was young – her smooth skin was the color of umber, her small eyes unlined and deep.

"Darna," Helen began, "please meet our new colleagues. They have brought us a marvelous discovery, and I would love for you to work alongside us in examining it further."

Darna looked around at each of us in turn. "Hello. Helen, I am busy."

Helen frowned. "Nothing should take precedence over this task, Darna… when I explain, you will see…"

Darna turned toward Helen aggressively. "*You will see* that Chuck is expecting a traveling device that prepares him for where he's going and *this*," she kicked the machine, "*thing*", kicked it again harder, "*won't*", one final assault, "*work*!"

Helen huffed. "Chuck does not yet know about what we have found, but of course I will inform him. And he will agree with my assessment."

"When he does, that will be a delight to me," Darna said gruffly. "I am not a historian, Helen, and this machine can only hold bits of information. He wants tutorials on his destination zones? *Read a book, Chuck.*"

Helen grimaced and turned toward the three of us. "Darna is our zone's top biologist."

"*Biologist*," Darna repeated, throwing her hands in the air. "Not historian. Not electrician. Not physicist!"

"We are… understaffed," Helen somberly noted.

"I have shelves of samples," Darna gestured toward the wall opposite her – indeed, there were rows of blood and other tissue samples atop shelves, "that I am supposed to be testing to ensure *he won't die*, but he makes me do this!"

"Is he sick?" I asked, wanting to know more about what Darna was both doing and supposed to be doing.

"I don't know!" she exclaimed. "With all the travel he insists upon, for all I know, the vortex is atrophying his cells. But I would have to *test the samples* to tell!"

Quentin narrowed his eyes. "Why would travel... I assume you mean time travel? He has access? Why would travel atrophy his cells?"

"I don't know that either," Darna confessed, "but in earlier samples I have seen evidence of unnatural aging. He travels often, so it seemed the logical explanation, though admittedly it is only a correlation."

Gerard piped up then. "To travel through time... he uses magic? He is a mage?" Darna nodded. Gerard eyed Quentin and me knowingly.

"What do you know?" Darna accused snippily.

I decided to see if Darna was worth her reputation. "Want to trade information?" I asked. "We'll tell you that, and you help us figure out why lentivirus makes vampire blood resistant to the sun."

Darna's eyes bulged, and widened as they were I could see their silky brown color. "What lentivirus?"

"Sample a136r," Helen said. "This fellow, Gerard," she gestured to him, "suggested its attempt, and it worked! Darna, it was magnificent."

Darna put her fingers to her lips. She began talking, more to herself than to us. "The mandurugo blood carries the genetic code to react to sunlight as a toxin, and overcompensates and destroys itself." *Mandurugo* was not a name for us that I'd heard before – I wondered what legends had called us that. "The lentivirus injects information into the host gene. Could it be suppressing the code to react to sunlight in such a violent manner?"

Gerard's eyes widened, and I thought I saw a small smile. "This feels beyond my years… and yet, what you say sounds plausible."

Darna, now invigorated with this knowledge, scurried to the far-left corner of the room where a desk, adorned with several colorful floral arrangements, sat, and she flipped through several stacks of paper. Finally, she pulled out one page.

"The language will be wrong, but we received this note from Zone 658.9. It describes what I indicated before, that lentiviruses have the ability to insert genetic code into host genes. Yet… our time now… I cannot isolate the process. Might this relate to DNA?"

Another redacted note from the future, giving them more to work with without revealing what they deemed to be too much. It was a risky game.

Quentin nudged me, and I looked at him. His eyes were bulging; he wanted to say something but couldn't. I'd have to teach him to put thoughts in people's minds soon.

Darna saw. "Do you know? Oh… are you…"

"From the future," Helen said. "They are." Well, Quentin and I were and Gerard wasn't, but I didn't correct her.

Darna nodded. "You cannot say what you know to me. I understand. But please do validate it with one another… and tell me what you can."

Quentin leaned in to my left ear and whispered so softly even Gerard couldn't hear: "RNA interference."

Yes… that could be it. The lentivirus puts RNA in the blood's cells that suppresses the reaction. It made sense.

I nodded toward Darna. "It could relate to DNA, yes."

Darna smiled, the first time since we'd met her. "And this reaction has occurred successfully in a live host?"

Quentin frowned, a little I-told-you in his face. "No," he said, "only in a test tube."

"Hmm…" Darna rubbed her hands together, "then we ought to develop a proper experiment to determine, indeed, how well it works in real life."

"Glad you are willing," Helen said.

Darna grinned. "Chuck can conduct his historical investigations on his own. This is fantastically exciting."

"Let's get started, then," I said, and, not forgetting my bargain, I put the thought in her head: *Mage magic is powered by the soul. So each time Chuck travels, he's consuming a part of himself. The more he travels, the faster he will die.*

Darna locked on to my eyes and stared as the thought finished. "Yes," she said, "let us begin."She put her note down and approached us. "Will one of you be a test subject? Or do you have another in mind?"

We'd never told her in words we were vampires. What had been her clue?

She must have read the question in my face. "A guess, really, that I gather is right? That you would know more of your own blood, secrets you might not reveal to others?"

I nodded. "A fair enough assumption. But we aren't particularly keen to use ourselves, and not anyone we know. Does your lab not have any willing subjects?"

Darna frowned. "None who are vampires. Mostly humans, in exchange for money or a service."

"Service?" I asked, thinking of Adelita and already knowing the answer.

"The sick desire cures," Darna confirmed. "When there is none known, they are usually willing to try more experimental options. They know the risks."

A modicum of consent was nice, I supposed, though I knew all labs were not that way. "Always?" I prodded. "All the known risks?"

Again, Darna read my face. She was more than book smart, that was clear. "Our scientists are supposed to inform of all known risks. Yet I would be lying if I told you all of them did. I have oft wondered why *she* has not punished them for the transgression. I fear she cares more for the ends than the means."

Helen scowled. "She is creating a better world for us all."

Darna sighed. "Yes. So we say. And while I am here, the science that occurs by my hand will be done correctly. Ethically. So there is that."

I pushed further. "How much oversight does she really have? From what Helen said, it sounds as though she only intervenes when great discoveries are made."

"Mostly, yes," Darna agreed. "But what more could you expect of her? Do you know how many regions we have? Because I do not. The number may be uncountable. It would be too much for one person. The regional managers are charged with ensuring their own regions adhere to the code she prescribes."

Yet Geoffrey did not adhere to the code himself, so how could one imagine his region did? We had learned something of value here already – the organization was thoroughly decentralized, with its leader overseeing only loosely, more of a fearsome figurehead to keep the secrets locked down, to keep workers in line. How great *were* her powers that they could do that? How much had her reputation exceeded her, so that what people knew of her was more the end result of a horror-themed game of Telephone than anything real?

Who was she?

But if truly decentralized, that suggested that their resources were as well. Funding sources, for one. If we could find the funding source for the office that had poisoned Adelita, that sanctioned the Energy Components Project, or the office that had directed the slaughter of Dohain, it might be possible to eliminate the worst parts. But were any parts *really* not-worst? Darna seemed ethical. But would that hold in action?

"Perhaps we can utilize the volunteers we have, Darna," Helen piped up. "Those same sick you mentioned… they would do *anything* to be well, would they not?"

I was struck by silence. She didn't understand the magnitude of what she was saying.

Darna squinted and rubbed her eyes. "Indeed. But you invite them to immortality only to perhaps destroy them the same night?"

"It's bad on both sides," I said, finding my voice. "What you said, Darna, that's right. Promise them forever, but what if they die? But there's also…" I lifted my arms in frustration at the enormity of it. "What if they live? What if they do survive, and now one or more of us has this new person to teach how to live, this new person who now gets *forever*. Are all your volunteers model citizens? Are they all people we would like, much less care for enough to invest the days, months, years needed to get them situated in a world where you need to *eat other people* to live? What sort of person would we be unleashing on eternity?"

There was silence as Darna and Helen seemed to mull that over. Helen, predictably, was the first to respond. "What of your existing progeny? Your investment in them may be finished, and they may have already lived beyond a human lifespan."

Uh, no. "Yeah, fuck off with that."

Helen looked… mildly apologetic, but not apologetic enough for someone who just suggested offering up our children for experimentation. "Surely one of you made one who is lesser than the others? Not all progeny are *model citizens*, even if you believed they would be."

I shook my head. "Are you asking if we have a *spare*? Fuuuuuuuck you," I replied matter-of-factly. The truth was… she wasn't wrong. I hadn't always chosen ideally. But that still didn't mean I'd offer her up for experimentation, even if I had any idea where she was.

Darna waved her hands in front of her, pleading for sanity. "Please… I imagine if there are humans who are willing to be the subject of experiments, there are vampires as well. Can you think of no reason someone would be interested?"

I looked at Gerard and Quentin. Gerard shrugged. "Many would be interested in the outcome. Immunity to the sun is no small matter. Perhaps…" He seemed to have an idea but didn't say.

"Perhaps…" Helen prodded.

Gerard sighed. "Living only at night has disadvantages for us all, but some more than others. A man who had a family, and underestimated the difficulty he would have being apart from them during the day. Or one who has no source of income, no employment that allows night work. Desperation could lead a man to seek out alternatives."

"Someone could grow to hate our way of life, too," I added. "We've all… done things we regret… and not everyone can reconcile that with themselves. But that person might not be able to kill themselves, either. Maybe seeing the sun again might make life worth living."

Helen was grinning, and Darna seemed pensive. "Do you know where we might find such a person?" Darna asked.

Gerard rubbed his chin. "I do not know of any."

"Well we cannot roam the streets in search," Darna scoffed.

"No," Quentin said, smiling. "But we don't have to. Someone will come to us."

Chapter Eleven

"Can we call it something else, though?"

Quentin twirled his pen and nodded. "Call it anything else," he said as he wrote another few words.

We were going to submit an advertisement to the New York Daily Mirror. It was mostly a tabloid, but it was exactly spaces of oddity that a vampire might look to for news about his or her kind. But we still couldn't just come out and say "Seeking vampire volunteer for medical experiment." We had to, as Quentin had put it, *"dogwhistle"*, meaning write something below normal perception, something so coded that no one besides a vampire could identify it for what it was. But the term had broader use, and I'd heard it used to describe how, in the early 21st century, Nazis would signal to each other with symbols and words that no one for a long time knew were their signals – a green frog named Pepe, for example. Anyone could dogwhistle, not just Nazis, but I didn't care for the association.

"What do you write?" Gerard inquired.

"Seeking person suffering extreme Protoporphyria for experimental treatment: COlumbus 5-4624."

"Whose number is that?" I asked.

"Darna's office," Quentin replied. "It should be a real medical office, to seem official. Plus, I didn't want to give out Gerard or Adelita's number."

"Thank goodness for that," Gerard said snarkily. It was a funny change… Gerard had for so long been polite, gentlemanly, and he still was, but… there was something else in him he was letting us see now, maybe because we knew him better? Something angrier, more impatient. I hoped that it really was just another side of him, and not the darkness taking hold of him. But I had lived in New York City for many, many years, and Paris for a century, and so I knew that most people needed no darkness magic to be snarky. And he could also just be afraid. So much was at risk, including someone he cared about a lot.

"And photo… whatever, that's about sunlight?" I asked. Quentin nodded. "If it's a real disease, don't you think someone with it might answer?"

"It's rare," he said, "but… so what if they did? Maybe this very same substance can help them too. Maybe the problems are related?"

Gerard rubbed his face. "I do not suspect they are the same. Porphyrias are due to a missing enzyme."

"Couldn't that be it?" Quentin pressed. "A missing enzyme causing it?"

Gerard frowned. "And the lentivirus inserts the code that generates the enzyme… yet our condition is so much more… acute. In porphyrias, the damage is over time. For us it is quite rapid."

Quentin shrugged. "Even if there's something else at play for us, we could still gain information from them, if they came. But I still think there's more of us than of them; that's how few of them there are."

"It's a big risk," I said, "for one of us to go to a medical facility. It could be hard to imagine that someone would really be looking for vampires, *and* aren't looking for us to put us in a cage. Why do we think anyone would answer this?"

"Desperation?" Quentin suggested.

Gerard scratched his chin. "What might we add that only one of our kind might say? If the intended believed the advert came from another like him, he might not feel hesitant to reply."

Now that was tricky. We were as different from one another as humans.

"We could say what we know that no one else does," Quentin said, seemingly finding this a much simpler affair than I did.

"Which is?" I asked.

He leaned back in his chair, twirled his pen in one hand and ran the other through his hair. "What does blood taste like to you?"

I pursed my lips. "Everyone's is different. But… if you mean what's in common… it tastes like…" How to put it into words? "Ecstasy. Relief. Peace. Bliss."

"Like a summer's night," Gerard said. "A light breeze, waves gently crashing, a soft lover's whisper in your ear."

It was a nice visual, but I wasn't sure what good any of this did. "So we're going to offer breezes and waves in a bottle?"

"Seeking person suffering extreme Protoporphyria for experimental treatment: COlumbus 5-4624. Possibility of permanent relief of photosensitivity and temporary relief of additional symptoms including unendurable hunger. May experience sense of personal ecstasy."

"Don't say ecstasy," I said. "You'll get dick pics." Quentin chuckled and Gerard frowned.

"What is a 'dick pic'?" Gerard asked.

"Just a part of the exciting future," I said, smirking.

"How's 'bliss'?" Quentin asked. "Your word."

I nodded. "I think it works. It's a really weird ad, though."

"Weird ads for weird people," Quentin said, scratching out the final words.

"In the future, people would read through it. You'd get responses from those people who think they're vampires."

Quentin nodded. "Secrecy is harder for sure. But now, in 1943, people still had the good sense to not want to be us."

Gerard's jaw dropped. "People want to *be* us? They wish to be as Dracula?"

"No," I said. "Well, maybe some, but not most. Unless you mean Gary Oldman Dracula…" I shook my head, realizing I was thinking out loud and not meaningfully responding to Gerard. "Never mind that – what I mean is that fictional depictions of us started to romanticize us. People have an easier time giving in to their desire for immortality when they get to be sexy too."

"No one concerns themselves with the monsters they would become?" Gerard exclaimed, aghast. "The *murderers*? That they may learn to live with the hunger but it is always there? That it becomes easier to take more life after each one?!"

Quentin chuckled. "They haven't been listening."

I smirked at the reference. It tickled me to watch the depictions of us regardless of whether we were scary or sexy or both. "And they won't. To be honest… in the 21st century I think that's the main reason for keeping ourselves secret. Not for our safety from their fear so much as protecting ourselves from their increasingly desperate attempts to become us."

Gerard's eyes would have dropped out of their sockets if they could pop out any further. "Has the human race been taken by some illness that affects their wisdom?"

I shrugged. "Maybe? I think we have enough evidence of failures of wisdom to make the case."

Quentin stood up and picked up the piece of paper on which he'd written the ad. "Ready to go prey on 1943's unwise?"

I nodded. "Let's do this."

As Quentin walked to the telephone, Gerard approached me, taking my arm and pulling me aside.

"I am concerned for Adelita's procedure tomorrow," he said, and his face made clear he meant it. "Is this the best approach?"

I sighed. "It's the only approach. The alternative was her living with extreme pain and a metal block inside her forever. She decided to have the surgery."

"But…" he began, looking frustrated, "does she understand what it means? To have a surgery, to have this organ taken away, to…"

I put my palm up. "Let me stop you there. She understands."

"But…"

"*She understands.* Gerard, she's a really smart woman."

"I know that, but…"

"If you know that," I interrupted, "then shh."

He looked at me helplessly, but nodded.

*   *   *   *   *

The ad first appeared the next day, Sunday, June 27 – the day of Adelita's surgery. When I arrived at the hospital, Adelita was healthy, the surgery successful. She was awake and very loopy.

"I cannot feel my stomach," she murmured, giggling and poking at herself.

"No no," I said, taking her hand and putting it at her side. "Don't poke your wound."

"Why is she behaving in this manner?" Scott asked under his breath.

"Morphine, most likely," Gerard suggested, "to stop the pain." He was sitting on the opposite side of her bed from me and had tried to hold her hand, but she was too wiggly.

Adelita giggled again. "I do not have any pain. I feel… fuzzy." She was grinning and I wished I had a camera to take a picture of her to tease her with later. I *did* technically have my cell phone in the Sphere, which since I hadn't been using it might even have some charge left, but I didn't think whipping it out in 1943 was wise.

"How long did they say you had to stay here?" I asked.

Adelita shrugged. "A few days, but I do not know exactly how many. They said they would observe me."

"It is major surgery," Gerard noted, "so I imagine quite a few days, perhaps a week."

Adelita leaned forward urgently but I pressed her shoulder so she would lie back. "Will you tend to Cori while I am here?" she asked. "Someone will?"

Coretta, who was standing at the foot of the bed, patted Adelita's feet through the blanket. "I will care for my namesake," she smirked, and I huffed.

"And... the research?" she asked urgently, her eyes and pupils wide.

"It's ongoing," I assured her. "We'll let you know if anything new happens. So far we're just waiting."

"It is possible no one will reply," Gerard noted.

"It is, but what else can we do?" I asked. "We wait."

*   *   *   *   *

And wait we did. For three days, there was no response. We were just starting to think that Gerard was right and maybe it wasn't going to work when we awoke to a message from Helen.

Scott was pleased to deliver it. "*Five* people," he reported. "I told the woman to have them come in at 10 p.m. tonight. Will that suit?" It certainly did.

We arrived at Darna's lab at 9:45 p.m. and the five people were already there. Darna had cleared the floor of her office, boxes and contraptions pushed against the wall, and seated the people in two rows of three like a classroom. The chairs were all the same kind of wood as you might see there too, though there were no attached desks. The middle seat in the back row was empty.

"Are you sure you can do this, Gerard?" I asked. "The mayor won't be mad you're away so much?" The experiment, and everything we were hoping to do, was going to take a chunk of time.

Gerard nodded. He kept his voice to barely a whisper so Darna, who wasn't looking at us, wouldn't hear: "I told him that I am investigating a security threat. Which is not untrue."

Darna was wearing a light blue lab coat today and held a small stack of paper. "I received their consent to participate," she said, shaking the papers and turning to us. "I am thinking we should administer a different dose to each, as we know nothing about quantity."

I looked the group over. There were three women and two men – an Irish woman with stark red frizzy hair; a slender Black woman with her hair cut short, near to a shave; another woman with taupe hair, or maybe it was just very dirty – her skin was dirty too but I guessed she was some sort of White – who was turning a small object over and over in her hands; an Asian man, East Asian probably, with shoulder-length black hair who fidgeted uncomfortably in his seat; and a saggy-skinned White man with dirty blond hair who looked deeply annoyed. But there was one thing they had in common – they all appeared some form of dirty, or disheveled, or too-thin. They were very poor.

"Do they know the risks?" I asked.

Darna shook her head. "I thought it would be better delivered by… someone who understands."

I sighed. "Okay… why are you here?" I asked them. "What do you hope to gain from this procedure?"

"A life," the Irish woman said, her lilting voice cracking.

They had to be young. Not very powerful, but… I understood, too well, how poverty can strip a person of a real life, but why were they *so* poor? Why couldn't they use their power, their talents, to earn at least a baseline living? Maybe they actually had the disease in the ad… but all five of them?

The Black woman must have read the questions on my face. "Our blood does not work."

"What?" I asked.

"It does not work. We have no powers, no ability to do anything. We are no more than humans who cannot walk in the sun."

I looked at Gerard helplessly. His eyes were wide, and he shrugged.

"We starve," the dirtiest woman said, "cause we can't get food this way. I gotta chase down rats in alleyways."

"So what," the White man grumbled in a gravelly voice. "we're just gonna let them poke and prod us like animals? We're *immortal*; we're better than that. We'll figure something out; we'll..."

"Now you stop it, Cliff," the dirty woman said, the object in her hands slipping out to dangle from her fingers – it was a cross necklace. "You didn't haveta come, and you didn't haveta sign that form. I'm done with livin this way. If I can't have no magic, then I'd liketa just live a normal human life. Find a nice man and settle down."

"I'll be your man, Berthy," Cliff replied tauntingly.

"Ah shove it, Cliff," Berthy said. "I don't want your pig ass." She looked me in the eyes. "He just mad cause he don't like bein a failure, not makin no money like a real man."

Cliff's face turned bright red and he turned aggressively toward Berthy. This was getting us nowhere, and I didn't feel like going down the rabbit hole of prescriptive gender norms at that moment.

"Everyone, please. You should all understand the risks here. We have a treatment that appears to have stopped our blood from reacting violently to the sun, but only in a test tube. We have no idea what it would do in a live person. It... it could kill you."

"Kill us?" Cliff exclaimed. "No, no, I won't do that."

"You don't have to," I said.

"Berthy, Shelby... this is crazy," Cliff said, waving his hands in distress. "Peter? 'Phelia?"

The others looked around at each other. The Black woman... Shelby?... threw her hands up. "I do not want to die, yet this is not living."

I moved next to Darna. "Can we take samples of their blood first? I want to see if we can understand why they can't use their powers."

Darna nodded. "I am interested in that as well."

I turned back to the five volunteers. "We will draw some of your blood first, then, and then we'll make sure you get fed. And then... we'll administer the treatment."

Darna nodded. "We will not tell you which dose you'll receive, so that we can be sure any effects are due to the medicine."

"No," Cliff grimaced. "I won't."

"Okay, then the rest of you?" They nodded. "Before we do this... how do you know each other? Did you have the same maker?"

"I am their maker," the other man said – Peter, I assumed. "I did this to them."

"No, Peter," Shelby said. "We asked for this. You did not know."

Peter's face sagged. "I have some abilities... I could never do much, but I thought it was only that I was young. Sometimes I can read people's thoughts. I thought my progeny would have at least that."

"You've brought us some food when you can, and I know it's hard providing for four. Means a lot to us," Berthy said as comfortingly as she could.

He shook his head. "Please give me the treatment first. If I should die, at least they might be spared."

Darna turned to her work – extracting blood samples one by one and labeling them. Cliff spoke up, saying that he wanted her to do that part to him so he could get answers too. Was Peter's blood already weak for some reason? And why had it passed on even more weak than that? I was no vampire biology expert, but there had never before been any evidence of a sort of dilution. Human DNA didn't weaken, whatever that would mean, as it was passed from generation to generation; why should our blood be any different?

We had planned for the feeding-them part but hadn't been expecting them to be this hungry... nor were we expecting five. (We couldn't see not feeding Cliff too.) I asked Darna if we could solicit donors from her lab. She told me that it wasn't unusual for laboratory staff and regular volunteers to provide blood samples for testing some new thing, so they probably wouldn't mind... but asking someone to let a doctor extract blood with a syringe was one thing; asking someone to let a vampire bite them and take an indeterminate amount of blood... that was something else. That had a fear and uncertainty element... and uncertainty is also fear, really... that what they were used to didn't have.

Darna retrieved five additional people – for seven total – who were used to donation for the task – and I made sure she led with the vampire-bite part, so they knew what they were getting into. I would supervise the feeding to stop it if it seemed like they were taking too much. I wished I had cookies or whatever blood centers gave donors – Coretta had told me about it once and we'd joked that we should carry Oreos on us.

That conversation hadn't happened for her yet.

We gathered the volunteers in a tiny room adjacent to Darna's lab. It had a table with several chairs, an unplugged lamp, and nothing else. Peter let his children feed first, and Cliff, not to be outdone, said the women should go before him. Berthy... Bertha?... fed first, and she was gulping so hard and fast that after a minute I had to pull her off of a large and wide man before she killed him. He stumbled upon release and I set him down into a chair. His face was white – not the race white, the crayon white.

The blood was still seeping out of his arm wound and the aroma hit me in the face. I bit my lip hard; if I dove on him, he would be dead in seconds. I couldn't blame Berthy for feasting; he smelled delicious. It was like... when I was human, and starving, and at work – at a restaurant, the irony of being surrounded by food and starving far from lost on me – it was like the way a good steak smelled while some rich douchebag ate it. The smell of the meat, of desire and longing and satiation and the only thing I could think about wanting in that moment.

I took a nearby towel and held it to his wound. "Hold this as tight as you can for a few minutes, and then you can tape some gauze over it," I instructed, and the man weakly nodded.

Were they all going to feed that way? I was glad Darna had found seven; we might need the spares.

Shelby moved in on a woman who was way too slight to have as much taken from her, so I watched more closely. But I didn't need to rip her off; Shelby detached herself in time, and the woman had the physical strength to seat and tend to herself.

"Should there be more," Shelby said, observing the vampire-to-food ratio, "I would like some, but let my friends take their first sip before then."

Ophelia, Cliff, and Peter all fed from medium-sized people with no ill effect, and Shelby then took the second slight female to even it out. The one volunteer who'd not yet been used, a slender man with spiky hair, glanced around the room.

"If you're done…" he said, his face tight and his hands trembling slightly, "maybe I'll go?"

Cliff eyed the man as though he were that steak. "I'd never be done, if I had a say." *A lovely contribution to eternity, Peter,* I thought.

"That's alright," I said, looking at the volunteer who was no longer wanting to volunteer and ignoring Cliff. "If you want to go, you can." He nodded nervously and rushed from the room.

On to part three.

After I was sure that the six drained volunteers were well, I sent them on their way and took the mysteriously incapable vampires back to the main area of Darna's lab. She was adjusting some syringes that were laid out on a desk with the test tubes on the back wall of the room. Quentin was seated on a small wooden chair – probably one of the ones the vampire group had been sitting on earlier – next to the desk, eyeing the vampires walking in with…

concern? Pity? He was hard to read in that moment. Gerard was holding a syringe at the ready.

"All fed?" Darna asked. I nodded. "Good. Vivian, you're the only one who doesn't know what's in each syringe, so I'd like you to be the one to assess results."

"Okay," I said, though something about making the study double-blind felt pointless. If they turn to dust, that's a pretty clear result.

"Who's first?" Darna asked, and predictably Peter stepped forward. He rolled up the sleeve of his light-blue collared shirt and held out his arm. His face was steel, locked into his commitment. Gerard walked next to him, did the tap-tap thing doctors do to get air bubbles out of the syringe, and took Peter's arm in his other hand. He injected the contents directly into his big elbow vein.

I watched, glancing between Peter's face and the injection site. The inside of his elbow turned a little red, but nothing else happened. Okay – so we knew that dose, whatever it was, wasn't lethal, at least not immediately. But we didn't know if it worked. I guessed that was Part Four.

Peter smiled wistfully at his children, fear deep inside his eyes that drooped and softened. He had lived, but perhaps only to watch a child die.

My stomach flipped and my blood seemed to turn to lava inside me. Is that something I'd be able to watch? Seeing it happen to him?

Cliff, emboldened by Peter's survival, leapt forward and put out his arm. "I'll do it," he exclaimed. "I signed the form; me next." So Gerard approached him with the next syringe, and it was much the same as Peter's result – a bit of redness, nothing else. So far so good.

Bertha stepped up to follow the men. She was resolute, unafraid, perhaps buoyed by the men's success, though her personality had seemed enough. Her injection did nothing, not even redness. She seemed dismayed by that – was she assuming that meant she'd received the lowest dose? It could be.

Ophelia followed, pressing her hands together anxiously as she waited for Gerard and her needle. Finally he came over and repeated his task.

When the syringe left her arm, at first there was redness, as with Peter and Cliff, but then I saw the spot of injection start to turn gray. The grayness spread quickly, shooting along her arm, covering it in ash. No… it wasn't covered in ash; it was ash – her arm was disintegrating.

Ophelia screamed, though whether it was pain or shock, I couldn't tell. Did it hurt to die? To evaporate? But it wasn't complete – the ashing took her whole left arm, her shoulder, and a chunk of her upper left chest, leaving a jagged edge of loose flesh so it looked like she'd had her arm bitten off by a large creature. It stopped there.

Rapid decomposition of extremities.

Ophelia kept screaming after the ashing stopped, and a terrified, horrified Peter ran to her side. He gingerly put his arms around her, avoiding the site of the wound.

"I'm so sorry, Ophelia," he mumbled, his voice thick. "I'm so sorry."

Shelby stared open-eyed, not blinking at all, at the space where Ophelia's arm had been. Would it grow back? Would it get worse? Time would tell. But Shelby stepped forward anyway and walked over to the table with the final syringe – five, meaning they'd guessed Cliff would change his mind. She picked it up and handed it to Gerard, who seemed shocked.

"Do it," she ordered. "If it's good for my sister, it's good for me." I wasn't sure anyone would say it was *good* for her, but I took her meaning.

"No, Shelby, no," Ophelia begged, reaching out with her remaining hand.

Shelby pushed her away. "Baby, we are in this together. One way or another." Peter looked horror-struck and helpless. I admired his willpower to not try to tell them what to do, and I empathized with his fear.

Gerard injected Shelby, and her elbow *started* to ash as Ophelia's had, and I thought this was going to be the worst one yet, but it stopped, leaving some scarring in a jagged circle around her elbow.

I turned to Darna. "So, the effect was: weakest, Bertha; Cliff and Peter were basically the same; then Shelby; then Ophelia. If that matches the order of the dose, we've found the sweet spot in terms of side effects… assuming no further effects later on."

"It does match the dose," Darna confirmed, "though Cliff got a slightly larger dose than Peter. It did not seem to matter. We will need to keep them for observation, for at least a day or two."

"And," I said, feeling the weight of what we were doing to them, "we will need to do the next test – did the desired effect even happen?"

Shelby rubbed the scarred spot on her arm. "Will we go into the sun? Is that how we test it?"

Darna shook her head. "I would suggest a controlled administration to limited parts of your body. We have an artificial sunlight lamp that we can use. You will wear an opaque black cape over the rest of your body and expose only one limb. If it works, we may expose more, but it seems needlessly dangerous to start there."

"Is there a better order?" I asked. "Ophelia is most likely to see it work… but…" I drifted off.

"She ought not lose her other arm as well?" Shelby finished for me. "I agree. I volunteer to be the first."

"Shelby…" Ophelia began again to lament, but Shelby raised her hand, and Ophelia stopped. From the look in Ophelia's eyes, I understood. She knew Shelby well enough to know that there was no point in arguing. It made me think of how I must have looked at Coretta at times.

I couldn't participate in this part; the lamp would harm me for certain. Darna escorted Shelby out of the lab to the room where we'd fed them.

Peter continued to hold Ophelia while the rest of us milled about silently. Quentin seemed lost in thought, and Gerard was gazing at the test tube of light-impervious vampire blood. That's when Shelby screamed, a shriek that seemed to shake the whole room.

Peter jumped up and tried to run the way Shelby had gone, but Darna must have locked the door and he didn't have the strength to get through. I could have... I thought about it, but letting the light in here didn't seem like it would help anyone, not even Shelby.

It didn't matter, though, because Darna opened the door shortly thereafter. The look on her face... I knew what she was going to say before she said it.

"I'm sorry," she cracked out.

Peter ran past her into the room behind, and we could hear his cry. "Shelby!" he screamed, and his voice was full of sorrow.

"It worked at first," Darna said, raising her hands in a plea. "When I exposed her arm to the light, nothing happened! It was extraordinary. But... the area of effect must have been limited to her arm; when she pulled back the cloak, she pulled too far, and..." Darna lowered her head. "I am deeply sorry."

Ophelia began to wail, a desperate cry for her sister, and Bertha hugged herself and shook. Cliff was furious.

"I told you!" he screamed, booming and deep. "I told you this would happen!" Tears slipped quietly from the sides of his eyes.

I had never really thought about what vampire blood smelled like before. Human blood, the aromas were part of the taste, as it had once been with food, complementing and enhancing the experience. But I didn't drink vampire blood... I was nearly certain I'd only had it the once... and so it hadn't occurred to me to notice its aromas. Yet now the scent was palpable. Tears dripping chaotically from eyes, hands smeared with them from wiping. And it was a cornucopia… perhaps each person's was different, or perhaps all such blood was incredibly complex; it was impossible to tell as it blended across person in the air and on their bodies as they embraced, and I dared not approach any one person more closely to find out. There was a light thread of copper, which was common in humans; I wondered if that was innate to all blood or if it was that these were less powerful, more ordinary vampires. But there was also… a berry scent, perhaps a blueberry, though I was hardly an expert on fresh fruit. Something oaky, like a whisky but without the harshness of the alcohol… and something floral… jasmine. Yes, definitely jasmine.

Flowers I had come to know better than fruit. Once you're a vampire, it's not that you can't taste food – you can; taste is a sense and in a very pure, objective way it too was enhanced, just like our hearing – but it won't be imbued with the joy food flavors had when they meant your survival. But flowers… those I could smell much better than before, and I had often taken the time to enjoy them, savor them, learn to pick out the minute differences in aromas among them. It was a simple beauty that was hard to find anywhere else in the world.

Sometimes Coretta had worn jasmine flowers in her hair. When we lived together, I would tie them for her, threading them through sometimes to look like a headband, and sometimes just one bunch on the side. She said that it added to her overall disarming appearance. Between the flowers in her soft blonde curls, her youthful face, and her sweet smile, people viewed her as nonthreatening and would open up to her, telling her anything she wanted to know, often even without the use of any magical persuasion techniques at all. That plus her intelligence and aptitude for business plans was part of how she'd built a powerful network of informants and funding sources regardless of what society thought about women that day. They had no idea of the gears churning in her mind, of the manipulative calculus going on at all times. And I loved it, and admired it. To all outward appearances she was an upstanding member of society, and that enabled her to privately, secretly, trash all of the rules when they weren't producing the desired results… and they so rarely did.

What were the rules of the game I was playing with the Society? Were there any?

Peter emerged behind Darna with ash all over his hands. His face was painted with his blood tears. "You should have given me the strong dose. *Why didn't you give me the strong dose?*" He seized Darna's arms and shook her.

Gerard rushed forward and put himself between them. "If you're to be angry with anyone, let it be me. I administered it to her."

Peter shook his head and sobbed. "It was supposed to be a gift. Eternal life. It was supposed to be a gift."

And yet here we were.

Darna backed away from Peter and moved to my side. She leaned in to my ear and whispered, "given Shelby's death, of course those with lower doses will die. Ophelia remains the only one for whom it may work."

"Even if it did," I whispered back, "the side effect is too much."

"Yes, but we would know. We would know whether it needs refining to remove the side effect, or if it simply does not work in a real body."

I side-eyed Darna. Her curiosity might be beginning to outweigh her ethics. I guess they'd signed the consent form.

"I hear you," Ophelia said. Perhaps her hearing was a power? It was one that was common to most of us. "I do not want Shelby to have perished in vain."

"No," Peter ordered, unable to bear more. "I won't allow it. I cannot lose you as well."

Ophelia looked at the space where her arm had been and sighed. "Peter, we must know. Please tend to the others." She started walking toward the room where Shelby's remains still lay, and Peter tried to block her path. "Peter. Please." Her voice was sad, desperate, pleading. He wept harder and stepped aside.

Darna rubbed her hands together. As she moved toward the light room, she called back to us, "Perhaps find some manner of container. We can give Shelby a respectful rest." And then she pulled the door closed, and this time I heard the click of the lock. A seemingly kind sentiment, but if Ophelia perished too, their remains might be a mixed, indistinguishable pile.

Peter began looking around the room, but his eyes kept leaking and couldn't seem to focus. I went over to him and touched his shoulder. "Sit. Rest – be with the others. I'll find something." He nodded gratefully and moved to Bertha's side, who put her arms around him.

A few minutes passed without any sound other than soft sobs. I recovered a tin that had some rubber gloves in it, dumping the gloves onto Darna's desk.

The door to the adjacent room creaked open and Ophelia stepped out. She appeared to be in one piece, short of her arm, and seemed dazed.

Darna stepped out behind her, grinning. "It's worked."

It worked.

There was silence for a long minute – there was a lot to digest.

Then Quentin spoke up: "For now. You said you'll keep them for observation, and you should. We don't know if the effect is permanent or not."

I nodded. "Or if the side effect is permanent." I could regrow my arm if I needed to – it would take a long time, maybe a few months, but I could. Could Ophelia? And if not, would it be because she was weak, or because something about the virus made the damage remain?

Darna nodded. "If all are ready, I can show you to a room in which you may stay a few days. I will have Shelby's remains brought to you."

It had to be better than their prior arrangements, so it wasn't much of a surprise that they agreed. Darna led them away, each still too morose to process much of anything that was happening.

I shook my head. "What do we do if this is real?"

Gerard frowned. "I would not attempt broader use until the side effect has been ameliorated."

"If it lasts. If the damage is temporary but the effect is permanent... who wouldn't take that trade?" I mused.

Gerard cocked his head to the side, seemingly in thought. "I have a difficult time imagining that the effect will be permanent in any case. To change her DNA in full, to strip every bit of her blood of the urge to disintegrate in the sun, would require a massive transformation. One syringe does not seem that it could be adequate."

"You're thinking a more prolonged exposure would be necessary?" Quentin asked. Gerard nodded.

"Maybe," I said, "but it didn't take prolonged exposure for vampire blood to completely transform our human bodies. Just a very aggressive single dose."

"Viruses can be aggressive, indeed," Gerard said, "but I have yet to see anything in nature with the transformative power of preternatural blood. At least, not anything that could do so without destroying the host."

And whether that would happen remained to be seen.

I sighed. "But that's not why we're here, right? Let's not forget. We're not here to try to see the sun again." I picked up a small notepad from Darna's desk. "Dear..." Um. We still didn't know her name.

"Would Helen prefer to write?" Gerard asked.

"I'm sure she would," I said, "but Helen doesn't know her name either." And our purpose also wasn't to feed Helen's career.

Dear fearless leader, I thought in jest, and then because I didn't have a better idea, I wrote it. *We have identified a substance that induces resistance to the sun in vampires, which is a promising step in undoing one of the biggest drawbacks of immortality. We will be glad to share more details with you if you are interested. – Darna's lab*

Quentin peered over my shoulder at what I was writing. "Helen will be angry," he suggested.

I shrugged. "We needed her to get to Darna so we could write a note like this. What do we need her for now?"

"Nothing, but what good is there in making her mad?"

I frowned. "Fine." I added + *Helen* to the signature.

Quentin laughed. "Do you think she usually receives curt letters?"

"I assume Helen's are worshipful," I agreed, "but it's the science content that matters here." I looked around the room. "Where should we leave it?"

As though her ears had been ringing, Helen entered the room behind us. "I hear from Darna that the experiment was a success?" she beamed.

Helen *would* think this was a "success".

"It's promising," I said. "I was just writing about it. Where do you leave letters?"

She knew what I meant. "Give it to me; I'll place it. There's a location in my office that she checks." I ripped the letter off of the pad and handed it to Helen, who skimmed it. Her eyebrows raised. "If you do not mind, I know her better," she said, which I imagined was only barely true, "so I shall rewrite this in a manner pleasing to her. As we wish for her attention, yes?"

I rolled my eyes. "Fine."

Helen retreated with the note, and I saw Quentin quietly chuckling out of the corner of my eye. I looked directly at him. "What?"

"She's right about our common goal," he said, shrugging.

"Eh," I muttered.

He smiled. "You have a problem with authority, I'm guessing."

"I have a problem with authority expecting deference. With it thinking it's better than me."

"We don't know for sure that she does. Only that Helen thinks that she expects deference. Or that she'll gain some brownie points from being deferent."

I sighed. "Yeah."

Darna returned from the hallway. "They are put to bed," she said, "and I've arranged for their breakfast. If you leave the tin with me I will see that Shelby's remains are collected."

I nodded. "Good. Should we return tomorrow?"

Darna nodded. "I'll inform you as to how they are, and whether Ophelia's immunity remains."

So she might be dead when we get there. I rubbed my eyes.

"I've told Helen of our findings," Darna continued, "and she was as pleased as you'd expect." Darna's lips were twisted; her opinion of Helen was not much different than mine, I gathered.

"Yeah, we saw her a minute ago. She's going to tell… her."

Darna nodded slowly. "Premature findings, but very well. Do you think she'll remember that I was involved?"

I laughed. "In her note? Who knows. But she'll be the clear inspiration for the project, I'm sure."

Darna rolled her eyes. "It is no matter to me. I don't need her eyes upon me. I only need the means to do my work effectively, and as yet I've not been denied."

"Thank you for your assistance," Gerard said, bowing slightly. "We ought to take our leave, as it grows late."

Darna bowed her head. "Until tomorrow."

Chapter Twelve

"What exciting news!" Helen read. *"My gratitude to each of you – especially my devoted Helen, whose commitment to our cause has produced this discovery."*

Had Helen even mentioned the rest of us in the note? Did *she* really think Helen should get all the credit? Or… was she playing Helen? Manipulating her, not unlike how I had at our meeting with Phillip. When you're as obvious about your intentions as Helen, it was easy.

"If you would proceed with the next phase, I would suggest Region 235.1, as they are working with blood and may find additional insights." Helen grinned ear-to-ear. "She has never written me directly before. Oh, this is a delight."

Quentin and I side-eyed each other.

We were alone with Helen in her office. Gerard had gone with Darna to run more tests, including understanding why the original blood samples were weak, and to inspect the newest batch of results. Ophelia was not dead, and Darna claimed that her immunity mostly remained, though her exposed skin had become a little pinkish, so it might be wearing off. Gerard wanted to sample Ophelia's blood over time to see if the concentration of the lentivirus was decreasing, or if the virus was mutating, or something else was going on. It was above my pay grade, so here I was with Helen.

I put my hand out for the note, and Helen passed it to me. The paper was grainy to the touch and off-white. At first, I tried to see *her*, to view the note's author as she wrote, but there was something stopping me. It felt like slamming my willpower into a wall.

She knew I would look. Interesting. But it taught me one thing about her for sure – her powers were no joke. I turned to more manual inspection of the letter.

There was no signature, and the script was made up of small, tight curves forming each letter. There was a lot of blank space at the bottom. The letters were *so* tight, it was as though it was important to leave that space. I ran my thumb over the bottom of the note and focused on it, trying to be as inconspicuous as possible. There was a message there… it wasn't for me; it would have activated when Helen first read it, perhaps through sound, or temporary writing. But I could feel that there was something, a message suspended in the vortex, attached to this paper. I asked the vortex to let me hear it.

In my head I heard a voice… it was familiar. A woman's voice I couldn't place, but I definitely knew. *"Do not fear to show her our work. The others may balk, and she may as well, but in time the others will fall away. She will come to us, alone, and change everything."*

I swallowed hard and passed the note back to Helen. "She didn't sign it."

"I was told that she never does, by others she has contacted," Helen confirmed. "Only those closest to her know her name. We will. Soon."

"Where is Region 235.1?" Quentin asked.

"1667, based out of the University of Oxford," she said. "A student of Dr. Richard Lower leads the unit."

"Not Lower himself?" I asked.

Helen shook her head. "I know not if he would have been interested in leading, but a figure as public as he would not suit our interests."

Lower was a big player in the earliest successful blood transfusions. Though at the time they weren't medically-necessary transfusions. Lower was interested in the pure science of it, for certain, but he also thought that the infusion of "new blood" and the removal of "old blood" was healthy. It was an idea with a lot of adherents in a lot of different ways at that time, particularly among the rich. And the truth of it was… they weren't entirely wrong. Transfusing the blood of the young and healthy into the old wasn't the trick, despite the Keith Richards rumors. However, restoring the blood *components* that age, that decay – stem cells, for example – could trigger the body into healing and regenerating tissue more like it did when it was young. It wasn't immortality, not even close, but it wasn't nothing either. It at minimum provided a better understanding of the mechanisms behind aging. But as with anything, people get a whiff of a scientific finding, misinterpret it or over-apply it, and next thing you know you have centers in New York where rich people get transfused with teenagers' blood.

I couldn't hate it too much. Another blood center was another group of people to get to know.

"And you want to take our findings, redact them to match the knowledge, terminology of the time, and give them to that unit," Quentin said, sounding as irritated by the potential time breach as he looked.

"Yes, precisely," Helen agreed. "Yet, I do not have travel authorization. We could recruit another to do it, yet… you are from the future, yes? You have a method of travel?"

"Yes," Quentin said cautiously.

"Could…" Helen began, her face bursting with eagerness that her face tried, and failed, to hide, "could we all travel together?"

Quentin's mouth twisted in displeasure. "Vivian and I could go. You don't need to come."

Helen frowned. "I am the only of us who is a true member of the Society. They will care more for my words than yours."

I rubbed my face. "Don't we just need to leave a note?"

Helen wiggled her head in a sort of… not a no, but not a shrug, somewhere in between. "We do, but do you know where to place it?"

I sighed. "No. Do *you*?"

"… I could give it to the unit leader. And he will believe that I am providing an authentic message."

I looked at Quentin, who looked incredibly frustrated. Would he let her come, even though he hated the thought?

He pressed his lips together tightly, and then finally spoke. "We will go directly there. No stops. After you give the leader the note, we will come right back."

Helen grinned. "As you wish. A moment as I pen something? You may verify that what I write is safe, if you like." We nodded.

As she wrote, my mind started to race, the softly-spoken words from the note from *her* sinking in. Was she planning to kill my friends? Leave me alone so I would come to her, confront her? Or did she think I would buy into her mission whole hog once they were dead and could no longer object? What did she mean by 'change everything'? I didn't think it would be hard for her to find powerful vampires if she wanted to. Why me?

Did she know about my other power? My fae power?

Why me?

I didn't know, and I couldn't, not then. But I would be damned if she would lay a finger on any of my friends. It wasn't going to happen, no how, no way. I was *not* going to lose anyone else. Not to anyone, and definitely not to her.

If there was a battle, I'd put myself in front. If there was a dangerous journey, I'd lead it. I'd do what I had to do to keep them out of harm's way. Now that I knew… well, had good reason to suspect, anyway… that she had them in her crosshairs, and that she wanted me, for something… she wasn't going to get either wish.

"It is finished," Helen announced, and held the note out toward us. Quentin snatched it quickly and turned to reading it.

"New research has uncovered that inserting transformative substances into blood can change its characteristics, much as blood into blood can change the host blood. Weaknesses of the blood of the undead may be overcome in this way. Seek the transformative power of the smallest lifeforms you can find." Quentin stared at the note, his brow furrowed. "There's nothing dangerous, I think, but..." he shook his head, "you've also *said nothing*."

"What more could I add?" Helen asked. "They know not of viruses then."

"And they won't for another two centuries," I mused. "So why did she recommend that zone? What can they really, meaningfully do?"

"Stick random things into people's bloodstreams?" Quentin said, frustration caking the words.

"Even if a random thing worked, they wouldn't know why," I added.

Helen sulked. "I do not know why she selected that zone, but she knows far more than I do... more about their work, and how it might coordinate with ours. She must have a wise reason."

Helen was sounding like she thought *she* was omniscient. I shook my head. It didn't matter. We were trying to get to *her*; that was the only reason for doing this. So if planting a useless note in the past would get us closer, all the better – no risk and all potential gain.

Quentin folded the note tensely and tucked it in his pocket. "Fine. I'll go get her and bring her somewhere nearby. Somewhere inconspicuous." He turned away brusquely and walked out.

I wasn't sure if I wanted to hang out here with Helen for an hour-plus, but he had said "I", so I took him at his word.

"Who is he retrieving?" Helen asked.

I rubbed my face. "He meant that he's going to get the time machine."

Helen frowned. "The time machine is a girl?"

I shrugged. "Haven't you ever heard a man call..." Hm, were cars that common yet? A boat? "Objects he likes... that he owns... by female pronouns?"

She snorted. "I have. Because objects are women, yes? Or women are objects."

She might be power-hungry, but the feminist part of her heart made mine almost think it could flutter. "Right."

"Yet you tolerate him saying such things? We are the friends we keep, are we not?"

I frowned. It was out of character for him. In all of his overt actions, he had always treated me, and anyone I saw him interact with, with perfect equality. But… could anyone really fully escape their programming? Did he even know what he was saying, why he was saying it, what it meant?

I'd have to mention it to him. I didn't want to believe that, if he knew the underbelly of the words, he'd want to be saying them.

Why hadn't any of this occurred to me before? I'd heard him refer to the Sphere as a "she" and "her" before. We even talked about it, and I made a lame joke about it. To what extent was *I* still programmed to be completely okay with women and objects being inextricably linked? To what extent did I still, unconsciously, buy in to the idea that I was an object in men's experience of the world?

I shuddered.

Helen put her hand on my left arm and I jolted again, her touch shaking me from my rumination. "We ladies must stick together, yes? Men will never be the allies for us that we will be for each other."

I didn't know that I agreed with that… moreover, I wasn't sure that was a practical approach. Without men using their privilege and relative power to create a more equal world, we'd have an even steeper uphill climb… a climb that usually felt like a Sisyphean task. But I took the sentiment behind her words. Women had to protect other women.

"Yeah," I nodded.

*   *   *   *   *

I peered over Quentin's shoulder as a gust of frigid air slammed me in the face. Only then did it occur to me how underdressed I was... not only for the weather, but for the time. But then again, a woman at Oxford in the 1600s would have been odd enough, whatever I was wearing. Would the Society's unit look at us oddly, or were they accustomed to out-of-time visitors?

When Quentin stepped out of the Sphere, I could see the view in full. The area was caked in fresh snow, that pristine picturesque vision of snow you see on postcards, in movies, in fantasies of Victorian London. In modern life, that vision quickly turned to yellow and gray sludge.

The campus surrounded us on all sides. The continuous gray building that wrapped us was mostly two stories. Straight ahead of us was an open arch that led somewhere I couldn't see. Arches were carved out all along the first story of the building, creating covered walkways. I'd thought there were towers here from pictures... but perhaps we were too early?

1667. I had lived in London for the better part of the 17th Century. It was a chaotic time. England had been a republic, temporarily, for about 20 years. In 1667, the country was only just emerging from the warfare preceding the restoration of the monarchy. Christ Church, this part of Oxford, had been a garrison in the battles, or so I thought I recalled.

It was so different then. Or was it? The public thirsted for a return to monarchy because of the failures of Parliament, the Lord Protector, and the army to get aligned and be effectual – grossly put, but it came down to that. And maybe it wasn't the best comparison to modern times because early republics were... first drafts, trials in democracy, not great examples of how one might work for the long term. But was the only alternative the safety of supreme rule, of having to take absolutely no action in one's own governance because you *couldn't*? How many times since then had people thrown their rights away for a demagogue, a boy-king, a cult of personality, in an effort to return to some "good old time" that never really existed, and was never so good for everyone? How many people had died because of it? How many still would?

Helen wrapped her thick beige coat tightly around herself. I didn't miss the harshness of icy air, that sense that one more breeze would freeze even your bones, turn your skin to solid rock. I never had a coat like Helen's, but with the way she shivered, I guessed it would only have helped so much.

She was looking around with more trepidation than I'd ever seen her have. I assumed she'd never time traveled before, and being outside of the time you knew could be jarring. Even when I traveled, it had been only to years I'd seen already, nothing truly new or unfamiliar, with the exception of Dohain. But Helen wasn't that old, so nearly all of history was new to her.

She looked toward me and Quentin and smiled. "Shall we?"

"Do you know where the right office is?" I asked.

Helen nodded. "It is not an office, formally. The university cannot know of it. It is a lab constructed behind the dining room. Others believe only a kitchen would be there."

"And you know where the dining room is?" Quentin asked.

Helen rubbed her palms together briskly – she had not brought gloves. Watching her I could feel the tight, frosted pain in the depths of my fingers, as though the memory of my mortality was alive in my flesh, a memory of hurting that my fingers couldn't forget. I squeezed my hands into fists.

"I believe so," Helen answered.

The closest door was to our left, so we walked there. When we got near to it, I could see dents and bullet holes in the wood. Helen reached down to the semicircle metal handle and opened it.

Inside, the very first thing that grabbed my attention was the fanned vaulted ceiling. True to the name, it appeared as though several fans extended from the walls to splay out open across the ceiling – not colorful fans with prints and designs, but rather what I imagined a bamboo fan might look like.

"Come," Helen said. "It is upstairs."

The staircase nearby was simple stone that matched the rest of the building in color. It wasn't particularly grandiose; I wondered if it had been replaced later. The railing made an attempt at intricacy with swirling leaf-like carvings between waist-high posts that were topped by something that looked like half a cob of corn with its husk partly peeled back. We ascended, meeting no one on our way – were classes in session? Were all the men – the boys, really – off at war? Or were they in other parts of the church hoarding munitions?

Helen guided us left through what appeared to be a functional bar – though again, no one was there – to what I immediately recognized as the dining hall from the Harry Potter movies. It probably wasn't, but the set they filmed in was definitely modeled after this hall. Three long tables, shiny and reddish-brown, stretched from one end of the room to the other. I didn't try to count the chairs, nor the plates set preemptively before them. Unlit lamps sat at regular intervals along each table. The room was covered, thoroughly on each wall, with portraits, mostly of rich-looking men in various poses. The ceiling here too was vaulted – though not the fan style, rather a standard arch topped in a point – with darker wood than the tables, more of a dark umber. We walked alongside the middle table toward the opposite end of the room, which did not, unlike in Harry Potter, have a dais. Rather, the table simply ended at the far wall.

Tucked in the far left corner was a door – unremarkable, nearly blending into the wall. Helen opened it and we stepped into a very-dark and very-narrow hallway stretching about ten feet. It ended in another door, this one silver steel.

Helen knocked on that door, which very much looked like the entrance to a meat locker. A few moments passed; there was shuffling, scuffling, and murmurs. Finally, the door opened revealing a tall, wide man topped with white-gray poofy hair, longish but thinning, and a matching long, flat mustache. He was wearing a long black jacket, a frilled white dress shirt underneath that stuck out only via frill, black pants, and shiny shoes. He took up nearly the whole doorframe so I couldn't see beyond him.

As I studied him, he returned the sentiment, looking over all of us, his eyes narrowing in suspicion. "What hath presented at my door?"

Helen's eyes were buggier than I was expecting. "Are you Lower's student, Paul Abelworth?"

"I am. Who are you?"

"I… have a note for you. From the… *Society*…" she rasped. "I am a member and bring this to you."

Paul looked at her skeptically. "You, a man of science?"

"I…" Helen stammered, "a woman of science."

"How may I know the truth of your allegiance?"

Helen cracked a bit of a smile for the first time in the conversation. "I have a note from *her*." Paul's eyes narrowed, adding wariness to his skepticism. Strange, he knew about their fearless female leader, but still couldn't accept women scientists? Prejudice is resilient.

Helen handed Paul *her* note, and as soon as he touched it, he jolted. What on earth was that? Had she marked the note with some power that only she had, that everyone knew meant it was really her? What could a power like that be?"

"So it is," he said, his nervousness increasing as he returned the note. He hadn't even read it; were they not allowed to read other people's notes? Or was something about the power she put on that paper too scary?

Helen extended her own redacted note again. "This one is for you."

Paul took the note and skimmed it. "What means this note? Shall I inject a man with ants?"

Helen's face was frozen, urgently searching for a response. The note said nothing, and Paul knew it.

"Am I to supply medicine to the dead?" Paul continued. "Shall I hasten them to bed and sweat their monstrosity from them?"

The Society had seemed pretty tolerant of us in the 1940s, but 250 or so years earlier made a big difference. Those who had already achieved a manner of immortality were an obvious path to longevity research, but if we're monsters, it's not a viable path for a faithful mortal.

I waved my hand. "Think not on the dead. An example only, that blood may be strengthened with scientific study. If a party be sick, think not to sweat, but to blood." Hmm, needed to be more specific. "Think… to the work of Dr. Lower. Think beyond powders, salves, waters." Ugh, my words felt twisted in my mouth. I had spoken all of the primary English variants from the mid-1500s through 2019, but my memory wasn't good enough to recall exactly which words and phrases to use for each particular year. At least I was doing better than Helen would. "Blood hath properties the eye may not see."

Paul nodded, seeming to grasp what I was saying, but he was continually distracted by my and Helen's dresses. He should see what I wore in the 21st century. "This clue you carry… through study, I must needs make the invisible appear, be part of medicines applied to lengthen life. Is this what you intend?"

I nodded. I cast my eyes over at Quentin, who was pressing his lips together. Did he think I'd said too much?

"I will take this advisement," Paul continued. "I pray it is most excellent to achieving the glory of our missive." He nodded graciously, and then shut the door in our faces.

Was that it? Just leave the note, a few words, in the past and go about our business? No harm, no foul?

What would await us in the future?

If *she* was right, there would be something. With those few words, we would have changed the path of the Society's science just enough to further their work meaningfully. Or, we had said the words we'd always said, and produced the work that had always been done.

When I emerged from my thoughts, Helen was beaming at me. "Well done," she said. "I am grateful; you supplied the words I could not find. Had you been alive this year?"

I nodded again. "Here in England, too. Though, not Oxford."

Helen grinned brighter. "You must tell me of it some time. It sounds so romantic. The renaissance, the birth of much knowledge, coffee shops and the free exchange of ideas."

I shrugged. "That's true, but there were a lot of ignorant forces too. There always are. And accessing all of that knowledge was harder as a woman… as I'm sure you've gathered."

Helen frowned. "Indeed. Well then, let us return to a better time."

Better? That I couldn't say. Every time was awful in its own way.

"Yes," Quentin said, finally detaching his lips from each other. "Let's go back."

Chapter Thirteen

I sat at the small wood table and ran my hand across its smooth top. Where was I again? Or, when was I? We didn't jump around that frequently, and I could imagine that if we did, it would be rattling. And people complained about adjusting to Daylight Savings Time.

We'd dropped Helen off at her office and then proceeded back to what seemed to be our home base, the yard in front of Adelita's house. What lawn ornament did others see in the Sphere's place? I would have to ask Scott. He'd never been inside it, nor even really had it pointed out to him as he went about his business going in and out of Adelita's.

We hadn't seen a note in Helen's office yet. Were we supposed to? How did it arrive? Did it just magically appear? Did a scientist, intellectually descended from Paul, stroll into the office and drop it off? Or did they leave it for *her*, and then she synthesized notes from across labs and distributed knowledge as she deemed appropriate? Was she educated enough in all of the relevant sciences – biology, immunology, virology, beyond – to be an effective arbiter?

"Hey," I said, and looked over at Quentin, who was inspecting the Sphere's display. I narrowed my eyes at him. "What are you doing?"

"Making sure she didn't touch anything," he said, running his fingers gently along the wiring sticking out of the back.

I chuckled. "She didn't. I would have seen."

He continued investigating.

"When you're done there… would you come here?"

He dropped the wire and looked over at me. "Everything okay?" What had my voice sounded like? I was a bit anxious. Maybe he heard that.

"Yeah. I just... sit, okay?"

He walked over to the other chair and sat, locking eyes with me. "What is it?"

I inhaled deeply. "Um... so, Helen noticed something and I... um... you know how you talk about the Sphere? You call it 'she', 'her', words like that?"

Quentin nodded. "Yeah."

"Right... and, I mean, you know a lot of guys do stuff like that, right?" I pushed my hair behind my ear on the right side. "Their cars are *she*s, and their boats are *she*s. But women never do that with stuff they own, right; you never hear a woman call her car a *he*." I kept looking at the table, then quickly and briefly back at him, then back to the table. "And I know you don't mean it that way. I know that. But it is a thing where, where... we're all comfortable thinking of objects as female, right? Because on some level we're comfortable with female people as objects." I pushed my hair on the same side back again. "And I know you don't think that or mean that but, I thought... if you were saying something that sounded like that, you'd want to know." I raised my eyes to look at him again.

He was nodding slowly, slightly. He pressed his lips together. "I do want to know," he said, finally. "And I don't want to sound like I think that." He nodded more firmly this time, and ran his hand through his hair. "I'll stop. I'm sorry. I won't say it anymore."

I exhaled. "And I mean, it's okay to say the wrong thing sometimes, right? It's okay. We all make mistakes. I... I didn't even think about it. Helen said it to me, after you left to get the Sphere. So I... we're all victims of our programming, right, and society's had a lot of time to work on us, so, we make mistakes."

He nodded again. "As long as we're trying to be better."

I smiled. "Yeah. Exactly." I looked at the table again, my hands pressing against each other restlessly. "And it's hard. You can think you're better, and then you realize that you're... not as better as you thought. That there's still this unconscious thing that you buy into."

"Sexism is a hard nut to crack," he agreed, and I looked back up at him. "I think... and maybe this isn't true, but it's what I've seen... that, of all the biases and prejudices out there, sexism is the one that has the most people, the most of its victims, who enforce it, whether they know it or not. So it sinks in more to the social consciousness. It sticks."

I nodded. "That might be true. Probably because of 'benevolent sexism', right? Sexism has done a good job of framing itself like it's some sort of woman-worship. We're delicate flowers that need protection. But flowers don't have intelligence, and they don't have opinions, and their wishes don't matter, and they're definitely not real people." I sighed. "Or because we're taught to hate ourselves in so many ways. No matter who we are, what we do, what we look like. For every woman there's a thousand ways she's taught to hate herself. And, from what I've seen, the number of ways multiply even more if she's also any kind of minority."

Quentin nodded. "And I didn't mean that it's women's fault. Men, and our culture, drill that into you from the day you're born. So if you *don't* buy in, that's... real strength. That's exceptional."

I shrugged. "Yeah... but I'm still not going to let complicit women off the hook."

"Nor should you. And neither will I let well-meaning men who do sexist shit off the hook. Not even myself."

I smiled softly at him. "A misspoken word. Not sexist."

"No, no..." Quentin shook his head and smirked. "Don't go easy on me because we're friends. What would Coretta say to me? What would she say to you if you unknowingly did or said something that was sexist?"

I could answer that from experience. "She'd verbally kick my ass."

"I'm sure." He folded his hands on the table and leaned in. "Thank you for telling me this. I hope you know…" he paused, his word hanging. "We haven't had anything I'd call a *difficult* conversation, right? Not until this, and I'm guessing it was hard to bring up, but I'm glad you did. So… know that it'll be okay? To talk about difficult things. If anything comes up."

I nodded and smiled. "Yeah. I know that."

"Good," he said, and leaned back. "Anything else on your mind lately that you want to share?"

I sighed heavily. Was I that obvious? "The woman… *her*, whoever she is. She… she wants me. Alone." I paused and shook my head. "She left a message on that note, the one she left Helen, at the bottom, a private message suspended in the vortex for Helen that I was able to crack. And she said…" I echoed the words that I wouldn't forget: "*The others will fall away.*"

"Fall away?" Quentin asked. "What does that mean? We're not going anywhere."

"Exactly. Not voluntarily. Which is why I'm scared she's going to kill you."

Quentin's lips twisted in thought. "That wouldn't endear her to you, though."

"If something happened to you… all of you, any of you. She doesn't know I know about the note. She might try to do it in a way I couldn't trace to her directly."

"Do you think Helen would try something?"

I shook my head. "The language was written that way for Helen, not me. She's not instructing Helen to do anything other than freely show me what they do. Their work in the lab. Which… I guess serves our purposes for right now. But… what does she want with me?"

He sighed. "I think you know that."

I groaned. "I know that she wants my abilities. I mean, I could guess that. But *why*? I barely even know how to use them. She could go kidnap one of the fae for that."

He shrugged. "Maybe there's something special about vampire plus fae? Something you could do that the fae can't?"

"Something I can do that a vampire standing next to one of the fae together couldn't? If there is such a thing, I don't know it."

Quentin pressed his lips together. "But maybe she does."

My teeth clenched and I involuntarily slammed my fists on the table. Quentin jolted slightly but didn't otherwise move. "Then she should *say so* and stop with the mystery. If she means to use me for something, she should fucking say what it is!"

Quentin smirked. "As though you'd let her use you."

I nodded, feeling my face tighten in anger. "I wouldn't. I won't." I tried to un-clench my teeth but they seemed to be sticking. "And I won't let her hurt anyone I care about."

Quentin put his hand on my left one. "No. We won't."

*　　*　　*　　*　　*

"Come on," I muttered, rubbing my thumb roughly and quickly against my pointer and middle fingers. Nothing happened. I rubbed my face and sighed.

It had been awhile since I'd tried anything new, but I was becoming impatient with just practicing what I already knew, trying to get better at those things when I had no idea of the practical limitations of those skills. I could rip the guts out of a person, compel them to nearly any action, any emotion. The only people I struggled to affect were very powerful people who could resist the attacks or heal extremely quickly… and I suspected *she* was one of those people. Still, I would keep trying to get better at those things anyway, but I decided I needed a broader set of abilities too. Never too old to learn a new trick.

Or maybe I was. This wasn't working.

But it had to. *Something* had to. *She* wanted me for my abilities? Well, she was going to get more than she bargained for. But I had to crack basic tiny flame first.

My frustration was interrupted by a knock on the Sphere door. "Who's there?" I called.

"It's me," Coretta's voice replied. I stood from my chair at the little wood table and went to open the door. She was wearing a new dress, dark blue, snug, and down to the knee. The neckline was straight, ending in short sleeves. She was holding a thick book with a dark red hardcover. "I'm not interrupting anything, am I?"

I shook my head. "Not really. I was trying something but it wasn't working. Come in."

I stepped back and Coretta walked inside. "Where is Quentin?"

"He's out getting food," I replied. We had come up with many sayings over the years so it all sounded very natural, and didn't sound like we were hunting humans. "What's in the book?"

Coretta laid it out on the table, flipping it to a page marked with the book's own fabric bookmark. "I have been reading some of Gerard's books," she said, "and I discovered something of interest. See, here," she pointed at a paragraph, and I leaned in to look.

"*Wards placed operate through the darkness' entanglement with the continuum,*" I read, and looked up at Coretta at the end of that sentence. "What continuum?"

"I believe it means the vortex," she said.

My eyes widened. "The *vortex?*" She nodded, and I went on. "*Dark is a force of nature just as is the continuum. One can sense disturbances in the other. The ward identifies threats in the near parts of the continuum and acts to block them.*" I thought about that. "Does that mean that darkness wards are a kind of timeline violation?"

Coretta shrugged. "No more, I suspect, than locking your doors if you know a killer is afoot. We all interfere with the future every moment."

I nodded. "But that's being proactive, versus deliberately changing known existing events. I guess. It's a fine line, though." Coretta shrugged again. "This is interesting, but you didn't bring it to me because of that."

Coretta smirked. "If this mystery woman means to harm those for whom you care, her plans are already in the vortex. Perhaps there are wards that may help?"

I'd told her my fears when we'd gotten back from Oxford, mentally, just about an hour ago. "Maybe… I could ask Gerard. Thank you for looking into it. How… how have you been? You don't come along to anything we do. Are you doing research? Do you want to go home? Do…"

Coretta put her hand up and I stopped talking. "I am reading, yes, and watching. I am fine. And you? What is this thing you are trying?"

The quick change in topic told me now wasn't the moment to press. "I was trying to create fire."

"Ooh, fire! But you did not? I imagine you could."

I frowned and sat down at the table. "Not yet."

Coretta sat down as well and took my hands in hers. "Do you remember when you first thought your voice could be more than beautiful?"

I nodded and smiled. "It could influence people to feel whatever I wanted. So I thought maybe it could be a weapon too."

"And you tried for weeks! You tried to 'influence' a pillow to tear. As though it was a matter of motivation, as it was with emotions."

"It didn't work. It couldn't. I was still using my voice but had to learn to do it differently. Rather than coercing or cajoling, I had to use brute force. Tear it independent of will." Was I looking at the fire problem wrong too?

Coretta squeezed my hands. "How have you attempted to create fire?"

"I thought I could enhance natural friction," I said, and rubbed my fingers together to show her.

"But you are not attempting to do something natural. You are calling your blood to spark a flame. What use do you have for friction between your fingers?"

I noticed immediately that she didn't say friction was the wrong approach, but rather that friction *between my fingers* was wrong. What if I created friction in my blood, between the cells inside of it? I took my right hand back from Coretta and stared at my fingers, focusing hard on the blood inside them. As I focused, I could feel my blood beginning to race around in my hand, and it felt warm. Coretta squeezed my left hand again, and as she did, I felt a burst of heat in the tip of my pointer finger, but it didn't hurt, and then the top inch of my finger was on fire.

It didn't burn. It was *my* fire. It couldn't hurt me.

Coretta grinned. "As I said."

I smiled. "You did. Now I just need to figure out how to make this useful beyond lighting your cigarettes."

"How are you tonight?" he whispered, even though whispering was idiotic. She was the one who needed to hide their conversation. Gerard was alone in Adelita's dining room. He had hoped to see Scott tonight as well, but he had been asleep by the time he arrived.

"Better," Adelita said. He'd arranged to have a telephone installed in her hospital room so he could check in on her. Yet if her nurses knew, they would surely hang it up and force her back to sleep. "I still do not sleep much, but the visions are gone. The pain remains, yet I can move around a bit more."

"You should not attempt it yet," he advised. "Do not rush. We will take care of you."

She sighed. "I appreciate it, Gerard. But I know my limits. I want to be better as soon as I can."

The door to the house swung open and Gerard turned his head to look. A moment later and Vivian and Coretta entered the room. Vivian saw him on the phone and wordlessly raised her hand in greeting. Coretta waved to them both and went upstairs, the stairs creaking like a haunted house with each step.

"You cannot be sure, Adelita," he continued. "Let the doctors be the judge."

"The doctors treat me like an invalid," she complained.

"They only worry for you, as I do. You are delicate now. Your wound tender. And they worry for your state of mind."

"My what?"

"You have endured a great loss," he explained. "It is understandable if you have clouded judgment. You cannot rush back to normalcy."

"Is that Adelita?" Vivian called from the other side of the room.

"It is," he confirmed.

She moved forward quickly and put her hand out for the phone, which he gave to her. She pushed back her hair, which in the dim room looked as dark as a void, and pressed the phone to her left ear. "Hi Adelita!"

He concentrated his hearing to listen to Adelita's side of the conversation. "Hi Vivian! How are things going?"

"Pretty good," she told her. "We're getting somewhere with the research. And I figured out how to make fire, so now I can literally burn the place to the ground when we're done."

Adelita laughed. Gerard tensed up. "Don't make her laugh," he whispered. "She might dislodge a stitch."

Vivian raised an eyebrow at him. "How are you?" she asked into the phone.

"As I was trying to tell Gerard, I'm improving," she said.

"That's great. Will they release you soon?"

"I think so. In another day or two."

"Good. We're looking forward to having you home. But it's late! You should get some rest."

"I will. Say goodnight to Gerard for me."

"Sure thing. Goodnight." Vivian hung up the phone, but didn't convey the goodnight message. "You shouldn't spy."

"How do you know I was?"

Vivian frowned. "A reasonable guess."

He stared up at her. It wasn't really her business, but then again she seemed to think everything was. "What brings you in the house at this late hour?"

She licked her lips and exhaled. "I want to ask you about darkness wards. I read that they can sense threats in the vortex. In the future."

That was a very simplistic way of describing it, but she did not know of what she spoke. "It would be very difficult to place such a ward. Wards in space, frozen in present time for the detection of physical movement, are challenging enough. But to make them *mobile in the vortex, enough to sense what is oncoming in a larger sense, is extremely advanced."*

Vivian raised her eyebrows, her blue eyes glinting in the bit of light. "Are you saying you can't do it?"

Gerard pressed his lips together. "I am not; I can. But there is no guarantee they will work, nor for how long they would operate. And it is not something I can do instantaneously."

She nodded. "Well... I'd appreciate it if you could try. I need a ward against..." she paused, her mouth open, searching for the words. "Death. I have reason to believe that the leader of the Society is going to hurt you. All of you."

There it was again. Everyone in her path in danger. At least she admitted it. "And you can do nothing to prevent it? To remove the weaker of us, at least, from the line of fire?"

She scowled. "I will do everything I can to protect all of you. Which is literally *why I am standing here asking you to do this."*

It was a very small gesture. "You must stop bringing Scott and Adelita into your plans."

Her eyes were shooting daggers at him. "They are adults who can decide what to do for themselves. Will you help or not?"

He stared at her for a long time. Would she take no accountability at all? Perhaps it was entirely up to him to save the others. "I will do the best I can to create a ward. Against the leader, you say? From killing our friends?"

"Yeah," she confirmed. "Or someone she'd put up to it."

"It is an abstract request. It will not be as effective as if you could be more precise."

She shrugged helplessly. "I don't know how she'll come at us. Only that she will."

He sighed. "Very well. It will take some time. I can commit an hour, approximately, each night to building it. It may take a week. Will that suffice?"

She nodded. *"Whatever is the best you can do. Thanks."*

"Of course," he said, turning his eyes from her. *"I will do* anything *to protect our friends."*

"What," she began, her voice sharp as a knife, *"is that supposed to mean."* It wasn't a question; it was an accusation.

"I think you know perfectly well."

She didn't say anything. He could feel her tense even standing a foot away from him. Finally she responded. *"I'm going to protect them too, Gerard."*

"That will be more convincing once you stop endangering them," he said flatly.

She stood by him silently for a long moment, seething, but then turned around and left the house. Her temper didn't restore his faith in her in the slightest.

He'd put up the best ward he could. He just hoped it would be enough.

Chapter Fourteen

We were set to return to Darna's lab at midnight that night. Helen had suggested the time, saying that she thought the lab would be busy earlier and by that late hour everyone would have gone home, or to bed if they slept onsite. It didn't surprise me that Helen wanted to keep most of what we were doing from too many other people – this was "her" project, and no one else should get the credit, in her mind. Not even Darna, who deserved much of it.

It had been... who knew, maybe a week? We'd spoken to people from the past, from a sketchy organization dispensing dangerous pills, and from a lab that seemed – on its surface – to maintain some ethics. We'd begun to scratch the surface of how oversight happened, how the structure held together. We'd started to see how deep the rabbit hole goes.

She had seen it.

Not *seen* exactly; she rarely came along to whatever we did, but she was part of our group conversations and she and I spoke, as we always had, every night. She knew so much now, and had come to see it voluntarily – insisted on it – but every new thing she learned was a lesson she'd keep from me for centuries.

Quentin put a thermos of warm blood on the table, which I was standing next to. He eyed me hesitantly.

"By the time this is done..." I started, mid-thought, "when we take her home, how much will she have seen? How much will she know?"

Quentin sighed heavily. He looked pained, as though he didn't want to answer my question despite having the answer. I waited.

He looked down at the floor. "How much does she already know?"

That was not what I was expecting to hear. "What do you mean?"

He looked at me wistfully. "When we came here, in the Sphere… you stood. You didn't fall."

"No," I began, "I've gotten used to it." He looked at me hard this time, urging on the churning of my brain. "Just like you said I would, and like you did…"

And then I remembered. We landed, and there she was, my beloved Coretta… on her feet.

He must have read it in my face. "She's seen a lot more than we know. Our futures – what's yet to come."

I sunk into the nearby chair, my usual spot now at the small table. "How is this possible?" I shook my head. "Five centuries… we always told each other everything. And now that's all a lie. She never told me anything."

Quentin sat next to me and took my hand. "She couldn't." I looked at him, feeling desperate for any words that could wash away the ache in my heart. "What would you have her tell you? The good things? And spoil them? Like knowing the ending to a great book midway through. Or the bad things? So you could try to change or avoid them, and make everything worse? How could she know in advance which bad things to tell you to change? How could you ever want her to carry a burden like that?"

I thought about the Twilight Zone episode where a woman travels back in time to kill baby Hitler. She kidnaps the baby, replaces him with an orphan, and drowns him. And the orphan becomes the Hitler that kills six million people.

She tried to change a clear, known bad – and became the one who made the bad happen.

"I wouldn't," I rasped out.

Quentin nodded. "And she bears a burden anyway. She has to carry the knowledge of what's happened, the good and the bad, alone. Because she'll never tell you. Because…" and then he chuckled, which was unexpected. "You two, you're so different.

Every pair I've ever seen… friends, lovers, it didn't matter. There was always some element of control. One would tell the other what to do because it was what was best for them. Or so that person thought. One would say, don't go, or come with me. But not you. You and Coretta put each other's autonomy first. I can't imagine either of you telling the other what to do, ever. And she knows that telling you what happens in the future would affect your choices, and…" his voice trailed off.

I picked it up. "Then I'd be less free." I sighed and took a long sip from the now-tepid thermos. "You're right. She and I led such different lives before we met, but… they were the same in the way that mattered. We weren't free. It's why… or at least part of why… she asked me to make her like us. It gave her a freedom society never would."

The funny thing of it was that we were putting into words things I'd always known, but never articulated. My entire friendship with Coretta was based around becoming free, helping each other be free… helping other women be free. Violating each other's autonomy would be the greatest sin of all.

"When I met her… I had become good at being alone. Independent. But the only relationships I'd ever had seemed designed to take my independence away. People only wanted to use me, treat me as a thing that was relevant only so long as I served their purposes. And I saw other people's relationships… marriages were prisons for women. Owned by their fathers, then owned by their husbands. The only way to stay free was to reject all of it and be alone. But with Coretta… it was never that way. Our friendship made us both more free." And it hadn't just been that I turned her. In my solitude, I had been a slave to routine, to living my ordinary life. She helped me be free to become bigger than the day-in, day-out of life… she helped me see purpose, beauty, what good there was in the world.

I stood up abruptly. "Where are you going?" Quentin asked.

"I have to see her."

"What are you going to say?"

I frowned. "She has had to hide what she knows – even that she knows, for… I don't know how long. And she'll have to hide it from her contemporary me for centuries more." I pushed my chair in. "She might not be able to tell me what she knows… but *that* she knows… she doesn't have to hide that from me anymore." Maybe, just maybe, if I could lift at least that burden from her, she could be a little more free.

I knocked on the unadorned brown wood door to the room Adelita had given her to stay in. When she opened it, she was wearing Adelita's brown dress with the gold shiny trim. They were about the same height, though Adelita was a little bigger in the hips, so the dress hung a bit limply off of Coretta.

When she saw my face… well, that was our way, too. Who needs words?

Her lips pressed together and eyes turned softer. "Come in," she said, and I did.

The room was mostly bare, designed for guests Adelita, I supposed, never had time or perhaps interest to entertain. There was a tall but narrow free-standing wood closet, carved on its front with floral swirls in the corners, and a matching shorter and wider dresser. We sat together on the blue-comforter-covered twin bed adjacent to the door and were silent for a long moment. And then, stupidly, I laughed.

"I should have known. How ridiculous." I turned to face Coretta, who was smiling faintly. "Only one question. Just one, and you have to answer." Coretta said nothing but raised her eyebrows. "Are you actually as perceptive as I think, or did you just get a copy of my biography before we met?"

And then Coretta laughed, her quiet, breathy laugh that lit up her face. There was relief there, and I was glad. "Only the abridged version," she smirked. And then I hugged her, and we stayed that way for a few minutes.

When I released her, she'd become serious. "But it doesn't matter what I know. And it also doesn't matter what I infer – and I am good." She smirked slightly again as she said that. "What matters is the one and only thing I know for certain, that is true no matter what happens in this time stream or any other. That I know you, Vivian." She put her finger out and gently rested it over my heart. "And that is all I need to know."

I frowned, a thought entering my mind. "*They* know you, don't they? It's why you didn't want to come when we met Phillip. They know you, but in a way that's outside the timeline... seeing you now would be out of order."

Coretta pressed her lips together. "That could be. But... Vivian... I need you to trust me. I know that there is much you wish to learn. And you will, but... with every step I take, or have taken... *out of order*, as you say... I have a responsibility to protect the timeline, and protect you, and your future, and your right to choose it. So please... do not ask me more. Trust me."

I nodded. "I can't promise I'll never ask anything. But I can promise that I'll always accept when you can't answer, even if you can never answer. And I will *always* trust you."

Coretta smiled. "And I, you, my love. Please remember that. Please remember..." she paused, a long, deliberate pause, and I wondered desperately and futilely what she was thinking. She pressed her lips together softly, her eyes narrowing. Finally, she exhaled heavily. "Please remember that those who love you will always trust you. It will help you to do what is right in your heart."

With those words, it felt as though my blood thickened in my veins, flowing through me like heavy sludge. "It will be hard, then. To do what's right."

Coretta's eyes grew soft, and a little sad. "Yes. More than you can possibly imagine."

I laughed, an act my body did reflexively from frustration. "So you'll tell me that? And that's all? Leave me there?"

She smiled again, but this time the smile was pained. "You told me I would."

I looked at her incredulously. "What?"

"A long time ago." She looked down at her hands. "I saw you, and you approached me, and you told me…" she laughed softly, the chuckle nostalgic and bitter at once, "a few things, much as I am telling you a few things now. Things you knew that I should know. I have carried them with me since."

It was hard to process what I was hearing. "I told you that you'd tell me that it would be hard to do what was right?"

She shook her head. "You told me that you found strength to act when it was hard because you knew I would trust you, because I told you I would."

I rubbed my eyes. "Did I tell you anything else?"

Coretta smiled and chuckled. "Yes." I looked at her beseechingly but knew immediately she'd say no more.

I sighed. "How long ago?"

Coretta said nothing for a long moment. She folded her hands together. "A long time."

"This is very bad science," Darna said, rubbing her eyes.

Gerard wiped his mouth. "Agreed. But what choice do we have?"

She sighed, leaning on the table and putting her head in her hands. "None, without violating the timeline."

He understood her frustration. They had been trying to determine the reason Peter and his offspring's blood had been so weak, but they continually hit a wall. They both suspected that they did not yet have the tools or the knowledge to answer the question. Would the future? Gerard strongly suspected it was some form of mutation to the DNA, but he couldn't prove it. How would someone begin to do that?

In the absence of that ability, they had taken to modifying his own blood, mixing it with all manner of substances and exposing it to a variety of elements, to try to weaken it. And the only way they could discern its "strength" was for Gerard to taste it and qualitatively assess its potency.

"Nonetheless," he noted, "this batch bears some weakness. The radiation seems to have been effective."

"Unless Peter was irradiated," Darna lamented, "that tells us nothing."

"It supports our mutation hypothesis," he suggested.

"It does," she agreed.

There was a knock on the door to the lab. Both of them swiveled on their stools to look toward the sound.

"Come in," Darna said. The door swung open and Helen marched in – and marched was the right word. There was something irritatingly arrogant about her.

"Are you near to done for the night?" she asked.

Darna rubbed her eyes again. "We may as well be. You don't need us? Are Gerard's friends not coming?"

Helen's lip twitched. "They are. Yet you won't be needed tonight. And... what are you working on?"

Darna leaned back on the stool. "We're trying to determine why the vampire Peter's blood is weak. We know that radiation reduces blood's potency. Beyond that, we're stuck."

Helen huffed. "You should focus your work on how to strengthen blood, not weaken it. You know our mission as well as I do."

Gerard watched Darna attempt to suppress anger, to no avail. "You can't see how the tasks relate?" she snipped.

Helen's brow furrowed. "Naturally they do, but the direction of effect is important. Do not waste our resources, Darna. If blood's potency can be decreased, it can be increased." Darna stared back at her, unblinking. "But that is for tomorrow. Go home. Think it over and return with a fresh hypothesis tomorrow."

It was an odd request from Helen, who'd never seemed to care much for Darna's wellbeing, but she did seem tired. "I can continue the work while you rest," he suggested. "Staying up late comes to me naturally, as you'd imagine."

"No," Helen objected, "you ought to take the night off as well. It would not be protocol to leave you here alone, as you are not truly a member of the Society. Not in our employ, properly. There must be much you've not attended to at home?"

Gerard felt his blood flutter in his veins. He hadn't 'attended' to Scott in a number of nights. Perhaps she was right. In fact, perhaps he ought take Scott out... away from the house, the work.

Helen smirked, self-satisfied, without waiting for his reply. "Then it's settled. I trust you can see yourselves out. Have a lovely, restful night!" With that, she spun on her feet and walked out the door, leaving it open.

Darna stared after her. "That was odd."

Gerard sighed. "Indeed. But she is right. I ought to take the night off. You as well."

Her hands were tense, balled into fists. "Something isn't right."

He put his hands on hers. "Many things are not right. But there is always tomorrow."

Darna wasn't satisfied by that, but stood up, adjusted her hair bun, and grabbed her brown satchel from the side of the table. "No," she shook her head, "not always."

Chapter Fifteen

When Quentin and I arrived at the lab, Helen was, as far as we could tell, alone. She greeted us at the door and walked us through the hallways to her office; we neither saw nor heard anyone else. Oddly, however, she didn't say a word either, only nodding at us with a smirk.

"Hi Helen," I tried.

"Hi," she replied, smirking again, her cheeks wrinkling where her smile dimpled them. She said no more.

It was very unusual and *very* suspicious. I called my blood to read her and… there was definitely something dishonest about her. But was it more than what we already knew, but she didn't know we knew? That she had ambitions to get *her* attention? That she had gotten a special, private note from *her*? I couldn't tell.

Once inside her lab she kept moving to the very rear-right of the room where there was a door. I'd seen her go into that room before but didn't know what was in there besides the note-leaving place. She entered, and even though I felt very much like I was walking into a trap, I wasn't sure what other choice there was. Quentin's face told me he was having the same thought. We cast each other a wary glance and followed Helen.

Inside, there was one long wooden desk to the right with books and papers strewn about – it looked like something Gerard might own. It also bore, less like something of Gerard's, a few small cardboard boxes with who-knew-what inside, but the pictures on the outside of the boxes suggested small gears.

To the left was… a whole bunch of contraptions. I didn't recognize most of them. Silver boxes with huge wheels, like old computer mainframes. A wide and short table covered in dials and switches, blinking lights all over. Several clocks, some large, round, and mounted to the wall, and some atop fancy wooden pedestals like some makeshift grandfather clock. Wires and plugs connecting everything.

But I recognized one set of things – large translucent tubes with something vaguely neon sloshing through them. Like something out of a 1950s sci-fi movie. Like *exactly* what Quentin had built in the Time Sphere. I didn't know what specific purpose they served, but presumably Quentin did, and when I looked over at him for his reaction, he seemed thoroughly annoyed.

"Yes, much gratitude," Helen said. "I was struggling with the last piece to connect to the vortex. When I saw these in your machine, I knew they were it. Brilliant, by the way. A conduit for the vortex to manifest and connect to the machinery itself. Truly fantastic."

Quentin did not seem enthused by the praise. "What are you doing with this? It won't travel through time."

"Oh, I know," she said, "not yet, not unless I place it in a vehicle that can generate the needed rotational velocity. But it is a start. Now – to more important news. I received a note!" And Helen's face lit up in the largest smile I'd ever seen.

"Oh?" I said. "From the 1600s guy?"

"No – from *her*. And she was so pleased." Helen went over to the long table and snatched a slip of paper from the top of the largest pile of paper. *"Dear Helen – the result of your communication to Dr. Abelworth was extraordinary. The cumulative result of this new knowledge, over more than two centuries, was that the genetic code within blood can be affected by a wide variety of factors. Viruses, as you found, but other components as well. Perhaps a combination of elements may lead us to success. I am immensely grateful to you, Helen, and your work. You have a bright future in our society. I will keep you in mind for further projects, and perhaps an enhanced role."*

That was… also uninformative. But maybe it was more informative to Helen? From a 2019 perspective, all of that was obvious. Was it redacted for Helen's benefit? Was the truth more complex? Did *she* already have a sense of what the other elements might be?

It reminded me again of the Energy Components Project that had so upset Phillip. *Perhaps a combination of elements may lead us to success.* Were these findings the impetus for the Project?

"Your knowledge from the future opened the door to her… made her see us, made her communicate with us… made her see *me*." Helen's cheeks lifted in a smile but her mouth stayed open, wagging breathily. And here it would be. We used Helen to get to the leader, to begin to understand the hand at the top, but never had delusions about who she was. She was doing this for herself. We had given *her* access to the leader too. So what would she do with that?

I decided not to respond. I would let her have her monologue moment.

"And she will be awed by me even more tomorrow than today. You put yourself in my time stream, and thus I might do to you what she never could. And she will surely reward me richly."

I looked over at Quentin, who seemed amused by this turn of events. "You just acknowledged that your contraption over there doesn't travel through time yet," he snarked. "So what difference is it if our streams overlap?"

Helen grinned. "It doesn't travel through time. But I did not say what it *does* do. The future is rich with knowledge, and particle entanglement gave me all the information I needed."

Quentin's eyes widened at that. She'd mentioned entanglement before, and it was still way too advanced for her. How had she learned about it? Who hadn't properly redacted a note?

"Yes, your machine uses entanglement. It moves when it wishes. And it moves when it is forced to. And machines are not the only things that can be so forced."

Quentin and I nervously eyed each other. No point in hiding it now. What was she planning to move?

"Typically, as you know, we have prohibitions against altering the time stream… but for this, she will make an exception. I know it." I suddenly noticed Helen was twirling a small object between the fingers of her right hand. "Say goodbye," she breathed, and I saw her thumb press down on the object.

Nothing happened.

Helen's eyes flew open; her grin vanished. She held the object – now I could see it was a button – closer to her face and jammed it several times with several fingers. Nothing happened. She looked at us, from one to the other, and threw the button on the floor. "It must have worked!" she screeched.

Quentin laughed nervously, obviously as relieved as I was. "I have to know… what were you trying to do?"

Helen looked at us in fury, then helplessly, then sank back onto the edge of the table, nearly sitting on it. "Destroy your team. Or, rather… prevent it from forming." Quentin and I eyed each other again, this time in confusion. "I'd forced your machine to entangle across two points in time. From the past to some time in its future. And I entangled you too." She cast her eyes at Quentin as she said that. "I had to store… more energy than I believed a machine could hold… perhaps it was not enough. It was to tear you from the moment you met… throw you into a separate future… so that you would not form this alliance that has so much of her attention. So that you would… *fall away*." She slammed her fists on the desk. "How? How is it that *all that energy* was not enough to tear you apart?"

I felt like I had my very first time in the Sphere… spinning, nauseated, having a very hard time staying on my feet. Centuries… all that time not knowing… not understanding what had happened or why…

She thought it hadn't worked. It had, and it had shaped the rest of my life.

My blood throbbed inside me and I was… upset, anxious… enraged. And then it started. The seeking… my anger, my fury longed to tear Helen's soul from inside her and consume it.

I wanted to let it happen.

But my brain wasn't completely lost to me, not fully, and I used every ounce of lesson Thomas had taught me to clamp down on the urge. I could barely process my surroundings, it took so much out of me, and when the urge was fully suppressed and I could return to the world, I saw… well, it was a scene.

Helen was on the floor and bleeding freely from her throat. She was unconscious, and Quentin was standing over her, his mouth dripping with her blood. With the seeking suffocated, my own thirst was free to return to me and I took a step toward her.

A bright light flashed in front of me, blinding me – for a moment stars danced in my eyes and I thought surely something had exploded. But instead, when the light dissipated, there was a man – dirty blond hair, tan suit, but not from the 40s… from the 1970s? He seemed shrouded in shades of orange-y brown.

He looked at me and Quentin urgently. He was so close to Helen he was almost standing on her. "Has anything shifted?"

Quentin wiped his mouth. "No. Not from our perspective."

The man cocked his head. "Yet her timeline disruption was… successful?"

I had to take a big gulp of air because small amounts were not going to get words out just then. "We don't know. What she wanted to happen happened. But I don't know if it was a disruption or just… what was always supposed to happen."

The man nodded sagely. "One may never know the truth of that. What I mean to say is, her intent was to disrupt the timeline as she believed it to be. And she completed the intended action." I nodded weakly. "Then she will be brought in."

Processing words was a struggle, but Quentin was able to pick up for me. "Your organization, for all it does, does punish timeline violators? I knew you didn't encourage violations… but you actively punish them?"

The man nodded. "Oh yes. Zoe cannot abide violations."

Zoe. "Is that… *her*… name?" I forced out.

The man eyed me with interest, and then seemed to come to a realization. "Apologies, I didn't know that you had not yet met her. Regardless, Zoe wants this woman, so I must be taking her." He paused, and then kicked Helen in the side, just strongly enough so that she rolled over, exposing the bitten and bleeding part of her neck. "Before I take my leave, take your pleasure, as you will." He stepped back out of the way, and I was in no position to resist.

When I sat back, Helen was dead.

"I'm sorry," I said mindlessly. "I killed her before you could get her to Zoe."

The man kneeled down and laid his hands on Helen's body. He looked at me curiously, and then smirked mischievously. "Her life was never what Zoe wanted."

Before I could respond, a bright light flashed again and when I could see, the man and Helen were both gone.

I was sitting in a puddle of blood, spreading out across the floor like the wreckage of my life. Quentin sat down beside me, not seeming to care that he too was now sitting in blood. We sat in silence for what must have been several minutes.

Then words came out of my mouth, unbidden, but unstoppable. "Did I do this to myself?"

Quentin sighed heavily and grabbed my left hand in his right. "I don't know. But… that's not the lesson here. Not for me, anyway."

I looked at him, his eyes soft and tired like my own must have been. "So what is the lesson?"

He squeezed my hand. "Magic. Science. Entanglement. Decades, centuries, miles. Secret cults. We overcame all of that."

He smiled, and I did too. I squeezed his hand back. "And here we are," I said.

He nodded. "And here we are."

The moment was broken by a man busting into the room, skidding across the wet floor on slippery black dress shoes before righting himself – I put him around 45, with a few light gray streaks in shoulder-length brown hair. He was breathing quickly and smelled of salty sweat. "You two all alright?"

Quentin and I looked from the man to each other and back. "Yeah," I said. "Who are you?"

"William Jenkins, miss, at your service. Mister Phil sent me, thinking Miss Helen was due to do something nasty to you. Seems I missed it," he said, and frowned.

By over five hundred years, yeah. "You work for Phillip?"

"I did. I work for the Society. Usedta work under Mister Phil, til he retired, per your advice, Miss… ah, he told me your name…"

"Vivian," I replied. "No 'miss' necessary. William… did Helen know you?"

"Sure did, as I worked for her a bit in the last weeks."

"Did… she know that you were going to try to help us, if she did anything 'nasty'?"

William shook his head. "No she did not – I count myself a good actor, Miss Viv, and she did not suspect a thing."

Quentin piped up then. "How much do you know about the Society? Its operations?"

William shrugged. "Not much. Only my day in, day out. I know where some o'that information is, but I can't get at it, not with Miss Helen in charge."

Quentin and I locked eyes, and then I turned back to William. "Right now, no one is in charge. If Helen were to have… died, say… how long do you think it'd be until her post was filled?"

William stared at me for a long moment, his brown eyes a little wide and buggy, but then ultimately shrugged again. "Not too long, but with Mister Phil and Miss Helen both gone, not too many in our unit left. Maybe Mister Nicky would be appointed, but it'd be a day or two I'd reckon."

"Then that's a day or two that the information you mentioned is open to you?"

William's eyes twinkled. "Wicked to spy on 'em... but I'm thinkin this Society's done enough wicked too."

I turned my body fully toward him and leaned forward. "William... you could help us learn some critical information, the last pieces we need to take them down, or at least begin to. Will you tell us what you know? What you can learn?"

He nodded firmly. "Mister Phil told me that I could help. Before he ran away. He talks to me sometimes now, but... magic talking, not on the phone or nothin' like that, so I can't talk back. He needs to be away, and I need to help." I was glad to hear that. I hoped Phillip could be happy, could be safe.

But William wouldn't be. "Are you sure you want to take this on? You're..."

"Miss Viv," he interrupted, "I worked for the Society most my life, and not all's bad. But lately I seen the bad. And it needs stopping. And if it's not me, who?"

I nodded. He got it, at least, whether or not he fully appreciated the extent of the danger.

But if he was going to help, I had to be clear on what we needed. "I don't think you'll find anything on this... it's research by the 51st street lab, and from what Phillip said, highly confidential... but if you can find anything on the Energy Components Project, that would be outstanding. Who works on it, for example."

William nodded to me. "As you wish. I'll seek it out."

Quentin started to stand up, but his left foot slipped on the blood on the floor. He caught himself on the desk in front of us, but knocked off a box covered in dials. It made a loud and sudden crash, cracking open and revealing its inner wiring. William screamed, and then blushed, chuckling at himself.

I felt as though all the blood had drained from my head. I knew that scream. It was a very-toned-down version of the one from my dream.

William was the one who would die.

Quentin must have noticed a change in my expression because he was staring at me. But he didn't say anything.

William rubbed his hands together. "If whatchou say about Miss Helen is true, I best be getting to spying now, while I can. Where can I findja when I got whatcha need?"

Was it safe to give him Adelita's address?

Quentin, likely with the same thought, mused out loud, "You're trustworthy as far as I can tell... so here." *Trustworthy...* he'd sensed that William wasn't lying. He took a piece of paper off of the desk, ripped off a section with no writing on it, and scribbled what I assumed was Adelita's address on it.

William took it, bowed slightly toward us, and then left.

Quentin turned toward me. "What was that?"

I sighed. "I..." I lowered my voice, "I had a dream. Of William. He's going to get attacked, with a sword, and I think it kills him. I heard him scream... it was horrible."

Quentin frowned. "You're sure it was him?"

I nodded. "I'll never forget that scream as long as I live."

"Okay," he mused. "Well, then, if he does help us, we'll protect him. Least we can do."

I nodded, but I felt... uncomfortable. I could still *feel* the scream, somewhere in my gut, and when I remembered it, I felt a bit of nausea too. I wanted to believe I could prevent it, but it felt so real, even then, even before it really happened.

"Come on," Quentin said, holding out his hand to help me stand up. "I think that's enough for one night."

It wasn't that tracking her through the vortex was hard. With her own powers, it was a simple matter. The challenge was that there was... so much of her. The woman had lived over a half-millennium by her own memory, and who knew how much beyond that. Which point to home in on? Which time, which location?

But her mortal friends were easier. She decided to begin with the woman, Adelita... the one she already knew something about. Adelita, after all, had been working for Judah in a misguided attempt to avenge her more-magical sister. She had no more to learn from Adelita's time in his service, and when the foolhardy girl put herself in battle against him, she had no more magical ability than before. Yet her timeline might point to other insights, about Vivian, or vampire magic, or many other possibilities. But time portals took a considerable amount of energy, so she would need to build her stores.

She drew her energy to herself and popped back a few years, landing as planned in the soul cellar. Judah was there, as he often had been, gazing upon the souls he'd collected. She glanced around herself quickly, spotted a can of air freshener, and scooped it up. When she sprayed it, he heard.

He had always been gullible. All she had to do to earn his favor was be just like him, but slightly lesser, always assuring him through word and behavior that he was the bigger, better magic user of them. His knowledge of souls proved useful, far more than he could ever have known. What he told her layered on to her own existing knowledge like a well-matched frosting.

When she laid with him, he showed her some truly adorable – and, admittedly, pleasurable – tricks with soul energy, but they were in no sense why she had come. She did not expend the energy she absorbed as she led him to believe, but stored it deep within her, a trick she doubted he knew. She could hold it indefinitely if she pleased, and perhaps would not need all of it now.

In the morning when she left Judah's company, she asked the vortex to show her how long Adelita would live. And through the web of time she gazed a woman near the end of her days standing before a no-different-looking Vivian, each on opposite sides of a doorway. Elderly Adelita handed Vivian an envelope. She focused some of her power and pulled the year 2017... that would make Adelita... nearly 115 years old. Few lived that long of their own accord... and then Adelita handed Vivian a jar. She focused more of her energy... Vivian was thinking that her own blood had been in the jar... that Adelita had survived on its power! Which explained her unusual longevity!

She grinned to herself. Vivian's blood extended her own life, she had known that, but it could also extend even a mortal life span. That was remarkable. And no one knew, not yet, what it could do coupled with the fae's soul healing ability. The power of the blood infused with the power of souls... it could be the key. The missing piece that made anything possible. Even...

She shook her head. First things first. Immortality for the currently-living was challenging enough.

She closed the vortex window and sighed. Don't get greedy, Zoe, *she thought.* Play the long game. *A resistant, angry Vivian was no good at all. A compliant, pliable one was a much better ally.*

Zoe reached into her pocket and pulled out the tiny diamond earring within. She turned it over in her hand, then closed her fingers on it tightly as though she could draw power from it. And in a sense, she could.

Vivian thought she was nothing like her. But people... they're all the same. Across time, space, and species. Motivated by the same hopes, dreams... and fears.

Chapter Sixteen

When we got back to Adelita's house, I wanted nothing more than to take a nap.

Again my life was swirling around me like an invisible tornado. What Helen had done had changed everything, or been the catalyst that made everything what it was. With one push of a button, she had set things in motion over centuries.

No one was there when Quentin and I walked in, at least not in the living room area. I rubbed my eyes absently.

"I'm going to wash up," I murmured, suddenly feeling the blood caked into my clothes. Quentin said nothing and nodded, so I lurched myself up the stairs toward the bathroom.

But I didn't stop there. I went one door more.

One push of a button.

Could I have stopped her? I didn't know. But I could have tried, if I had known it was coming.

I grabbed the doorknob and threw it open, storming in and slamming it behind me. She was there, sitting on the bed, staring blankly ahead. Like she'd been *waiting* for me.

I felt my blood racing through my body, creating an enormous amount of pressure in my head. "*This*," I snarled, "you couldn't have told me *this*?"

She said nothing. She didn't shift her posture at all.

"You talked a big talk about how telling me the future would be taking away my choices. But now *not* telling me took away my choice," I railed. "How could you *do* that?"

She pressed her lips together for a moment, her eyes shifting their gaze to the ground. Her blonde curls slipped over her right shoulder. "What would you have chosen?"

I rubbed my face. "Maybe I couldn't have stopped her. But I'd have *tried*. I'd have tried, and if I stopped her, it'd have changed *everything*." My voice was cracking now, and I could feel myself starting to shake.

She nodded without moving her eyes. "Yes. What would have changed? What would have happened then?"

I huffed and turned away from her, staring toward the window that had a thick black textured curtain taped over it. "I don't know. Everything." I started to imagine what might have been. He might have taught me how to live, so I didn't have to figure it out on my own. Would I have killed fewer people with his help? Or at least been able to target better, at the beginning.

We would have seen so much. Centuries more traveling… where would he have taken me? Other planets, other countries? A life unhinged to any place or time. I'd never have spent nearly a century wandering Vienna mostly alone, nor…

My stomach clenched and twisted, and I felt like the floor had dropped out from under me. I grabbed the window frame as though I could catch myself.

My voice came out hoarse. *"I'd have made the wrong choice."*

Was the room spinning? I could feel Thomas' words in my mind. Stupid emotions, making stupid choices.

She spoke then: "You have no idea how much I wanted to tell you. Even though I knew. I wanted to give you the choice you deserved."

I turned around again, and her eyes were wide and shiny, her mouth tight, her hands clenched on her lap.

"But I couldn't," she continued. "And maybe I was glad that I could not. Because I am a little selfish. But I couldn't, because it would have been a…" and she cleared her throat and mimicked Quentin's voice, "*massive timeline violation*".

I slid forward, kneeling on the carpet in front of her. "It would have been the biggest mistake of my life. I'd always regret it."

She smirked and shrugged. "If you would remember enough to regret."

I grabbed her hands in mine. "I would. Somewhere, somehow… some part of me would always know what I'd done." I started to shake again, but this time it was a deep horror at myself. I would have been so consumed with undoing what I perceived as a great wrong in my life that I'd have actually undone the greatest thing that had ever happened to me. I'd never have settled down in Paris, never begun charity work there, never met Coretta. And my life wouldn't be worth the timeline it was written on.

She leaned forward and kissed my forehead. "So you forgive me, then? For, this once, making you a little less free?"

I squeezed her hands tighter and leaned my head against hers. "You made me more free. Not this one act. *You.* You did. By existing in my life." I felt tears starting to trickle down my cheeks. "Will you forgive me? For what I would have done?"

Her eyes were an inch from mine and their deep brown seemed to twinkle. "I knew who you were when I decided to love you. It's why I love you, and I would not change you, not even for what you would have done."

I squeezed my eyes shut in a futile attempt to stop my tears, like I could turn them off at a valve. "Thomas was right about me," I lamented. "I am too emotional."

Coretta chuckled, that soft chuckle I loved, and I opened my eyes again. "Nonsense. Was that not the reason you took pity on a poor homeless girl and her son? Was that not the reason you tried to save him? Emotions make you prone to mistakes, but they also make you prone to kindness, and to love, and to the very best of yourself."

I sighed. "And the very worst."

Without pulling her head away, she nodded, just slightly so her skin pressed against mine. "Yes. Both. It's so for us all. Do not think yourself special in that."

I reached up to wipe my face, and then we separated, each sitting up straight. "Still. I need to get myself in check. I don't know," and I glanced up at her then, "if I'll have other opportunities to make terrible, emotion-driven choices."

She laughed deeply, a belly chuckle. "Oh, plenty, no doubt. That isn't a spoiler, my love; that's life. You will make many absolutely *awful* choices due to emotion." She shrugged. "But then again… how awful depends on who you ask."

I laughed weakly, more of a release of breath than a true sound. "I only care what you think," I said, and it was true.

"Oh, well that isn't terribly reasonable, is it?" she said, grinning, her eyes lightening. "I'll forgive you nearly anything."

She thought she was being funny, but it was also true, and it was more than I could bear at that moment. I wrapped my arms around her waist and laid my head against her chest. She put her arms around me too and stroked my hair, as was her way, and it was almost like we were back in Paris, in that small apartment in the city center with centuries ahead of us, centuries that seemed like they would be without end.

Quentin heard a door upstairs slam – a violent sound that shook the whole house, and shook him, too. It was a more aggressive sound than he'd expected at the moment. He heard, muffled by the wood and plaster of the house's floors, walls, and ceilings, Vivian's voice raised in anger. He could have heard her words if he'd wanted to, but he had decided not to pry. She would tell him what she wanted to, if she wanted to. He sat at Adelita's dining room table and found he could quiet the noises that weren't his to hear with his own thoughts.

Quentin had long ago become accustomed to the humming of the vortex inside him. His parents had told him that with enough travel, you could start to feel it. And more and more he felt like he could sense… minor things, shifts, machinations of time manifesting in subtle ways. When that man from the future talked about Zoe, there was something unsaid. There was more.

But what? Neither of them had met him before. But he knew Vivian. He knew her, and Zoe did too. How much did her timeline cross with Zoe's? And how much did Coretta's?

Enough to mess with Vivian's nightmares. He knew she had them. Usually they had slept apart, of course - she in her apartment and he in the Sphere. But whenever they slept in the Time Sphere together, he woke earlier than her and, some nights, saw her toss and turn. Sometimes she would bury her face in her pillow, or the blanket, clutching either in her hands and speaking into them, something muffled and sad. And once, just once, she'd rolled close to him in her sleep and clutched his shirt instead, and he could feel the word vibrate against his chest: 'mercy', in old German, how old he couldn't be sure. A single word uttered as though to no one; a desperate plea spoken knowing full well no one would listen.

He never told her. Dreams were deeply personal, and he didn't think anyone should be held to account for what their brains did without them. But he hoped one day she would feel that she could tell him what it meant.

Still, it was always the same nightmare, or at least the same tossing, turning, and plea. This thing with William, that was different. That was some other thing intruding on her mind. She seemed to think it was some sort of prophecy, and maybe it was. But if her timeline crossed with Zoe's, and Zoe was in any way responsible for William's death, perhaps it was less of a prophecy and more of a memory, but out of order. But would Zoe have to send her the memory? And why would she do that, if she could? To deter William's involvement? Or something else?

Quentin scratched his head and leaned back in his chair. All he knew for certain was that their lives and Zoe's life were far more intertwined than he had ever guessed. But what that meant...

Chapter Seventeen

When I woke up, Quentin was already dressed, wearing a dark gray suit and black shoes. "William is in the house," he said as I sat up and rubbed my eyes. "He brought us something."

I got up and walked to the closet. The bag I'd brought with me was tucked in the corner of it, largely unused. I hadn't been expecting 40s clothes then, when I packed it. I pulled a blue dress with a silver belt from the rack. "How long has he been waiting?" I asked.

Quentin was facing the Sphere's door, his back to me. We had developed a rhythm for getting ready in the evening that didn't need words. "Fifteen minutes, maybe. Or at least it's been that long since Scott told me he was there."

"You could have woken me up."

He shrugged. "I didn't think you'd be asleep too much longer."

I zipped up my dress. The store had contained dresses with both zipper and button closures. Had the zipper been around long in 1943? I didn't think so. I walked to the bed, sat down, and started putting on my shoes.

Quentin turned to face me. "I have a puzzle for you," he said.

"Oh?"

"When you travel through time, the past and the future become... fuzzy. Relative. Right? There's your future and my future, but it's relative to us, not absolute."

"Mhmm," I agreed, sitting upright.

"So... what's the difference between a prophecy and a memory?"

I leaned back on my hands. "One is a vision of the future… things that haven't happened in your relative timeline yet. The other is a vision of the past, things that have. But… they're both visions of points on your timeline."

He nodded. "Right. And if your future, say, is someone else's past…"

"Like Coretta's," I suggested.

He shrugged. "Sure. Or like that guy, who took Helen's body. Or like Zoe."

That was something. "Then my dream could be… Zoe's memory. That's what you mean?" He nodded, and I felt my muscles tense. I shook my head and stood up. "But it's not my memory yet. And it won't be." I sounded more confident than I felt.

"No, of course not," Quentin confirmed, "but… dreams are… activations of nodes in your brain, right? Sometimes memories, or sounds, or thoughts, or any tangentially linked things that get strung together. But you can't activate a node that's not there yet. So how do prophecy dreams happen?"

It was a good question. "Maybe something with the vortex? Maybe because I've traveled through it, my brain can access parts of it?"

Quentin rubbed his chin. "I hadn't thought of that. Maybe."

"What were you thinking?"

He sighed. "I was afraid that she, or someone, put it there."

I frowned. "For what? To warn me? That seems like a silly thing for her to do."

"Yeah, I guess it would be." His forehead was scrunched in worry.

I walked up to him and touched his arm. "Whatever the reason, we've been given a heads-up. We can work with that." He nodded, and I started toward the door.

But he didn't follow. "Is it okay if you talk to William?" he asked. "I need to... do some research on the vortex."

"About this?" I asked, and he nodded. "I don't think you need to..."

"I just need to look for a few things," he interrupted. "Okay?"

The look on his face told me that he wasn't going to stop worrying until he did whatever he had in mind to do. "Okay," I said, and I left him to it.

Inside Adelita's, William was seated on the recliner that Coretta had previously lounged on. He was wearing a brown suit with a frilled white undershirt that looked about a century too old. He smelled better today, perhaps wearing a musky cologne. Besides the cologne, the room smelled unpleasant, like an old sock. There was an unwashed plate on the dining room table – the books had been shoved to the side – and a few sticky empty bottles lying about.

"Miss Viv," he said, standing up as soon as I entered the room. "Good evening."

"Good evening, William," I said, moving forward to shake his hand. "Thanks for coming. What did you find?"

William handed me a thick brown folder. I turned it over, untwisted the string that latched it closed, and pulled out the contents, several manila folders, each labeled. As I flipped through them, it was... incredible. Hierarchy charts. Financial information... bank accounts. With this, we could find out who funded their work. And where that money was being funneled. There was nothing on the Energy Components Project, but I hadn't realistically expected anything from that.

I looked gratefully at William and... realized that he was one of us now. Working with us. With *me*. I had already gotten one person killed and another one stripped of her uterus. And I had a clue as to what could happen to him.

"I want you to know, William... this work... I'm so thankful for it. I know it puts you in a lot of danger. And... you need to know we'll protect you. I will." I thought back to my dream. It was his voice, no doubt about that. And he had screamed in *agony*. "If it's in my power at all, I'll make sure nothing bad happens to you. I promise."

William looked at me kindly. "Grateful for the sentiment, miss Viv. M'thinks we'll protect each other." I nodded, smiling, and William took his leave.

After watching him leave, I turned around to see Coretta standing in the doorway to the kitchen, leaning against the frame, looking at me with... an expression I couldn't quite identify. Distress? She was wearing a much-better-fitting dress, a lavender knee-length one that was appropriate to 1940s fashion; when had she gone to buy it?

"Why did you say that to him?" she asked softly.

I sighed. "I had a dream before I met him... there was a flash of a sword... and I heard him scream. It was horrible, Coretta. And I couldn't see much else but I felt... a way I never want to experience awake. I have to make sure that doesn't happen."

Coretta's face didn't shift while she listened to me, nor after. Why was this bothering her? What did she know?

I stared at her, and didn't say anything for a long moment, and then... I don't know what happened. Maybe she couldn't hold it in anymore. Her firm expression softened, just a bit, but I noticed, and her eyes became sad.

I bit my lip. "I can't save him, can I?"

Coretta pressed her lips together. "No. I don't think you can."

I sat down on the floor and shook my head. "You can say that. I don't need to believe it. Not for now, anyway. I can try." Coretta nodded slowly and smiled softly. "In the meantime," I wiggled the manila folders in my hand, "he's given us a treasure trove. Want to go through it with me? Even though I'm sure you know what's in here?"

Coretta grinned. "I do not, in fact. Not specifically, in any case." She came into the living room and joined me on the floor. I laid the folders out in front of us.

I flipped the one on top open and involuntarily laughed. It was an organizational chart. Phillip's name was at the top bearing the title of Unit Supervisor, and was roughly scratched out with "Helen Smythe" written in its place – by her hand, no doubt. Directly reporting to her, connected with lines, were Nicholas (Nicky, I assumed) Dade, Medical Director; a new name, Wendy Karloff, CFO; William Jenkins, Office Manager; and Chuck Flanigan, Interregion Communications. The latter was surely code for "time travels to other offices and shares redacted information". Hopefully redacted. Helen had reported to Phillip, and her title at the time had been Research Director, but that was now crossed out too and reassigned to no one. Darna Moreno, Senior Biologist, reported to Nicholas – not Chuck, though I guessed that any of her superiors could give her orders – as did a few other scientists: Jason Stevens, Chemist; Antonio Carrera, Virologist; and June Li, Immunologist. Why did they report to Nicholas, instead of Darna? Lila Brooks, Participant Acquisitions, had reported to Helen but was now assigned to Chuck. Patricia Mostino, Human Resources, reported to Wendy.

"This is a much smaller organization than I was expecting," I said. "There's no way this includes anyone from the chapter Adelita visited. But we know Phillip worked there."

Coretta scooped up the other three folders and flipped through them quickly. She stopped at the end of the second one and put the others back down. "Look at this," she said, and pulled out her page of interest, resting it on top of the folder for support. "Phillip may have worked for this group and the other, but they are completely separate financial entities."

She was showing me some kind of financial statement. I skimmed the numbers and got the gist of it – money in, money out – but that was it. The funding sources seemed mundane enough – grants and the like. "How can you tell that from this?"

"This report has to show all activity. The numbers are too small. There is no way possible that these numbers include the other facility's activities."

I frowned. "Does that mean their research projects are separate too?"

Coretta shrugged. "They could collaborate, as can any set of researchers, but they may not."

I thought about the implications of that. "Does that mean that Helen also led the other office? Or did someone else take over Phillip's role there?" I flipped through the folders and didn't see any other organizational charts, so I answered my own question. "Someone else must be working at the other facility now. Helen would have had that chart too if she worked there." Had that been Phillip's intent? To completely segregate the facilities with his departure? If so, why? Or was there some other remaining connection between them?

"If I try to escalate the research…" I began, thinking out loud, "I could talk to Nicky more, and see what he knows. Their lab is small, and maybe I could ask if the other facility has more resources, and try to get him to say if and how they work together. Or if they don't, if that's because of Phillip." Coretta nodded. "And if Nicky replaces Helen… it doesn't seem like any of them have met *her*…" Wait, I don't have to say it like that anymore. "Zoe. I don't think any of them have met Zoe. I need to understand how everything ties back to her."

Coretta shrugged again. "Speaking with this Nicky may be a sound idea. You know not what you may learn." I raised my eyebrows at her, and she laughed. "Nor do I! Not specifically." She grinned.

I smiled too, but then returned to the folders. "I also haven't met the researchers whose work made Phillip feel so much remorse. I have a hard time seeing Darna doing that work. So I have to get an in into the other facility."

Coretta nodded. "If Nicky takes a liking to you, perhaps he could get you to speak with Adelita's doctor there. So you might learn what pills they gave her."

My blood quickened inside me. "That's a fantastic idea. I can't undo what they did, but I can learn what they were trying to do."

"Longevity, no doubt," Coretta said, stating the obvious. "Metal will outlast flesh, and so if her uterus was making her sick, turning it to metal would save her."

I huffed. "It's practical. Totally removed from the consequences, but for the precise problem of survival, practical." I shook my head. "So yeah, that, but I mean… she only took one. What was pill two going to do? What was the next phase? If pill one got her to 'survival', what would pill two do? It couldn't turn more organs into metal. You can't have a metal bladder, or a metal heart, unless it was metal with gears and stuff. Some organs do things that create survival. A more durable replacement couldn't just be a metal hunk."

Coretta continued to nod slowly. "All excellent questions."

"Okay, so that's one next step." I turned back to the folders. What else was in there?

Most papers were administrative – a building lease, a certificate of incorporation for "SFL-546" – was that their region number? No decimal for once? Salary lists – Darna was being decently paid, at least. I had to give the Society that – there didn't seem to be any differences in pay by gender, or by my guess at ethnicity based on the names. Pretty big deal for the time. Pretty big deal for future times. Did Zoe mandate pay equity? Were there any cross-region mandates?

Ugh, getting distracted again. The final folder was the thickest. This one contained write-ups of ongoing research projects. The first one was our own – *Toward the elimination of light toxicity in vampire blood*. What I could understand of it wasn't surprising – all of the findings I already knew were there. But the rest was too technical, too jargony. I'd have to share this with Gerard.

There were two other projects described. The first I'd also heard about, and reading the write-up of it made me laugh. *Creating a preparatory device for introduction to other time regions.* Poor Darna, the biologist-who's-not-an-electrician, or a historian, or anyone who should be building that sort of thing.

The second was... intriguing, to say the least. *Reducing human rejection of external intervention.* From what I could gather through the jargon, this was an effort to stop the body's immunological response to foreign substances, such as injections or transfusions. The introduction seemed to suggest that one of the biggest obstacles they encountered to increasing longevity was the body's own defenses, rejecting outright in most cases the changes they tried to make to increase survival, and in some of those cases reacting violently and destroying the body instead – being so riled up in defense that the body attacks its own parts.

Decomposition of extremities.

There was a lot of promise in work like this. It related to our own research – our body's response to sunlight is itself an overreaction, a rejection of a perceived dangerous external substance. But it was also tremendous for humans. If you didn't need to worry about blood type in transfusions, or compatibility in organ transplants, those procedures would save even more lives.

However, as with anything, there was area for misuse. Shutting down the body's defenses so that it accepted whatever "external intervention" the Society wanted to do to it could kill as often as it could save. Again, how the research was used was everything. And I had no idea what Helen, or Zoe, or anyone, had in mind for this.

The work was in its early stages and they hadn't had much success yet – the project, led by June, was still experimenting in artificial environments like petri dishes and nowhere near human subjects. I was glad for that. Maybe I could learn more about this work from June before it could hurt anybody. And get a sense of June's ethics, while I was at it.

Coretta had been reading along with me, but she was a bit faster so was done a few moments sooner. When I looked up, she was staring at the floor in thought. She noticed me looking at her and turned to me. "When you see Gerard at the lab, will you tell him that his boyfriend is becoming insufferable?"

I frowned. "How so?"

"Without Gerard here to amuse him, or to study with, he is restless. But rather than channel that into a useful activity, he has begun consuming bottles of beer, and as he eats and drinks this place has become a mess. Adelita used to clean, but without her here, Scott makes dreadful comments, the like of which you can imagine. Insinuating that I ought to be his maid. Adelita ought not have had to clean up after him either, but as this is her house I could understand the behavior. I will do no such thing."

I remembered, before we went to meet Phillip, Nicky, and Helen in the Bronx, wondering at Scott's behavior. I had meant to raise it with Adelita, but then she became sick, and we started our experiment with Darna, and it just fell by the wayside. It seemed that my concerns weren't unfounded.

Would Gerard actually tell Scott to clean up after himself? Or would he just hire a maid until Adelita came home?

"If Scott should continue this way," Coretta went on, "I will need to speak with him. Yet I do not know what I would say. I…" she let her voice trail off, and her brow furrowed. Finally she shook her head slightly and sighed. "I did not know he had been this way."

It took me a second to grasp what she was saying. It was an unusual turn of phrase. "You mean… he won't be. That somehow he becomes a model citizen?"

Coretta laughed. "I would not say model citizen, but he becomes much more of an ally. I do not know when, or what changes him. I wish I did."

I smiled fondly at her. "I bet it's you. Something so fabulous you'll do that he can't relegate us to housemaids anymore."

She laughed again. "More nonsense," she said, smiling.

I scooped up the folders and stood up. "Well, if I'm spouting nonsense, then there's no time like the present to go see people I might need to lie to."

Coretta didn't get up but looked up at me. From this angle, her face looked heart-shaped, with her cheeks blushed rosy. "You do not lie to them much."

Had I told her that? Was that true in the future? Or was she just reading that in my face, or my words, the way she always had?

I was overthinking this.

"No," I said, cocking my head, "but I haven't had to. They've mostly been… obliging."

Coretta squinted a bit, and I could tell she was going to say something provocative. "What do you think Darna would say if she knew about Dohain?"

I hadn't thought of telling her about it. "I don't know. I *hope* she'd be horrified. But…" I couldn't be sure. "Do you think I should tell her? As a test of character, maybe?"

Coretta shrugged lightly, her smirk and teasing eyes saying everything I needed to know – she wasn't going to tell me to say anything, but it was definitely a good idea, and certainly a minor spoiler.

I shook my head and laughed. "You're being bad."

She leaned back and put her legs up in front of her, pulling them close to her chest. "Perhaps. You are not the only one who's allowed to make poor decisions due to feelings."

My heart swelled. She was the best person this world had to offer. I'd cut the timeline open if I knew how, if it could save her.

I swallowed hard and looked up at the ceiling. I didn't deserve her. I didn't deserve her loyalty, her love, any of it. In her whole life she'd only ever loved two people and I didn't deserve to be one of them.

She stood up next to me, put her hand on my chin, and physically turned my face toward her. She didn't say anything, but just stared hard at me and shook her head.

I swallowed again and nodded. It was her way of reminding me to stop my spiraling thoughts. "I wish you could come with me. It can't be fun being cooped up in this house all the time."

She seemed to reflect on that. "I could go with you to meet Nicky."

"Yeah? He won't meet you in his future?"

She shook her head. "He's a minor player in all of this, Vivian. But he can likely get you what you wish for now."

I nodded. "But you can't meet Darna."

Coretta shrugged again. "She is not a minor player."

That was… interesting. I hadn't thought of Darna as being more than our scientist-of-the-moment. "But… she hasn't met you yet. Right? You've met her, but how would that impact your ability to meet her now? It's not a spoiler as long as you don't say any."

She shook her head. "We meet in your future. It is too dangerous to alter that."

She wasn't going to budge. "Okay. But Nicky. You could come for that."

Coretta narrowed her eyes. "Could I be sure I would not encounter others?"

I thought about that. I couldn't guarantee it… but wait. I could.

"No, but I can make you invisible until we get to his office," I said.

She grinned. "That will be suitable, then." She paused for a moment, biting her lip. "This Nicky… is he cute?"

He'd received the note sometime during the night, stuffed under his doormat. He didn't have a phone. He couldn't. He had to stay off the grid.

The note was from William, saying that he'd successfully gotten the vampires the files. That was good to hear.

The vampires had seemed to think that he would retire quietly, and perhaps initially he'd thought he would too. That he could finally have peace. But peace was not to be. His remorse ate at his soul like a parasite. How could he leave the consequences of what he'd done for others to fix? No, he may have retired and thereby lost his standing in the company, but that actually gave him an advantage. They couldn't supervise him all the time anymore. He was off their radar. And he could still use what he knew to help stop them, to at least somewhat undo the horrors he'd had a hand in.

It was terrifying to think of what he'd enabled for the lofty goal of stopping death. It started small, little moral issues he could set aside – that woman was sick anyway, or was losing an eye that big a deal when it meant you'd live a few more years? But it got bigger over time, and then when they brought in the Nazi research... when he read their findings, he'd thrown up. He would never forget one report on the violence they'd visited on two identical twin girls. Different "treatments" for each, to see the difference in genetically identical bodies. It was a nightmare. It dawned on him then that what he was doing, what the Society was doing, was not really so different. And it only became worse as the Energy Components Project progressed.

He started to cry again thinking about it. His hands balled into fists involuntarily. He would spend every remaining day of his life atoning for his role in the Society's work. It hadn't all been bad – there was a lot of good research, in addition – but the bad was there and he had not stopped it.

He would now.

Phillip... no. No more new name to blend in, to disappear. Pinyah went to his dresser drawer, a tall nearly-black wooden column, and removed from the bottom drawer a box. He sat down on the floor crosslegged and opened it.

The things inside were the man he had been before. The man who hadn't yet learned to hide, to be afraid. To give them what they wanted, to be terrorized. He took from the box a silver pendant, a Star of David, its arms layered and crossed so as to appear more three-dimensional. He held it, touching it softly, and then put it on. He reached back in the box and removed his simple black yarmulke and a few black bobby pins and adhered the cap to his head. Finally, he removed his mezuzah, a beautiful piece with Hebrew letters inscribed in aqua blue. He would hang it up again.

Pinyah put the box back in the drawer and stood up. Next, he would help the vampires get access to the other lab. When he had retired, he'd ended the dual-leader role he held in the hopes that Helen's, and now Nicky's, lab could do real good without the taint of what the other lab was doing. He didn't know if it would work, and now it was harder for the vampires to get access to where the problems were, but it wasn't impossible. If Nicky was willing to make the necessary introductions, it would be enough, and if he wasn't, William could try to persuade him or seek other ways of making the connection. And this was only the beginning. He would do what was necessary to cut out all the rot.

He closed his hand tightly around the mezuzah. "Barukh ata Adonai Eloheinu, melekh ha`olam, hagomel lahayavim tovot, sheg'molani kol tov." He was unworthy, but God had blessed him with the ability to atone, and to bring light into the world, and he would.

Chapter Eighteen

Coretta and I got to the Society around 10 p.m. We'd made a pit stop to feed on some men we found having a late dinner in a diner's outside seating area – Coretta claiming the one she thought was "cutest", and me not particularly caring.

Before we entered, I took her arm and called my blood to hide us from the world. Once we were invisible, I decided to try something out – I released her arm. She stayed invisible, which was what I had been hoping for. Next step – I made myself visible again, releasing the energy from myself. She stayed invisible.

"Okay, great," I said. "We'll go in, and you just follow close."

"As you like," her disembodied voice said. It wasn't that strange – I was used to hearing her disembodied voice in my head; this was just more external. "So you know, my love, while your skill at this is quite proficient, I am… holding on to the cloaking energy, so to say. Should you attempt this with others, they would likely need to be able to do so."

I nodded. "Thanks for the tip." I opened the front door and held it. "After you."

First stop would be Darna's lab where Gerard would be, and hopefully where I could find out where Nicky's office was. Or would he be using Helen's office now? Hopefully Darna would know.

I had brought the folders William gave me with me in a gray shoulder bag, more like a body pouch than a purse. I wanted to give the research findings to Gerard, preferably without Darna knowing. Fortunately, when we got to her lab, she wasn't there, but Gerard was.

"Hi Gerard," I announced myself tersely. I hadn't forgotten our last conversation, but now was not the moment. He hadn't been entirely wrong, anyway. "How's Ophelia?"

He was seated at the test tube desk, poring over a few samples. "Hello Vivian. She's well. Though sadly her arm has not returned. And the lentivirus concentration wanes each night. Her immunity is nearly entirely gone."

My heart sunk. "So she lost her arm for nothing."

Gerard nodded. "It would seem so. Yet Darna had an idea, that if we could in some way disable the body's tendency to reject foreign materials, that the lentivirus could take root in a more permanent manner."

Right. "Yeah, about that… please check these out when you get a chance." I pulled the research folder from my shoulder bag and held it out to him. "Don't tell anyone you have this."

Gerard eyed me skeptically but nodded and took the folder. He placed it inside a briefcase at his side, black with a crisp silver buckle that clacked when closed. "Where is Quentin?"

"He's doing some research on the vortex," I said. It was as specific as he'd been… of course I knew more about it generally, but it didn't need saying.

Gerard seemed to accept that explanation. "And you came to bring me the folder?"

"Not only. Where's Darna?"

"The washroom."

Okay, I could wait for that. "Good. Hey, while I'm waiting…" How was I going to deliver this? "I've heard through the grapevine that there've been some… uh… problems at home while we've been gone."

Gerard looked at me questioningly. "Problems?"

"Yeah. Apparently Scott's in the habit of expecting whatever woman is around to clean the house. He's not taking care of himself, nor picking up after himself."

Gerard frowned. "That is unfortunate. Adelita had always performed those tasks, so he was not accustomed. Yet… he ought not expect it of you, or Coretta. And he ought not leave a mess for her return from the hospital. She should return to a clean home. She should be cared for." The look on his face… his furrowed brow, dimmed eyes… he thought of Adelita as a daughter-figure. His eyes screamed that sort of love. I felt myself getting misty and bit my lip to stop it.

"Gerard," and that word came out cracked, and I felt an invisible hand on my arm. I cleared my throat. "It's wonderful that you have this caring relationship with Adelita. But she's an adult, and an intelligent woman, and you should be cautious that your paternal feelings for her don't translate into treating her like a child."

Gerard's face fell at that. "Does she say that I do?"

"Well, not in so many words. It's… the evolution. That I've seen basically the whole of society take, in parts, and fits and starts. First men think we're objects, then they think we're people but servants, then we're people but mental children. I want you to get to the people-and-adults phase. And maybe you've treated me differently because I'm not human, or because I'm physically strong, or whatever reason, but human women are adults too."

Gerard looked at the floor. "Have I done this to her?" His voice was full and moist.

I stepped forward and touched his shoulder. He looked up at me, pained. "Your daughter is a brilliant woman. It's not too late to show her you know that." He nodded, and pressed his lips together in a half-smile.

It was then that Darna walked into the lab wearing a very-loose-fitting baby-blue dress that was cinched at the waist with a shiny silver rope. "Hello Vivian!" she said cheerily. "Nice to see you. What brings you here tonight?"

"Hi Darna," I said, thinking about Coretta invisibly watching this woman she knew more about than I did. "I have two questions. One, where is Nicky's office?"

She laughed. "Nicky? Are you on personal terms?"

I realized that I had been using the familiar nickname and laughed myself. "Sorry, that's the name I heard him called when I met him. Nicholas, then."

"He's moving into the unit leader office right now. You can probably find him coming in and out of there."

"Great, thanks. The second question is harder. I wanted to tell you about the research that led us here in the first place."Gerard side-eyed me at that, but I kept going. "Do you know about what was done on the planet Dohain?"

Darna shook her head. "No. I gather you mean what the Society did. What did they do there?"

"They massacred the entire population. They experimented on them with no safeguards as far as I could tell, nor any regard for what happened to the people. They achieved some longevity but the people either disintegrated into living sand or killed themselves."

Darna listened, her face not reacting while I spoke, but once I stopped she softly nodded. "They committed genocide on the population. Did they even learn anything of use?"

"No. What we extrapolated from the findings... it was guesses, Darna. We got lucky."

She shrugged. "Much of science is about getting lucky. But... why do you tell me this story? Do you want more promises that I will not commit genocide on my patients? I won't. This lab won't. We do not work that way here. And Nicholas will not change that; he is a good man. I fear it less in his leadership than I did in Helen's."

"And the other Society lab? The one on 51st street?"

Darna's mouth opened, and closed, and she exhaled. "That lab is made up of monsters."

"Do you know what they've done? What they do?"

She shook her head. "I know a bit. I learned about some of it from Phillip, but he wouldn't tell me much, and always said that I should never put my hands in that work. He wanted me apart from it. He wanted me… morally clean. I only visited there once. I don't want to return."

I nodded. "I'm going to ask Nicholas to introduce us to the other lab. I need to know more about what they do there." How honest should I be? I was close to telling her the truth of why we were here, but could I?

If you wish to say it, you need not fear, I heard in my mind. *You may trust her.*

I exhaled heavily, bracing myself. "When I saw what they'd done to Dohain, I knew I had to stop it. What you do here, Darna, is good work, but… you know other Society labs aren't good. Labs across time and space wantonly committing genocide. That's why I'm here. To learn about the Society so I can stop it. And your lab… hasn't given me that much to go on because you are doing good things. Except for Helen, who…" Got me closer to Zoe than I could have hoped? Maybe. "Anyway, but the other lab has to be stopped. They gave my friend pills that turned her uterus to metal. I need to know what else those pills did, or are doing, or would have done if she'd taken more. I need to understand how regions are linked together – you all seem to work so separately; is there any connection? Any oversight? You have ethics but some do and some don't. So if there's no oversight, beyond… beyond timeline violations, and punishing those, what does…"

Darna didn't know her name. This was a big deal. I felt like I was on Trenzalore. Do I say it? Do I keep it hidden?

I closed my eyes to center myself, and opened them again. "What does Zoe do, if not oversight? Why does everyone fear her? If no one knows anything about her, what are they fearing? Why is she doing this? Why is she allowing the bad? How do I stop her?"

I stopped. Darna was staring at me. I had thrown a lot at her.

She blinked, finally, and took a deep breath. She reached behind her head and pulled off the thin pink band that had held up her hair, which now fell loose around her shoulders. She wrapped the band around her wrist, and then looked up at me.

"You know her name."

I nodded. "Only as of recently. But yes."

"And you told it to me."

"Yes."

"Does anyone else here know it?"

I shook my head. "Not that I know of. I haven't told anyone else."

"How? How did you learn it?"

I laughed involuntarily, tension trying desperately to leave my body. "Do you know why Helen isn't boss anymore?"

Darna nodded. "They said she committed a timeline violation and was suitably penalized."

"Did they tell you what 'suitably penalized' means?"

Darna's eyes widened. "Stripped of her title... but... more?"

"Yeah. I killed her. It was my timeline she'd violated."

Darna grabbed a stool and sunk onto it. "Why would she do that?"

"Zoe told her that I would come to her when my friends all 'fell away'. Helen took it upon herself to try to speed the process. She tried to alter the timeline to tear us apart."

Darna's laughter caught me off guard. She waved her hand in front of her. "Apologies, that isn't funny, but it's... that was Helen, wasn't it? Anything to impress the leader."

I nodded. "Yeah. It was her alright."

"But," and she looked concerned now, "you're well?"

Now I laughed. "I'm as well as I've ever been."

Darna gripped the stool top with her hands on each side of her. "You still haven't said why you're now telling me all this."

"Because I think I'm going to need your help. An ethical insider? The more of those the better."

She frowned and sagged. "I can give you information. But… if I do anything too direct to stop them or interfere in other labs' work… if I lose my post, I can't help you. I could also lose my life."

"I know. I know it's not small, what I'm asking. I don't want you to do anything too direct. You should stay behind the scenes. At least for now." I walked closer to her so that I was standing right in front of her. "Do you think they would kill you?"

She shrugged. "To answer one of your questions… I only fear Zoe because everyone does. She's a mystical all-powerful person who made this Society and monitors it. She gets our notes and responds and orchestrates communication between regions to improve the science. But beyond that… I only fear her because she's so unknown."

I put my hand on her shoulder. "So let's dig in to all this – learn as much as we can, and get to know her." Darna nodded, and I was glad she was on board.

I turned to Gerard. "Show her the folder."

Gerard raised his eyebrows. "*'Don't tell anyone you have this,'*" he mimicked.

"Yeah yeah," I rolled my eyes.

He retrieved the folder from his bag and handed it to Darna.

"Oh, the research reports," she said. "I wrote the one on our work. We have to track our findings."

"That's fine," I waved my hand. "I want Gerard to read it though, so we can be sure you're on the same page on the technical stuff. Okay?"

Darna nodded. "Of course, that is fine. He won't find any surprises." She smiled, closed-mouthed, at him.

"I want to ask you, though, about June's study."

Darna looked up at me in surprise. "I do not work on that. But her work could help ours, if…"

I waved my hand again. "I know, if the body could stop rejecting the lentivirus long enough for it to have permanent impact. Makes sense, but you grasp that there are huge dangers in shutting down the body's defenses, right?" She nodded, pressing her lips together. "So I want you and Gerard both to read her report. So that we can know if there's anything… inappropriate… going on."

Darna nodded. "How did you find the reports? They are supposed to be for the unit leader's eyes only."

I shrugged 'innocently'. "Don't worry about it."

Darna smirked, her eyes dancing. "If reading research reports is a way I might help, then you've enlisted the correct person."

"While you two do that, I'll go speak with Nicholas. I'll let you know if he'll help."

Darna pressed her lips together tightly and looked at me hesitantly. "Their lab's resources would aid in our study. But… know what that means. They have a machine that permits one participant to receive multiple treatments, one in each limb, without any mixing of treatments within. It is the perfect control to see the real differences in effects. But it…" she shook her head, her eyes turning sad. "I have seen it operate. They strap a person in, limbs splayed, as in the famous medical image, vitruvian man. They use a tourniquet on each limb. They inject what they will in each… and the effects are observed. If the person should suffer, they do not care. They watch the person scream; they watch the limbs decay. Should the injections affect the torso, threaten the life, they do not stop. No matter how the person may protest, or beg. They have no concern for consent." She sighed heavily. "Should you work with them… you will see that. They will use methods such as that for our experiments."

I bit my lip. "I know. But I don't mean to work with them more than I have to. I just need to know what they know."

"Even if you shut down that one lab," Darna said, "there are thousands more like it."

Thousands. This was every bit as expansive as I'd thought. Did I have a bigger plan? Yes. It was a loose plan, and a catastrophically bad plan, but it existed.

"If I shut down one lab, where no one else has – Zoe will come to me. And I stop her, maybe I can stop everything. And if not, we can take each bad lab down one at a time."

Darna laughed. "That sounds ambitious. And dangerous."

I shrugged. "At least, if I meet her, I'll know what we're dealing with."

*　　　*　　　*　　　*　　　*

Darna directed "me" to Nicky's office, and "I" stood in front of a plain wood door with a small placard hung on it still bearing Helen's name. Darna took her leave to return to her work.

"You here?" I thought to Coretta.

"I am," she thought back.

I knocked on Nicky's door, and his voice called back: "Who is it?"

"It's me," I said, and then realized I'd met him all of once, "Vivian."

"Come in," he said, and I opened the door. I walked through and held it open long enough for Coretta to grab it. As I moved forward, I heard the door close behind me. I was struck by the smell of disinfectant, as though Nicky were trying to erase any evidence Helen had ever been there. It was a much smaller room than the others, but it was an office, not a lab, so it didn't need much. There was a silver rectangular desk with a calendar and three open boxes resting on top. Nicky was sitting in the chair behind the desk, and behind him was a window, the moonlight coming through it casting a glow that made him seem haloed and twinkled on the desk. There was exactly enough room for one additional piece of furniture, a bookshelf along the left wall.

His eyes were focused on the door. "I do not know *you*. You are?"

I glanced behind me. Coretta had dropped her invisibility – had she done it as we were walking in, or did she do it in a way Nicky could see? If the latter, he didn't seem fazed by it.

"Coretta," she said, gliding forward in front of me to shake his hand.

He took her hand, but rather than shaking it, he kissed it. "A pleasure to meet you."

Coretta smiled her usual seductive smile. "The pleasure is all mine."

Nicky smiled. "To what reason do I owe this visit?" He was looking at her, and I wasn't sure there was a point in my being there.

"Oh, Vivian would describe it better," she said, and they both looked at me expectantly.

I rolled my eyes. "Nicholas, you may know that our research has produced some promising findings, but we've hit a roadblock. Several, in fact."

Nicky nodded knowingly. "The side effects are too large. And the effect is only temporary."

"Right," I said. "I don't think this lab has the resources to solve those problems."

Nicky raised his eyebrows and sat back in his chair. "You mean to say, our lab doesn't have the moral latitude to solve them."

I sighed. So he knew too. "I don't exactly mean that. I don't know what they have. I just know it's more. More equipment, more staff."

Nicky nodded slowly. "Your request would have been easier when Phillip was here. Before he retired, his last act was to sever any business ties between our labs. We had shared a Unit Leader to coordinate our activities, but in practice we rarely worked together as it was. Darna found their work distasteful, and Phillip of course agreed. So with his final act he allowed us the freedom to operate completely independently." He leaned forward and folded his hands on his desk. "Thus it would not be simple to transition portions of our work to their lab."

"What if you don't have to do anything?" I suggested. "Just make the proper introductions and help get them on board. Quentin and I alone would do the portion of our research in their lab. Nothing Darna or anyone else here does has to be contaminated with anything they do."

He pondered that. "Your team knows everything Darna does?" I nodded. "It could work. But when you say... get them on board... I would need to compel them to participate in our lab's research. Which is a form of endorsement."

I shrugged. "Not really. Just get them to meet with me and hear me out. You could say that you know a scientist, one who doesn't work in your lab, who's interested in working with them. I promise we will not do unethical things in the name of this work. And they should be interested; it all serves the Society's goals, right?"

He twisted his lips. "I do not know if it does." He nodded slowly. "Very well. I will consider it. Come back tomorrow and I'll give you my answer."

"Okay. Thank you." I paused. "Is there anything else I can do... tell you, maybe... to help sway you?"

He shook his head. "No, it's not you I need to consult. Now, if you please."

"See you tomorrow, then," I said.

He looked at Coretta. "Will you return tomorrow as well?"

Coretta tilted her head. "I may. Though I need not return if I am still here?"

Nicky's mouth opened. Most men reacted the same way, shocked by her brashness. It didn't much matter what year it was.

How will you avoid Darna? I thought to her.

She bit her lip. *He won't need to work with her today,* she thought.

"Oh... yes," Nicky muttered. "That... is true. Yes, stay."

I chuckled and shook my head. *I'll tell Gerard to keep her away.*

She glanced over her shoulder at me and gave a small nod. *Worst case, I think I might be able to disappear again. I know what it feels like to hold on to it now.*

She probably could. *Okay. See you tomorrow.* Then I realized that I didn't need to say that part secretly. "See you tomorrow, Coretta," I said out loud, and turned and walked out.

*   *   *   *   *

I decided to take a peek in Adelita's house before going into the Sphere, with my new knowledge curious what Scott was up to. Cori started barking nearly instantaneously. She usually stayed in one of the upstairs bedrooms, napping or playing with whoever was home, but now she was darting around the first floor and wagging her tail furiously.

"Okay," I said, leaning down to pet her soft fur, "I'll get you some food." I walked into the kitchen and went to the bag of dog food in the far right corner, underneath a wood utensil block. I opened it up and immediately caught a whiff of it – it smelled like dried barley. "Gross," I told the dog, who seemed uninterested in my assessment of her food. She was still wagging, now her whole body wiggling adorably. I reached down and scratched her behind her ear. "I'll put some of this in your bowl for now but I'll make you something better too, okay? So don't fill up on this crap." I grabbed a handful of food pellets and transferred them to her bowl, a circular light blue one with a picture of a white bone on the inside. She didn't hesitate to dive in.

In the meantime, I went to see what was in the ice box. I sifted through for a bit and came upon a halfway-decent-looking steak. It was frozen though, so I put a pot of water on to boil so I could quickly defrost it. I didn't know if this was the best or preferred way to do it, but it's what I knew.

As the water came to a boil and I carried the pot to the sink where the frozen steak lay, I heard footsteps behind me. "Cooking?" Scott's voice said hopefully, but also uncertainly.

"For Cori," I said, beginning to slowly pour the boiling water over the steak. The water splashed up at me, singeing my arms.

"You are cooking a steak for a dog?" He sounded annoyed, and I began to hear what Coretta was talking about.

"Yup," I said, continuing to pour.

I heard him huff and pull out a chair at the small, round, marble-topped kitchen table behind me. "Adelita will be home tomorrow, correct?"

Oh, no, that wasn't going to happen. I put the now-empty pot down on the counter and turned to Scott, who was sitting. "She will, and she'll still be recovering. From *major surgery*. And you know, Scott," I walked toward him until I was standing right in front of him, and I leaned forward so my face was close to his, "she was very, *very* good to you for a long time. Cooking for you. Cleaning up after you. When *you* were a guest in *her* house. And now that she is injured, I *fully expect* that you will make it up to her by treating her with the same kindness."

Scott frowned. "I do not know how to cook. And besides, Vivian, she is much better suited to it. Women are predisposed to such tasks."

I felt myself beginning to sneer. "Oh, how convenient – men, the *superior gender*, suddenly become inept in the face of a stovetop. Amazing, how you are the best at things you want to do but somehow 'less well suited' to tasks you don't want to do. Well Scott, I don't care if you really believe that bullshit or if you only say it because it serves your purposes. You *will* take care of her when she comes home. You *will* treat her hospitably. And if you *don't*, and God forbid you expect her to lift a finger in household chores, I will see to it that you hurt in ways you didn't know were possible. And if you think I'm afraid of Gerard, I'm not. Let him come at me."

I knew all I needed to know about how I looked from Scott's face – his wide eyes, pupils dilated, slightly agape mouth. His breath was quick and sharp. I leaned away from him and stood up straight. Finally I unlocked my eyes from him, retrieved the defrosted steak from the sink, and went back to the stovetop, removing a pan from the cupboard below.

"If you want to learn how to make a steak, watch me," I said, not looking over my shoulder.

I heard him stand up and slowly walk over. "How did you learn?" he asked softly, cautiously.

"Watching other people," I replied. "Restaurant cooks. Who were mostly men, by the way, because men suddenly figure out how to cook when they're being paid for it. I never got to taste it, though. It was easy to steal a few vegetables or potatoes here and there. But you give someone a steak with a chunk taken out of it, they get cranky." I shrugged. "The smell tells me if it's right. If it starts to overcook it smells… rougher, like charcoal. If it's not cooked enough, it just smells like dead, bloody flesh." I flipped the steak with a spatula. "A steak this thickness only needs a few minutes on each side."

Scott continued to watch. "Does Adelita like steak?"

I smirked. "I don't know. You can ask her."

When the steak was done, Scott retrieved a plate for me and I cut it up into small dog-mouth-size pieces. Cori had started paying attention to what I was doing when the steak began to sear, letting the characteristic juicy smell out, and was eagerly waiting while I cut. I threw the bone away and put the plate down for her, and she scarfed it up.

I didn't know if Scott would comply with my order. I hoped he would, and if he didn't, I'd make good on my threat. Adelita deserved for him to treat her better.

*   *   *   *   *

With Cori fed, I returned to the Time Sphere where Quentin was sitting at the table, lost in thought.

"So what did the vortex research tell you?" I asked, not beating around the bush.

My voice must have broken his thought; at first he looked at me in confusion, but then came to. "Oh, hi. Um… I'm not sure. It's complicated."

I rolled my eyes. "Are you going to tell me?"

He frowned, and then sighed, running his fingers through his hair. "Sorry. Okay." He leaned back in his chair. "I was looking to see how much your timeline crossed with Zoe's."

I raised my eyebrows. "And you found…"

He exhaled heavily. "It's not… it's not a *lot*, but… it's crossy, at least in the near parts. I couldn't see the moments themselves, but… when that guy, that servant guy or whoever he was, talked about Zoe… there was something he wasn't saying. There are parts of your future, your not-too-distant future, Zoe has seen. And… that's not all. Her timeline crosses with Coretta's too. And not only because your timeline crosses with Coretta's. There's interaction there, too."

I rubbed my face. It wasn't that surprising. Coretta knew more about the future than I'd ever know. So okay, she knew about Zoe's future too. Or Zoe knew about hers, but I did too. But how and why did my and Zoe's timelines cross?

"Why did you feel the need to be so evasive about that?" I asked. "I knew basically what you were looking for."

He looked remorseful. "I was afraid of what I'd learn. Turns out… I didn't learn much. Only what I could have inferred. I'm sorry I didn't tell you. I was worried, but you had a right to know."

I sighed and walked over to the table, sitting down next to him. "Whatever. Next time tell me though, okay?"

He nodded. "How was your day?"

I laughed involuntarily. "I told Darna everything we're doing. And I asked Nicky… Nicholas… to introduce us to the evil

Society who hurt Adelita so I can learn what they did to her and how to stop them."

Quentin nodded, pushing out his lower lip. "Not bad for one day. Why did you tell Darna everything?"

"In a rare moment of disclosure, Coretta suggested that I see if I could trust her. She said Darna is a major player in what's to come. And when I told Darna about what they did to Dohain, to Adelita, she was disgusted. She wants to stop the bad labs too."

"And Nicky agreed to help? Does he know everything too?"

I shook my head. "He'll tell us if he'll help tomorrow. I didn't tell him anything beyond wanting to further our study with the other lab's tools."

"Do you think he'll do it?"

I nodded. "I do. If only because people don't say no to Coretta," I chuckled.

Quentin grinned. "She came with you to ask him?"

"Yeah, she dodged Darna though. Apparently they meet in the future."

"She told you that, too?" His eyes widened, and I empathized with his surprise.

"Yeah. Weird, right? I guess she's being strategic about what she reveals. Or, what she feels like she has to so she's not disruptive. What she thinks we need to know."

Quentin huffed, not in exasperation but in acknowledgement. "Did she say anything else?"

I shook my head. "Not really. Only that Nicholas isn't a big player in what's to come, but Darna is."

Quentin cocked his head to the right. "That seems like a big deal."

"Not in any way that's meaningful. Why is that the case? How does that happen? She said exactly enough to let me feel safe to reveal our plans to Darna. Which I was glad to do. And I'm glad to know we have an insider on our side, one who's a brilliant scientist no less. So I guess that's *big*. But we still need to figure out what exactly she can do for us."

"Or," Quentin began, his voice going slightly higher to indicate something tempting, "what *we* can do for *her*."

I raised my eyebrows. "Such as?"

"Giving her a chance to change the world. In a more productive way than before."

I hadn't thought of it that way. "Hm… maybe."

"If we get into the other lab… what's the end goal?"

"Learn what they did to Adelita. If there's anything that can help her. Learn what we can about the Energy Components Project, and who's behind it. Take them down. Take the whole lab down if we have to. And if we learn anything about Zoe and her relationship to all this in the process, all the better. One lab down is good, but there are more."

Quentin nodded slowly. "It's a direct approach. No more sneakiness, or beating around the bush."

I sighed. "What reason do we have to be indirect now? Zoe knows us, for fuck's sake. The jig is up."

He pressed his lips together and leaned his elbows on the table. "Then I guess we wait to see what Nicky will do."

"Nicky," the voice in his mind intoned. "It is good to hear from you."

"The same, Phillip," Nicky said quietly. It was dawn and Coretta had gone to sleep. He didn't know what it took to wake a vampire during the day and didn't want to find out. "The lab is far emptier without you. Metaphorically as well as in actuality. Have you heard that Helen... misbehaved?"

Phillip sighed. "I knew she would. Yes, I know. It was only a matter of time with her." He cleared his throat. "Nicky... since I left... I have made some decisions for my life. May I ask you to call me Pinyah? It is the name my mother gave me."

Nicky felt a stirring in his heart. He had a sense of Phil... Pinyah's past. That he'd cast much of his identity aside to assimilate safely. But things were different now. Nicky could relate.

"Of course. Pinyah."

"Thank you." Nicky could hear the gratitude in his voice.

"I need to ask your advice. The vampires, the ones that came to us in Crotona Park. They wish to take our research, some findings they uncovered as a result of Geoffrey's insights, to the other lab."

Pinyah didn't say anything for a long moment, but Nicky knew him well enough to know that he was deeply considering what he'd said.

"Will you allow them?" Pinyah finally asked.

"That is what I wished to ask you. If you thought it wise."

"Wisdom is for philosophers. I think it necessary."

"You do." Nicky exhaled. "May I ask why?"

"This must escalate. Everything must escalate. That is all I can say."

'Escalate' was an interesting way to put 'furthering research', but it would in fact do that. "I am glad you say so. I did *not want to refuse them. Their work is promising. Terrifying. But promising."*

Nicky could almost feel Pinyah nodding. "That is an excellent way to phrase it, Nicky. Terrifying and promising. It will be that way for some time, I expect. But you will keep the labs separate? Only the vampires will take the work? I do not want Darna's good name tainted."

Nicky nodded as though Pinyah were there in the room with him. "Completely separate. Darna will never walk through their doors, nor have her name linked to any of that research."

"Excellent. Thank you, Nicky. The best of luck in your new role, and in all you do. I wish you, Darna, and the others all the good life has to offer." And with that, Nicky felt the connection close.

He'd take Pinyah's advice and get the vampires what they wanted. He only hoped more good would come of it than bad, because it was sure to be both.

Chapter Nineteen

It wasn't long after I woke up that I started to hear the whistle and pop of fireworks. Quentin was already on theme, wearing a maroon button-down collared shirt. Alternately, he might have just chosen a red shirt for no reason at all. A dark brown suit jacket was draped over the back of the chair he sat on, and he was reading the newspaper, an act that seemed funny to me. What could possibly surprise him there?

I stretched and stood up. What should I wear? I did have that red dress I'd worn when I went to meet with Phillip. Might as well make use of my purchase.

As I opened the closet, Quentin rotated his chair away so his back was to me. "Ready for explosions?" he asked, face in the newspaper.

I laughed as I pulled off my nightgown. "I hope you mean fireworks. I've had enough metaphorical explosions lately."

"I can't promise anything," he retorted, and I could feel him smirking even though I couldn't see his face.

I pulled on the red dress and stretched my arm back to zip myself. A loud whistle went up outside. "Well, better hurry. We don't want to miss the good stuff." I slid on matching shoes and approached him. When I reached his side, he put the newspaper down and looked up at me. "Anything exciting?" I gestured toward the paper.

"Nothing," he said, "which is what I was hoping for." He stood up, adjusted his shirt, and swung the brown jacket on. "Shall we?"

We went outside to find the sky sparkling. It was lit up on all sides, streaks of colors from across the whole rainbow. Adelita was sitting on her porch wearing a very loose dress, reclining so as not to put tension on her wounds. She smiled at seeing us.

We went over and I waved. I was glad to see her doing well. "How are you feeling?" I asked.

She shrugged. "Some pain, but it is greatly improved. They gave me pills I like."

I sat down to her right, and Quentin to mine. "Have you had a chance to say hi to Cori?"

She grinned. "Yes, earlier. Now she is hiding. She fears the fireworks. I've set music playing in my room to hopefully soothe her."

"And the others?" I pressed. I wanted her to say how Scott had behaved.

"Yes, all but Gerard, whom Scott tells me is busy at the lab," she said, and she giggled. "He misses him, I believe. I hear it in his words."

They had been apart a lot. "I won't be able to help with that, sadly. Our work is only going to grow. We're going to visit the other lab, I hope. The one that hurt you. Whether or not Gerard comes, Scott should never go there."

Adelita nodded. "No, they would recognize him. In addition to the danger. But… I cannot say what he has seen, what small parts, is all for the bad. Perhaps it has made him softer? He made me a *steak* when I arrived home. An odd choice of food for someone just from the hospital, but it was good, so I could not complain. And my bed was made and tidy."

I smiled. Good. At the moment I didn't particularly care if Scott took anything I said to heart, only that he was acting the way she deserved.

"Did Dr. Harrison have any additional insights about…" I let my words trail. I wasn't sure what to call it.

She shook her head. "No. He remains as confused as ever." I wasn't surprised. It was way above his pay grade.

We sat quietly, watching the explosions of color that were like miniature big bangs, clouds of twinkling lights bursting forth from a single point. It was always breathtaking to me. I'd come over from England around 1680, laying out what was a pretty penny at the time for passage. Sometimes it seemed to me that everything the history books said was wrong. Maybe not *wrong*, but… incomplete. High-level stories designed to inspire patriotism, love of land and country. Stories that took a rather upper-class perspective on everything… such as 'no taxation without representation', which wasn't something the poor gave two shits about because they didn't have much to tax in the first place. A revolution by the rich, for the rich, that found… creative… ways to enlist the largely-disinterested poor.

I had no strong feelings one way or the other at the time. Neither the colonists nor the mainland British were particularly friendly to anyone besides rich men, and as slavery took off in the colonies, anyone besides rich white men. Yet there was some hope in the idea of something new. A government not based in royalty… still upper-class men who were effectively appointed by other upper-class men, since nearly everywhere only propertied white men could vote, and also mostly only propertied white Protestant men… but it was different, so it felt marginally more hopeful. But only marginally. Early America was every bit as firmly against women and many others participating in government as anywhere else at that time.

Yet change started to happen slowly… so slowly, but in my lifetime I could see it all. The world lurching toward progress like a slug. A slug that got stuck sometimes, and then some guys would drag it backwards, but then it lurched along again.

Coretta would tell me about similar occurrences in Paris, though Parisians were of a different mindset than colonists. The spirit of fight in them had always resonated with me. France's revolution was more accurately begun by the common people than America's, and was sparked by its women. Coretta was thrilled to be involved and we would talk for hours about the space she would carve out for her work in the new world, the new opportunities for helping women there would be.

Yet whatever might be said of the American revolution, the country's experiments with representative democracy over the years, and the fights to include more people in that representation, were encouraging. Finally the catch phrases of the revolution meant something to everyone. It was an uphill battle, of course, and the powered forces tried to stop those who might vote against their interests in ever-more creative ways even until the present – my present, 2019. But that only meant there was more fight to be done.

When I watched the fireworks, I thought about that fight, and I thought about the victories so far, and everything still left to do, and I felt energized, and sad, and grateful, and ready.

Around 11 p.m. the fireworks began to taper off, and it was time anyway. Quentin and I called a car and went to meet Nicky. We were there by midnight, as seemed to be our pattern.

When we entered his office, he was seated in the same place as the night before, and Coretta was sitting next to him in an identical chair that had not previously been there. She looked up at us and smiled as we walked through the door.

"Good evening," Nicky said. "I see you've brought another companion. This one I have met."

Quentin nodded. "Good evening to you as well. I trust you've been well since we last spoke?"

Nicky snorted. "To the extent that one can be well with so many changes in leadership. I was not keen to ascend to this role so quickly. Yet, here I am."

"A better person for the role than the last," I added, and Nicky smirked. "So, have you made your decision?"

He leaned back in his chair. "Yes, as promised. I will introduce you to the other lab, to a scientist whom I believe can help you dig more deeply into your line of work. Yet... I feel I should warn you. This person is... unscrupulous. Darna met her the one time she was there, and was not enthused."

I nodded. "I expected to meet that sort there. Thank you. I understand who I'm going to meet."

Nicky shook his head. "You believe you do. Yet… well, there is no point in discussing further. You will see what you will see."

"So I will. When will you introduce us?"

Nicky shrugged. "Tonight if you would like. I see no purpose in waiting."

"They're still working at this hour as well?"

He smirked again. "Those who work with the supernatural often work odd hours."

Coretta stood at that. "Then I shall take my leave, as I need not attend the other lab." She looked down at Nicky. "Thank you for a lovely evening."

He smiled and kissed her hand. "I could say the same. Take care." He paused after releasing her hand. "Will I see you again?"

Coretta tilted her head in thought. "I do not expect so. But then again… who can know?"

Nicky nodded. "Until… whatever comes next, then."

She nodded too and wordlessly swept from the room, squeezing my hand in passing as she left. She didn't ask me to turn her invisible, so I gathered she had faith she could do it herself.

Nicky picked up his phone. "I will summon a car for us, and alert the lab to our coming. I hope one person I know in particular will be there. He is… more agreeable than most."

*   *   *   *   *

When we entered the lab, it was, on first glance, a standard medical office. White hallways with various mundane pieces of art hanging on the walls. One looked like something a child might have made while splashing paint. Another was a cartoonish picture of a brown duck.

We walked along, turning left, then walking past four or five office doors with similar insides – medical beds, desks with stethoscopes and tongue depressors – then turning right and continuing further past a bathroom and a non-medical office – a desk covered in papers, bookshelves lining the walls interspersed with diplomas. Our shoes clicked quietly along the shiny tiled floor. For a moment one could believe that we were really here for a check-up.

But I'd never had one of those, and certainly had no need for one now.

At the end of that hallway was another white door, this one with a translucent window to what was beyond – exactly cloudy enough so that the figures there couldn't be identified. There was a numeric pad right above the silver door handle, and Nicholas punched in 1473, each number emitting a beep in turn. He pushed on the handle and the door opened.

Inside was something completely different. One very large room stretched out in a big square, with archways along the walls that opened into other hallways leading who knew where. Maybe fifteen people, some in lab coats, others in straight pants and button-down shirts, bustled about around the machinery. And the machinery… I saw it, but it took me a minute to process what I was looking at.

A woman, no more than 30 years old, was strapped in to a big metal asterisk, her legs splayed against the lower two arms, her own arms adhered to the middle two, and her head lolling uncomfortably between the top two. She was conscious but only barely. She had an IV in her left arm that connected to a drip, and her bare legs were bruised and puffy. She was clothed in a dark blue short-sleeved robe that came to mid-thigh.

While I watched, a tall man with dark brown hair and golden tan skin, wearing thick black square glasses, approached her right arm with a syringe. "Sample 24," he said in a booming voice, and a shorter man with close-cropped hair standing behind him scribbled something on a pad of paper.

"What are they doing to her?" I whispered, not taking my eyes off of the activity. Darna had warned me about this but… it was different to see in person. The horror was real and undeniable. It was suddenly not as hard to imagine these same scientists conducting the Energy Components Project.

I could see Nicky shake his head in my peripheral vision. "I do not know which experiment this is. It could be anything."

The tall man... the main doctor, I guessed... took a blood sample, and the woman didn't flinch. He turned to his left and then seemed to observe us.

"Nicholas!" he said, and smiled. "To what do I owe this pleasure?"

Nicky smiled at the man. "Vivian, Quentin, I would like you to meet Frank."

I glanced at Nicky and put the thought in his head, *is this the man you were hoping would be here?* He nodded ever so slightly.

Frank shook Quentin's hand firmly and then turned to me. I put my hand out to shake his, but when he took it he tried to turn it so that my hand was horizontal. I held it steady so he couldn't move it and forced him into a firm shake. He pressed his lips together.

"And who might you two be?"

"We are leading a research project. We were conducting it in Nicholas' lab but... we need to take it further. We understand you have more resources?"

He nodded. "What manner of resources do you seek?"

I opened my mouth and then closed it again. "I'm not sure. Maybe if we tell you the findings, you can advise us?"

Frank nodded sagely. "Perhaps. Tell me of your research."

I glanced over at Quentin to see his reaction. He was looking at me sideways and slightly bobbed his head.

I began. "We've identified a... lentivirus... that seems to temporarily create resistance to the sun in vampires. But in the dose required to induce that resistance, it also causes limbs to decay, and they don't seem to be able to regrow through usual healing." Quentin pulled a tiny vial with a sample of the lentivirus from his pocket – Gerard had given it to us on our way out, suspecting we might need it. Its contents looked pearlescent in the lab light.

Frank's eyes widened. "Remarkable. It would truly be impressive to create a more perfect immortality. It might also tell us more about how to drive longevity in mortals. Perhaps there are other lentivirus strains that might work similarly, offering resistance to human illness." He rubbed his chin, stroking its light stubble. "And you are flummoxed at how to eliminate the side effect? Or how to make resistance permanent?"

I nodded. "Both. I understand that you have more advanced machinery that might aid in the study."

He nodded. "I must consult my team, but we may."

Time to get answers on one of our real questions. "I thought… we injected the lentivirus, which is a quick and direct exposure. What if we could create a pill that contained the active virus? A… delayed release pill. Lower exposure over a longer period of time?"

Frank wagged his head up and down, smirking. "It would be less likely to activate the body's resistance. And increase the chance of longer-term changes. Though it remains to be seen if the changes would be permanent, or if the pills would need to be taken indefinitely."

I breathed deeply. "Do you have any ongoing pill experiments we could model? That have had success in permanent transformation?"

Frank's mouth twisted knowingly. "Come with me."

He led us past the strapped-up woman, and I couldn't help but ask as we walked by, "What experiment is this?"

He glanced over his shoulder at me, not reducing his walk speed. "She has leukemia. We are attempting to turn the cancer into a weapon against itself, as well as other illnesses."

A noble end goal. But… "She agreed to the treatment?"

"Oh yes," he said. "She agreed to be treated and we've tried many variations since then."

His phrasing was interesting. We walked past more white tables with beakers and books, more scientists bustling about, writing and examining chemicals. "So you said you'd treat her, and she agreed, but you didn't tell her what the treatment would be?"

Frank laughed as we reached the archway directly behind the woman. "That would not be a very sound control, would it? She cannot know which treatment is which, so we can see what truly works."

So Adelita wasn't the only one not told what she was given.

Through the archway was a short hallway, white as the others but no paintings, and another door. Frank entered a number on the key pad – I couldn't see what he was entering as he was careful not to show. But I heard a faint whisper in my mind, a male whisper, though I couldn't pin down the voice – "2242". Who was telling me the code? I glanced over at Quentin, who didn't seem to have heard anything, though maybe he was just better at hiding it.

Frank opened the door and inside was a small, square room lined with white desks, each with wire-bottomed shelves above them. On those shelves were hundreds of pill bottles.

"Are you using all of these?" Quentin asked.

"Not at the moment," Frank said, "but we have plans to, or we did recently. Some have shown promise." He grabbed one bottle off of the right-hand shelf, turned it over in his hand, and held it out to Quentin, who took it, holding its label so I could see too. It was called 'Immunaboost', and said to take once per day. "This pill has had some success in enhancing the immune system's fighting power without it attacking the body itself. Not perfectly, as yet, but we are tinkering with it." He moved to the back of the room and grabbed another bottle, handing it to me. 'Stemithan' was to be taken twice a day for two weeks. "This reactivates the growth of new tissue in older individuals. It helps in cellular regeneration, but the overgrowth has caused cancers in some."

Tread carefully. "Tissue is always going to be vulnerable, though. Short of turning everyone into a vampire, what could we possibly do to protect against that?"

Frank nodded and reached in the far back of the right-hand shelf. He held out what he'd retrieved, something called Amplifirm. "This is from a different line of research. The others are designed to improve human tissue, bolster the existing body. This takes another approach, assuming what you have just said, that human flesh will always be weak and imperfect. It is one of the slowest-release medicines we have, and may be a good model for your work. It alters the raw DNA, bit by bit, to transform flesh into a more durable substance."

"What substance?" Quentin asked, having trouble keeping some growing anger out of his face.

"An alloy, turning the organs, bones, and eventually the skin, into a metal-organic composite."

Quentin pressed his lips together, and I stared at Frank hard. "Has anyone ever completed the regimen?" I asked, already knowing the answer.

Frank shook his head. "We have not yet gotten the new metal formations to adequately provide the functioning of the original organs. We are adjusting the formulation and hope that soon they will."

I held out my free hand and Frank put the bottle in it. "Is there a way to reverse the effect? Once you saw the metal wasn't working?"

"No, unfortunately. It is quite permanent."

I turned the bottle over in my hand. They'd given it to Adelita in a baggy. Did they think she could track the name? Were they worried she'd out them? "Yes," I said, "this could offer us a good model."

"If you want to take that approach, I will have to bring Sheila in to the discussion. She is our unit leader and expert in extended-release pill administration."

I side-eyed Nicholas, whose eyes narrowed at Sheila's name. Was she one of the unscrupulous ones? Frank didn't seem overly scrupulous as it was.

"Did she... order... the Amplifirm study? Or conduct it?"

"Both," Frank asserted. "She oversaw the development of the formulation, and then assigned scientists to run a double-blind study."

Maybe that was why Adelita got hers in a baggy? Otherwise they'd have to print up identical bottles for the placebo too. "Nicholas," I said, "thank you for taking us here and introducing us to Frank, but I think we can take it from here. You probably have a lot of work to do." I didn't want him to be associated with anything we would see, do, or learn next.

He glanced at me gratefully but... he was worried. That was clear. "I do. My thanks. Good evening, all." He nodded at us and swept out of the room.

Once the door shut, I turned back to Frank. "Okay. Now." I looked up at him inquisitively. "What have you really seen come from these pills?"

Frank raised his eyebrows. "I was not lying earlier. Are you seeking a more direct answer? Their organs turned to metal and ceased to work."

"And you continued trying them on more people after that?"

Frank's lips twisted. "Modified formulations. Improvements. Do you critique our methods?"

"Oh, no..." I said breathily. "I'm impressed by them. The tenacity. The focus on the goal. You'll find answers no one else will. Tell me..." I stepped toward him; now we were about a foot apart. "Did anything... other research... in other countries... help in making these pills?"

Frank bit his lip and nodded. "I believe that work goes too far. We always treat willing participants. Yet... yes, we have learned from it. It helped us understand toxic dosages for some medicines."

I had to suppress the urge to gag. How many innocent people had died to find that dosage? "Willing… at first. That woman in the main area before… she can't consent."

Frank shrugged. "She consented when she was conscious. She can't revoke consent now."

That was rapist logic. I turned toward Quentin so I'd be facing away from Frank for a moment. "Quentin, shall we meet Sheila? It sounds as though she can meet our needs."

Quentin pressed his lips together firmly. "That's a good idea."

From behind me, Frank's voice answered. "She is not in the lab at the moment, but she is due in soon. Would you like some coffee while you wait?"

I raised my eyebrows and Quentin smirked. "No," he replied. "Thank you. If I have it now I'll never get to sleep tonight."

I bit my lip.

"Ah, I understand that," Frank commiserated. "I barely ever sleep. Would you follow me back outside? There is a seating area where you may wait."

We followed Frank back into the main experiment area, with that poor woman still strapped in and being poked at. He led us around her to the other side of the room from where we'd originally entered, where we could now see four red-cushioned wood chairs against the wall.

"Please, take a seat. Sheila ought to report within the hour." With that, Frank retreated around the strapped-in woman to, presumably, his other work.

Sheila was "to report" – it felt so formal, militaristic. Reporting for duty.

I looked over at Quentin, who was leaning his elbows on his knees and his chin on his folded hands. He side-eyed me and exhaled heavily.

I thought to him: *You know how when you know someone really well, you can communicate without speaking? You just look at each other and somehow through your body signals and glances tell them what you want to say?* He nodded. *Putting words in people's heads is a lot like that. But instead of willing the person to understand you with looks and gestures, you will it with thoughts.*

Quentin peered at me curiously. Then he sat up straight and adjusted himself in his chair. He turned toward me and stared at me hard. His eyes bugged out a bit.

No, you're still doing it with your face. Resist the urge to communicate that way.

He sat back and flattened his expression. He started to raise his hands, but then folded them in his lap. I waited about 60 seconds but heard nothing.

"That's okay," I said out loud. "It takes practice. It's a different kind of connecting. We're used to relying on visual and audio cues so much. To will yourself to connect with another person through thought… it's really different. You'll get it."

He nodded and licked his lips. "Thanks for the tips. It would be handy."

We sat there mostly in silence until Sheila arrived. I tried to get a view of what the scientists were doing to that poor woman, but they were on the other side of her. Occasionally I saw someone walk past with a test tube, a syringe, a notepad, or trays of medical equipment. I also noticed Quentin looking at me every so often, and then not looking at me, and then rubbing his head. It had taken Coretta a bit to get it also. A day? Two? But she practiced nearly constantly.

After awhile, we were finally approached by a woman, strawberry-blonde hair and the whitest skin I had ever seen in a mortal human. She was wearing the standard white lab coat, and a light green dress poked out from underneath. "Hello – Frank tells me you are Vivian?"

I stood up. "Yes, and this is Quentin," I gestured to him.

Sheila nodded. "It is good to make your acquaintance. I understand you are interested in another extended-release pill study?"

Hmm... did it have to be another? Or could this be a way in? "I don't know if the information we offer would be better used in another study, or to supplement one already ongoing. Perhaps I'll tell you about it, and you can advise?" Sheila nodded, her eyes narrowing curiously. "There are two important findings that might inform your work. One – we've identified a strain of lentivirus that shows promise in eliminating vampires' vulnerability to the sun. But it has side effects... limb decay, and the effect isn't permanent. But we've only administered it in single large doses, so a slower, delayed-released administration might help. And Frank thought this strain, or a similar one, might reduce vulnerabilities in mortals too, like illness. Also..." This was dangerous to reveal, but... so was everything. And we had to stop the Energy Components Project. I had to give Sheila whatever would convince her to let us in. "There's another study in very early stages on how to pause the body's immunological response to foreign substances. Between a slow release to gradually change the body, and creating more receptivity to change in the body..."

Sheila's eyes were wide. "We could have a breakthrough in our work. My God. Vivian, you may have done it."

I wasn't sure how I felt about that... again, depends how it's used. But we were almost where we needed to be. "And the lentivirus, or a similar one, could be the missing ingredient in the Energy Components Project."

Sheila stared at me open-mouthed. "That... that study is confidential."

I rolled my eyes. "Yes, so I've heard. But if you don't bring us in on it, how can you get the lentivirus? Only we know what it is."

"I..." she stammered, a sheen of sweat starting to form on her forehead. "I suppose in this case... it has to be permitted."

Was she afraid of what Zoe would do if she found out her experiment leaked to us? In a way, I appreciated that her commitment to the science was greater than her fear.

"Good! I'm glad we can work together on this," I said.

"What combinations have worked best so far?" Quentin asked.

Sheila pressed her lips together. "As I've said, it's confidential. Let us discuss in my office."

She led us through yet another passageway from the main room, this one just to the right of where we'd been sitting. The hallway was very long, curved in a semicircle, and had no adornment whatsoever. There were no doors, no windows, nothing. The hallway's only function was to lead to the door at the end, another one with a punchcode lock. Sheila cupped her right hand over the pad and pressed four numbers with her left. Again, as the pad beeped, I heard in my head the numbers: "7382". The voice seemed familiar this time but I couldn't place it… it was too much of a whisper. The door beeped approvingly and Sheila pushed it open.

Inside was the messiest office I had ever seen. The room had long gray desks on the left and right walls stretching the length of the room and three rows of brown shelves on each wall above them. Every shelf and both desks were covered in stacks of papers and books, strewn about such that I couldn't imagine how Sheila ever found anything. On the far wall was a machine that looked like a standard late-1990s printer – was it actually from then? – except that its wiring was transparent and had a familiar gloppy substance floating through it.

Quentin noticed it too. "You've turned the printer into a time travel device?"

Sheila smiled. "Yes. It allows me to send and receive documents through time. Very efficient for sharing knowledge."

A little too efficient. "So… tell us about the project."

Sheila inhaled as though she had to brace herself. I guessed that she was the woman Nicholas had described as unscrupulous, but she didn't seem anything but nervous now. "We have advanced through many phases of the study. We learned that vampire blood heals some mild-to-moderate wounds rather quickly, and can even heal more severe wounds over time. But... you knew as much, of course."

I glanced quickly at Quentin, who saw me looking at him and shrugged.

"The lentivirus' compatibility with your blood is very promising... as you say, it may eliminate your sunlight sensitivity, and I could imagine it supplementing your blood's ordinary healing, applied correctly." That was an interesting hypothesis... I wondered what led her to think that. "We have combined vampire blood with strains of stem cells, stem cells plus magic. Some more promising results but far from perfect."

"What kind of magic?" Quentin asked.

"A mage healing spell," she said, which was probably obvious.

"How did you merge that with the stem cells?" Quentin pressed.

Sheila shrugged. "I placed the spell inside the pill. It held it."

So Sheila was a mage as well as a scientist, like Phillip had been. How did a spell stay inside a pill? The energy that drove the spell had to be locked in there somehow... and if it was a mage spell, it was soul energy. Stem cells and souls.

"Our most successful attempt to date was combining vampire blood, proteins extracted from young human blood, a particular line of stem cells, and... a variant on the healing spell."

"Are there a lot of kinds of healing spells mages can do?" I asked. For me, when I healed with blood, healing was healing.

Sheila stared at me for a long moment before responding. "I'll say no more. But this attempt did induce sunlight sensitivity in patients, due to the vampire blood's potency. So the lentivirus presents an exciting possibility!"

"How are those patients doing now?" I asked skeptically.

Sheila grinned. "Fantastically. Would you like to meet one?"

Quentin and I traded glances, and then both nodded.

Sheila led us back out through the central room past *another* archway, this one to the left of where we'd been sitting. This hallway was just as long and curvy as the last but had many metal doors, each with tiny barred windows near the top. Their patient ward looked like where they kept prisoners rather than those undergoing medical experiments.

Five doors down on the right hand side, Sheila stopped in front. She fished in her lab coat pocket and retrieved a small skeleton key chain. After flipping the chain around until she found the right long silver key, she inserted it into the lock, turned, and pushed the door open.

Locked doors are a clear sign of consenting patients.

Inside was a young man, perhaps 25, with matted brown hair and burnt orange skin. He was seated on a twin bed with a dingy white comforter and wearing a beige sweatsuit.

"Charlie," Sheila said, "these scientists have come to see you. They wanted to see that you're well."

Charlie looked at us hesitantly. "My body is healthy, yes."

"Charlie had the good fortune to participate in our study once we'd refined the pills to eliminate some minor side effects," Sheila described. "He came to us because he had a stroke. He had lost complete use of his right arm and leg. He agreed to be treated, and we devised a plan to truly test the pill in the most informative way possible. We wanted to understand if it would heal different forms of injury. So, we removed Charlie's left arm, and applied a tourniquet to his left leg until it decayed from blood loss."

There was that unscrupulousness. It had to come out eventually. I looked at Charlie as she spoke. The words didn't move him. His eyes were dead.

"We then began the treatment, 100 mg extended-release pill twice a day for a month. And it was astonishing! In one week, he regained use of his right-side limbs. In the second week, his left arm began to regrow, a little stump at the time. By the end of the month, his left arm was fully regrown and his left leg had spurred back to life! It's still a little gray in spots, but the pill's effects are still in his body so it may yet heal that too. We are keeping him for observation."

"For how long?" Quentin asked.

Sheila shrugged. "Until we feel the pill has run its course. And all that – that isn't even the most impressive part. Charlie – tell them how old you are."

Charlie didn't look up from the floor. "Fifty-two."

I hated myself a little for being really impressed by that. Even vampire blood didn't reverse aging; it just froze you wherever you were at the time. "You look half that," my lips said, unbidden. Charlie nodded, still not looking up.

"And there were no side effects of note," Sheila beamed. "Except for the sunlight sensitivity, so that is another reason to hold him, until we can attend to that. You may have brought the answer!"

I loathed the thought of Charlie enduring any more "treatment", but I did want him to see the sun again. He had a whole lifetime of mornings to see ahead of him.

"Will you give me the lentivirus sample so I may add it to our formulation?" Sheila asked. Quentin nodded and held it out to her. She took it eagerly. "If you'll excuse me, it has been a long day for me, but I will turn to this first thing in the morning. It will be ready by the evening, if you'll return after dark?"

Quentin nodded. "We'll be here."

Sheila grinned. "I'll walk you out."

*　　*　　*　　*　　*

We were silent most of the way back to Adelita's. We had learned what pill they'd given Adelita, and that there was no known cure. We had begun to see the Energy Components Project in action, but she'd of course shown us their "success case", not the failures. And we hadn't gotten to asking who had ordered it. And that was critical. We knew Sheila ordered the Amplifirm project, but that was small potatoes compared to this. Without knowing the power brokers, it would be much harder to take the Society down. I still suspected that it was either Sheila or Zoe, but we had to know which one, or if there were still more power players pulling the strings. We had to know if it was really just a matter of knocking down a figurehead, or if she had a cabal of insiders who would need to be stopped too.

Finally, Quentin broke the silence. "I've been thinking about what Helen said," he mused, twisting his hands. "She entangled me, and the Sphere, across time. But she didn't know to where, so that means that... the vortex, it's like... it's the same as the mind. So much of the physical world is built around similar patterns. So, in the mind, it's familiar things that are linked together, right? Related things. You hear a song from your childhood, or smell a food you ate at your grandma's house, and you're right back there in your mind. It's like that with the vortex. If she didn't target anything, that means it probably entangled us to things we're connected to, or things relevant to the situation."

It was a departure from talking about the Energy Components Project, and I really didn't mind. "So," I offered, "it entangled you to where the Sphere would eventually be, where you could find it?"

He frowned. "Maybe. Or..." he looked up at me. "It could have entangled me to where you would be. Think about it. What would be more relevant?"

He was stolen from the moment he made me like him... so it was returning him to me. It could be. It felt too egocentric for me to buy fully, though.

"I guess, but I had gone to that time and place because it took me there. Because that's where you'd be. So I still think it's more that it wanted you to find the Sphere. It just needed my help."

Quentin shrugged. "Either way, it makes sense. But why was the Sphere entangled to… where did you say?"

"2017, a storage room in a restaurant in Paris."

"Why there? What link does the Sphere have to a Paris restaurant?"

"None," I said.

Quentin ran his hand through his hair. "You said Coretta was with you when you found it?"

"She was the reason…" I paused, and then restarted. "She was the reason we went there. To feed from a guy she knew."

"So… it could have entangled to her."

I thought about that. "I guess it could have. A place she knew well."

Quentin frowned. "Do you think if I ask her about it, she would tell me if she knew anything?"

I smirked. "I think she would tell you veiled commentary that told you absolutely nothing until you figured it out on your own anyway."

Quentin laughed. "Probably. But I have to try, don't I?"

I nodded. "I get that. Go for it."

As soon as we got back, we went to Coretta's room and knocked. "Come in," she called, and we did. She was in a nightgown, dark brown, frilly, and too-short – her calves stuck out more than they should given the intention of the clothing. I should have offered for her to bring clothes when we came here. She was lying on the bed thumbing through one of Gerard's notebooks. Did he know she had it?

"Hey Coretta," Quentin said, lilting his voice so it was obvious he was there to ask something. "What's up?"

She laid the book at her side. "If you've come to ask me where the Time Sphere went after Helen did her deed, I do not know."

He frowned. "As if you'd tell me."

Coretta sat up and adjusted her nightgown underneath her. "I would not, but I would tell you that I couldn't tell you. I am telling you instead that I do not know. I know, thanks to Vivian's lovely spoilers to me some centuries ago, that it was this entanglement, which I still do not understand, really, by the way, that pulled you apart, but I do not know where it went."

"Well, but..." I began, and then realized what she'd said. "My spoilers?"

"Yes, yes, which is itself a spoiler I suppose, apologies. You tell me quite a few things in your future. It was charming, really."

She'd mentioned before that I'd told her things, but I realized I didn't know anywhere near the extent of it. "What else do I tell you?"

She chuckled and grinned. "You'll see. Or, hear, when you say it."

I shook my head. "So you really don't know where the Sphere went. Or how it got where we found it?"

"*We* found it?" she asked, and I had said too much already.

I sighed. "Yes, okay, fine." I turned to Quentin. "Could it have been linked to her, and things she liked, without her knowing?"

He nodded. "Of course." And then he smirked at her. "Ha ha, you don't know something."

She grinned. "Perspective is everything, Quentin. Once upon a time, I knew nothing and you knew many things. And that time will come for you. Such is the life we've chosen, hm?"

He ran his hand through his hair. "I suppose so."

"Now," she continued, "have you learned anything of use at the monster lab?"

Had I ever called it that to her, or had she coined that on her own? "A lot. We found out about the Energy Components Project, a bit about the experiments they've run, and what they learned from them. We're... inside now, and hopefully can learn who ordered the study soon. We also learned what pill they gave Adelita. And who ordered that study. And what it does."

She nodded. "It hardens other parts of the body as well, yes? Turns bones into metal?"

I sighed. "Why did you ask me if you already knew?"

"I only found out tonight. When Adelita found out."

My heart dropped. "What?"

Coretta giggled. "Oh, it isn't bad. Seek her – she will certainly show you."

Quentin and I immediately made our way to Adelita's room, but she wasn't there. We went downstairs but she wasn't in the kitchen, nor the living area. It was then that we heard a bang, the sound of wood cracking, from the basement.

We rushed toward the sound, through the kitchen and around the right corner to the short brown-carpeted staircase that led down. When we got to the basement, we found Adelita standing over a shattered pile of firewood. She was wearing a loose gray shirt, a flowing knee-length black skirt, and a smile.

"Vivian! Quentin – look what I can do!" she exclaimed, gesturing at the wood.

"You... broke that?" I exclaimed.

"With my hands! They are... so strong. My arms, through to my shoulder, feel so strong and sturdy. Vivian, do you think that my bones have turned to metal?"

I sighed and nodded. "We found that out today. The pills are very slow-release. They would have eventually turned your entire body into a metal alloy. Your bones must have transformed since your surgery." It would be an odd thing for doctors to miss.

Adelita's face fell. "Is it done? Or... will more of me go this way?"

I shook my head. "I don't know."

She scowled. "It matters not, not now. I have this gift, and I will not let it sit idle. For however long I survive."

She had to survive. And not just for practical reasons. "Let us know if you sense more changes. We'll act as fast as we can to stop any bad ones."

Adelita nodded. "Do you know who made these pills?"

I nodded too. "I do. We met her. She is..." I shook my head. Amoral? Cruel?

"If you want to practice," Quentin offered, "get stronger, more skilled at fighting, I think we would all be glad to help. V is probably best at it, but I could help too if you needed. If you promise not to hurt me too much." He grinned.

Adelita smirked. "I would be gentle." Her face fell then, and she looked down at the firewood. "Could it be reversed? If it got worse."

I bit my lip. "No. I'm sorry. They don't have a cure."

She nodded slowly, her eyes flat. "Then yes. Help me learn to fight. So that if I get the chance, before I die, I can kill them."

The moon was full and bright, its face staring down on Coretta and the city of lights. She flipped another page, this one more boring than the last. She hated reviewing the financial reports, but it was necessary, and so important to running an effective charity.

Oh well – if she had to read them, she could do it outside, in her backyard, out in her purple spotted bikini on a lawn chair striped with orange and yellow. The women of Paris seemed to love to sunbathe, and Coretta found moonbathing a perfectly adequate substitute.

As she read the list of 2014 donors, she felt the hairs on her arms begin to tickle. She put her papers down and looked around. Suddenly, behind her, the Time Sphere appeared.

She was surprised, but not unhappily. She hadn't thought that she would see Vivian again, not before 2017 at any rate, and certainly not in the Sphere. She got up, went to the door, and knocked. A few seconds passed – no answer.

"Vivian? Quentin?" she called. Again, no response. She pressed her ear to the wall but could hear nothing inside, no talking or walking or anything.

She put her hand on the wall and closed her eyes. She called to her blood to tell her the Sphere's recent history; from where had it come? In her mind she saw a grassy area... a forest of some kind, and silence except for some birds twittering away, and then... it was a tearing asunder, the Sphere catapulted through the vortex.

And it had landed here.

Coretta laughed. Entangled to her indeed. She returned to her lawn chair and picked up her cell phone, punching in a number she knew well. A familiar voice answered: "Hello?"

"Tahar? It's Coretta. I'm going to need a favor." She smirked as she studied the Sphere and marveled at the circles of time. "And a locksmith."

Chapter Twenty

Before heading off to our respective labs and tasks the next night, Quentin and I told Gerard about everything we'd learned from Sheila.

"Everything you say makes a good deal of sense," Gerard mused. "Our blood heals, and is able to go so far as to regrow body parts. Stem cells have healing and regrowth properties. Proteins drive cellular regeneration. It is an excellent lead."

"And maybe Nicholas will know what kind of healing spells to try," Quentin suggested.

Gerard nodded. "I will share this with Darna. The findings are valuable."

I huffed. "I've heard this conversation before." I remembered Nicky's arm around Phillip on Crotona Park's steps. "I'm counting on Darna to come up with a way to use them ethically."

When we arrived at the monster lab – I decided I was going to call it that now – a young woman no older than 20 with bouncy, chestnut-brown hair met us at the door. "Good evening! I am Clara, a resident here. Dr. S is in the OR," she informed us. "She has asked me to bring you to her upon your arrival." We nodded, and off we went down yet another archway, this one to the still-strapped-in woman's right side.

This hallway had several doors with translucent windows, but like the front door to this part of the lab, too translucent to identify anything on the other side. A few doors down on the left, Clara opened one to reveal the OR, and it was everything I'd expected an operating room to be. Stretchers scattered throughout, patients in white nightgowns plugged into beeping monitors. Sheila stood next to one patient, a woman of around 60, taking her blood pressure. When we stepped in, she looked up at us and grinned.

"Vivian, Quentin, please, come in." She unstrapped the blood pressure reader and tossed it onto the adjacent counter covered in charts, glove boxes, syringes, some medicine bottles, and cutting instruments.

Clara left, and we approached Sheila and her patient. The patient's small eyes fluttered groggily. Her blonde-gray frizzy hair rustled against the rough mattress as she shifted ever so slightly back and forth. A warm-looking dark-gray blanket covered her, though her right arm, from which Sheila had been measuring blood pressure, dangled lamely over the side of the stretcher.

"I was hoping you would arrive soon. The pill is ready to administer," Sheila explained.

"What's the matter with her?" Quentin asked.

"She came to us with stomach and intestinal cancer," Sheila described. "It was advanced; the cancer was all throughout, and so we had to remove it surgically." She pulled back the gray blanket to reveal… they had removed it, alright. But not just the cancer. They had removed her *intestines*. "Naturally, she would die this way, but with our pill, she may live anew. I'd like you to watch the administration?"

I shook my head, flabbergasted. "How is she going to digest the pill properly without her intestines?"

"She still has her stomach," Sheila said flippantly. "The cancer was not so widespread there, so we cut out as much as we could find. We will see if the pill can take care of the rest! It should completely dissolve with little to no waste product. And she will receive nutrients intravenously, so she does not strictly need her intestines as of now."

I didn't say anything, and neither did Quentin. Sheila moved to the countertop and picked up a medicine bottle. She opened it and dumped what must have been the only pill in there onto her hand. She turned back toward the patient.

"Open wide, Ruthie," Sheila cooed. Ruthie squirmed and looked at me helplessly. The horror of it was that this pill really was her last chance after what Sheila had done to her. She opened her mouth, and Sheila dropped the pill in. Ruthie swallowed.

"Give her some water, shouldn't you?" Quentin said, his eyes furrowed in distress. "She'll choke on it."

Sheila nodded and rushed to the other side of the room where I could now see a sink. While she filled a small cup, Ruthie groaned.

I stepped closer and stroked Ruthie's hair. I tried to put soothing power in my voice: "It's going to be okay, Ruthie… she'll get you some water, and the pill will heal you."

Ruthie's eyes grew sadder still. *"Help me,"* she whispered.

I pressed my lips together. "I'm trying," I whispered back. "I'm going to help you, and everyone else going through what you are."

Sheila returned and slowly poured the water into Ruthie's mouth, a gesture of bizarre gentleness considering. "And now we wait," she announced as Ruthie took the last sip. "We will monitor her for the next few weeks."

"And you'll record results? Where do you keep them?" I asked.

"Yes, in my office – you saw it yesterday."

"And who can see those results?"

"Only the scientists directly involved in the project, and the project executor."

"Oh? Who is the project executor?"

Sheila narrowed her eyes at me. "That is classified."

I sighed. "Sheila, there's no need to protect this person. We're working with you on this! We just want to meet her, or him, and find out about the larger plans, what inspired it, what more we can do…" I let my last word hang in the air.

Sheila shook her head slowly. "Vivian. It is classified. Please, leave it alone."

I frowned. I could force it from her, of course, but she would know I'd done it. And then we'd be locked out of the lab. No, if I was going to use powers on her, we'd have to have an exit plan first.

"Ruthie will be monitored and cared for," Sheila continued. "You are free to stay, but there is nothing you can do here. I suggest you return to your normal lives and return in a few days to see the progress."

I looked at Ruthie again. "Are you giving her something for the pain?"

"Oh yes, of course."

"Could you put on a radio for her? Some form of entertainment?"

Sheila contemplated that. "We could play music. That would be nice."

"And when she's well enough… they're not contagious. What if the patients could play games with each other?"

Sheila pressed her lips together. "I'm not sure it's ideal for them to discuss their experiences. We need to maintain control over the tests."

I scowled at her and she went silent. "They don't know what you did to them. It won't affect your results. Sheila, for god's sake."

She looked at me for a long moment but then acquiesced. "Very well," she nodded. "But supervised games. So we can be certain."

We turned to leave, and it was fine that she thought we would come back in a few days. Maybe we would. But maybe it would be sooner. We knew enough about the studies now. The good intentions and the horrific ethics. But we *still* didn't know the power players besides Sheila. We needed a plan – for how to get that information, whether or not Sheila wanted to provide it. And what exactly we meant to do next. High-level "taking the lab down" wasn't enough anymore. We needed details, and we needed them now.

Gerard pulled on his dark gray suit jacket. Scott stood behind him, watching.

"I should have said something before, when you had misconceptions of Adelita," Gerard said. "I know you only worked among men when you were with the police. And you've not said anything about the household in which you were raised."

"I have a sister," Scott said. "She required constant care from my mother. I haven't spoken to her in years… we had nothing in common."

Gerard tightened his black-and-white striped tie. "Women are as varied as men in their interests. I hope as you live longer you will see more of it. Adelita tends to her home because it is her home, not because she is suited to housekeeping or enjoys it. You are a guest in her home, and should act the part."

"Gerard, if women are not better suited to housekeeping, then why are they always found doing it? Why do we not see women in droves seeking out other activities?"

Gerard turned to face Scott. "If you look, you will see them. You will see them try to receive education and be scorned by men for the attempt. You will see them display their intelligence in all manner of work and receive none of their due. If they desire to engage in activities other than housekeeping but do not pursue them, it is because men have made it too difficult." Gerard hoped and believed that Scott's attitudes were a matter of exposure, not a negative opinion of women. He had only seen Adelita's intelligence and envied it, and perhaps he did see Vivian and Coretta as outside the human sphere. "Would you like to meet someone else who has pursued her desired profession regardless of men, and proven to be the equal of any man… and the better of most, if I must say? Adelita is not unusual. She is one of many."

Scott scratched his chin. "Do you mean your lab partner? This… Darla?"

"Darna," Gerard corrected. "Yes."

Scott smiled sheepishly. "If it means I get to go to work with you tonight, then gladly."

Gerard sighed. "It would be unwise to bring you to the lab unannounced. But I will speak with her and we will find a time to gather. Does that suit you?"

Scott sulked. "Yes, that's fine."

"And in the meantime... please treat Adelita as you would treat a male friend. I... I have much to learn as well," Gerard admitted. "She is a bright woman, our equal in all senses."

Scott nodded. "I do think well of her. It is only that the way she behaves seems... unnatural."

Gerard laughed. "You say this to me?"

Scott laughed too. "I take your point."

Chapter Twenty-One

We arrived home earlier than usual since we had done so little at the lab. But a quiet evening was not to be had. As soon as we entered Adelita's house, I heard a loud crash coming from the basement.

"Stop this!" Scott's panicked voice cried out.

THUD.

"Please, Adelita, you'll harm yourself…"

CRACK.

I reached the bottom of the stairs in time to see Adelita, standing next to a giant crack in the wood-paneled wall, turn on Scott viciously. Quentin was close behind me.

"If I wish for your opinion, I'll seek it!" she screamed.

"Hey!" I yelled, getting their attention. "What the hell is going on?"

"Nothing!" Adelita railed. "Nothing you ought concern yourself with." It was a snidely-put phrase.

"Is… is it something I did?" I asked. I thought I saw Quentin shake his head at me, but I ignored him.

Adelita was breathing heavily, but seemed to slow down. Her face fell. "No. I apologize. To both of you."

Scott tenderly touched her arm. "No need."

But should she be apologizing? *Was* this my fault?

"Look on my skin," she said, and held out her right hand. I approached and took it – it was solid, hard like skin-colored brick. And it wasn't bloody, despite her having, I assumed, punched the wall, and plenty enough splinters were sticking out to cut.

"Are you stronger now?" I asked hesitantly.

She shrugged. "Stronger. Yes. And stronger in that I cannot seem to break or bruise my skin. But..." she exhaled heavily, "I can no longer feel any sensation either."

I rubbed the back of her hand. "You can't feel me touching you?" She shook her head. "You didn't feel the wall when you hit it?" She shook her head again.

I was out of questions. It had transformed her so much that her nerve endings were dead. Even the transformation to being a vampire didn't do that much change. It was all wrong... you wouldn't know if you were hurt, or on fire, or if you were freezing to death, or if you were being hugged.

"That sucks, Adelita," Quentin said. "Maybe it's temporary?"

Or maybe it was part of her journey to being a machine. Maybe the next step would stop her heart.

"I'm done," I said plaintively, and I dropped her hand.

The others all turned to look at me. "Done?" Adelita asked.

"Playing around with them. Pretending. We have all the information we need except one piece. She's going to tell me who's in charge this time, or I'll see how many limbs *she's* willing to sacrifice for the secrecy."

Quentin frowned. "If we attack them, they'll attack back."

I shook my head. "Not most of them. Most of them are just scientists. And I don't have to confront her in public anyway. I'll isolate her in her office, and you distract the others. If I need to do anything to get information out of her, and they want to avenge her after that, they can get through all of us."

Adelita raised her eyebrows. "You mean for me to join?"

I shrugged. "If you feel like punching people who deserve it?" She pressed her lips together and nodded.

Scott looked directly at me. "May I join as well? I still have my old pistol."

Did I think he could help? I did. They really were mostly mortal scientists, unarmed, untrained in any sort of fighting.

"Yeah," I said. "You too." He grinned sheepishly.

"And if we are concerned about potential mages," Adelita said, "we can invite Gerard."

I nodded. The team would be together again for another stand. But this time the odds were in our favor.

"And the patients?" Quentin asked. "Well… we could turn them over to Darna's care."

"That's a good, but complicated, idea," I mused. We really were talking about finally taking the whole lab down. "Darna doesn't have room in her lab. So we'd have to not only stop Sheila, but also turn leadership over to better hands. Do you think Nicholas could take on both?"

Quentin shrugged. "Phillip handled both before."

That was a good point. "What about William? I *don't* want him in any fight," I shuddered, "but he could help with reorganization, or restaffing, after the fact."

"How much restaffing do you think we'll need?" Quentin asked. "Maybe some might like to work under more moral bosses."

It was a good question, one that made the strategy we needed more clear to me. "Okay, here's what we do. Quentin, you and I go there like normal. Adelita, Scott, and Gerard will hang back. I'll give you the door codes you'll need. I'll get Sheila alone in her office and confront her. She'll either tell me the truth, or I'll make her. Adelita, Scott, and Gerard can come in then and corral everyone into the main room, and if they make trouble, between a fist, a gun, and the literal darkness, I think we can manage. And Quentin, you work on charming them so that they trust you, and maybe they don't attack, and so they tell you the truth about their intentions. You can learn who likes the way they work and who doesn't."

Quentin nodded. "I can start corralling them too, to get a head start while you go with Sheila, and then call the others in. And the scientists who don't like the current system can stay and work under Darna, or William or whoever. And the ones who don't want a change, or might go to Zoe?"

I felt something dark and hard coalescing inside me. "Between Adelita and Gerard, I think they can... go away."

Adelita scowled. "I will deal with them. How many people are there?"

I shrugged. "Fifteen?"

"That will suit," Adelita said, her lips twisting.

"Are you sure you should talk to Sheila alone?" Quentin asked me.

"I'm not afraid of her," I said. "She knows about mage healing, but there's no reason to believe she's particularly strong or old."

"You cannot know for certain," Adelita noted.

"She could be keeping her true power under wraps," I agreed. "But I do know she's not older than me. Or even close. So the odds are in my favor."

"Does age always equal power?" Scott asked.

"No... but if we assume she studied every moment of her adult life, I've still got her beat by orders of magnitude," I explained. "It equals power because I clocked a lot of hours."

Scott seemed to consider that. "Are there many vampires who do not study their craft?"

I shrugged. "I don't know. I'd guess as many as there are humans. I haven't really spent a lot of time getting to know others. The ones I met over the years... well yeah. They varied like humans. There was a general who had studied fighting techniques, was insanely good at every aspect of it. No one could beat him in combat. And then there was another who had only ever mastered some weak mind manipulation, and just went around using it to exploit humans – more than just feeding; he robbed them and… more than that. He was about a century old, I think, and he was very easy to take down."

Adelita nodded. "There are always some people who settle into what they are and never try to improve themselves."

"Or want to improve," I added.

"Do you think you could beat Zoe so easily?" Scott asked.

I grimaced. "I have never met her to see, but if her reputation is at all accurate, I bet she's outdone even Judah in using souls to extend her life… and her power."

Now Adelita grimaced too. "By orders of magnitude."

*   *   *   *   *

"The Society for Longevity," I announced to the desk clerk, a new man at the job with a short chestnut bob and a dark gray suit. He scanned me and Quentin with suspicious eyes. "We work with Sheila?"

His eyes narrowed more. "One moment," he said, and lifted the phone behind the desk. I pressed my hands together and thought I could hear Adelita's breath behind me. *Stop breathing so hard,* I thought, though not to her.

Gerard had managed to cloak them with darkness, creating an interesting spotty pattern of shadows across the room. The desk clerk had looked at the darkening room but seemed unperturbed, probably blissfully unaware of supernatural activity at all. It was better than my invisibility power, which seemed to require them to be touching me unless they could hold the energy, and I doubted Adelita or Scott could.

"Mhmm. Yes. They say they work with Sheila. Yes." He cast uncertain-but-less-suspicious eyes up at me. "Your names?"

"I'm Vivian," I said, "and this is Quentin."

"Mhmm." He looked down at his desk again. "Yes, it's them. Yes of course. As you wish." Finally he hung up and looked at us. "Take the third elevator up."

"Thank you," I said, and we walked toward it, very soft footsteps behind us. Could the humans hear it at all? Or could my better hearing listen through the darkness?

After the elevator ride, we stood outside the door to the Society. The plan was to go in as usual, the others still cloaked. Once we got to the deeper door to the real lab, Quentin and I would go in and the others would wait outside for their cue. I would get Sheila in her office alone, and Quentin would gather the rest for interrogation.

It was a good plan but precarious. Our inferences about their power had to be right. And Gerard's darkness had to hold up and not arouse suspicion. I felt good about it, though, and I thought the others did too.

Into the lab we went. We walked through the standard-medical-office portion, nodding hello to the usual people we'd come to recognize. Finally we arrived at that deeper door, punched in 1473, and Quentin and I entered.

Sheila was there waiting. "Good evening! I'd not expected you tonight. Did you wish to check on progress? It is too early to see much, but no adverse effects as yet."

"No," I answered, "we came because I have questions. We're involved in this work now, Sheila, and to work effectively I need to know what's going on. Who's doing what, where, and why. Let's go to your office to talk. Just you and me." I looked her dead in the eyes. *It's important that we align on Zoe's plans.*

Her eyes widened, mouth slightly open, but then she nodded and her face settled. "Very well." She gestured toward the hallway, and we went.

I cast a glance back at Quentin as I followed Sheila. This *had* to work.

Quentin listened for the sound of the door to Sheila's office, closing his eyes to focus. Footsteps down the hall. Tiny beeps on the doorpad. Then the door opened... and closed. Good luck, V, *he thought.*

He opened his eyes and surveyed the room. Five scientists milled about. They would need all of them together here, but they had to be gathered discreetly so as not to alert Sheila. What would bring them out? *Quentin wondered. But it didn't take long to realize the answer – they all worked here for one reason.*

He selected the woman tending to the patient in the middle of the room, adjusting her drip. Her auburn hair was tied back into a tight bun, her eyes enormous and out of focus through her thick glasses lenses. He approached her slowly until he got her attention.

"Can I help you?" she asked.

He held her gaze and summoned all his charisma, directing it at her. She smiled wide and lowered her chin slightly so as to look up at him more. "There's been a huge development in the Energy Components Project. Could you gather everyone here for an announcement?"

Quentin hadn't thought her eyes could look any larger, but yet they bulged more. "Ooh," she cooed, "what is it?" She stepped toward him, her eyes skimming him up and down.

He took a small step back. "I'll tell you when everyone is in the room," he assured her. "Would you please get them all now? Except Sheila; she is busy in her office and knows to join us."

The woman nodded eagerly. "Happy to help," she breathed. She began walking out of the room, but kept casting her eyes back at him.

When she was out of the room, Quentin looked around again, running his hand through his hair. It would take a lot to attract the entire room. And... he didn't want to hurt them if he didn't have to, but he also wanted them to know how serious they were before Adelita got her hands on any of them. Maybe he could use a combination of love and fear.

As the woman brought her colleagues in 1, 2, sometimes 3 at a time, they all started to talk to one another curiously. They were tantalized by the findings they'd learn, but didn't ask Quentin about them, instead occasionally casting inquiring eyes at him. Frank, the only one whose name he knew, stood alone, shifting on his feet. Was it a question of hierarchy? Or was he not friendly?

It was convenient either way. He was the only one Quentin suspected might have any mage powers, and was probably second in command under Sheila whether he did or didn't.

Finally bun-woman approached him again and said "That's everyone," her voice unnecessarily breathy and deeper than before. It was time. They were all staring at him now, standing directly in front of the strung-up patient.

"Thank you all for gathering here," he began.

"Where is Sheila?" a scruffy-looking man with barely-visible eyes asked.

"She will be here soon," Quentin lied. "But for now, I'd like Frank to join me over here, please." Frank seemed a little surprised but moved forward anyway, coming to stand at Quentin's side. For a moment, Quentin felt Frank's height and human instincts took hold; he questioned what he was about to do, but cast that thought aside. Height wouldn't matter at all.

"You have all been working here for some time with the noble goal of helping people live longer. We all want that, to live longer and see those we care about live longer too." He called up a light allure for the crowd... just enough to let them hear his words without reacting badly, but not so much that he would be spent afterward. "But your methods here are... questionable at best. Some of you know that, I think. We want to help you. There is so much good you could do, but it doesn't have to be like this," he gestured to the woman strapped in behind him. Some eyes in the room lowered, and other mouths sagged. They had assessed these people right. But some eyes became sharp instead. Well, that was what the next part was for.

"You all can choose what comes next," he went on. "You can decide to do the right thing, the right way. Or you can not. It's up to you. But if you decide to resist..."

He didn't need to say it.

Come in now, *Quentin thought to Adelita.*

As the door behind the gathered crowd opened, Quentin grabbed Frank by the hair and yanked his head back. Frank yelped at the sudden motion, eyes popping out. His hands flailed and pushed back against Quentin as he moved in on him, but he wasn't strong enough. Quentin pulled his head closer and bit hard into his neck. It was then that Frank shot something into Quentin's stomach, something that felt like fire, but it wasn't strong and subsided as his blood took care of it. So he was a mage, but not much of one.

The crowd started screaming in panic. Quentin couldn't see what was happening, but since the sound didn't move farther away, he knew his Scooby Squad was keeping them gathered. He hoped Gerard had gotten the darkness cloak up so Sheila wouldn't hear.

Frank's blood had a certain oomph to it – not a lot, but mage blood always had a little something extra. After the last drop was gone, Quentin pushed Frank's body to the floor and turned back to the crowd.

Gerard had created a sort-of darkness snake around the group that they couldn't get past. Some struggled to, but always got pushed back like they'd hit a wall of rubber. Adelita was breathing hard and ready to pounce. Scott had his gun out in front of him, ready to shift right or left as needed.

Quentin called all that fresh, powered blood inside him to his task. "Now you'll tell us. Honestly. What you think of this lab. Whether you want to continue this work as it is; if you think the ends justify the means. Or if you want to try another, more ethical way. One at a time, please."

They all froze, the poor hapless humans. Their eyes glazed over, and he knew it had worked. He pointed at them, and one at a time they confessed their truths. Eleven had been morally conflicted.

Some had stayed because they had bills to pay, families to care for, but hated the methods. Some struggled daily with their tasks, forcing the worst from their minds because it was for a good reason... but they wanted another path. Some were morally repulsed by themselves but had family or friends who were sick, and whom they desperately wanted to cure.

The other five – there had been sixteen plus Frank and Sheila, so eighteen total actually – didn't see a problem with the methods. Three did think the ends justified the means, and two didn't object to the means at all – the patients had "consented", of course.

After it was said and done, Quentin looked at Adelita specifically. "What do we do with them? I think you have to decide." She was the only one personally impacted by the lab's actions, after all.

Adelita looked around at the crowd. "Leave the five to me," she snarled.

Gerard cast a glance at her that was... sympathetic, but also worried. "I know they hurt you, Adelita," he said, "but do not become the dark thing that they are."

Adelita's eyes narrowed, and she didn't look at Gerard. "I did not say I would kill them all. I've not yet decided their fates."

Quentin looked at each of the five in turn. "Go with her," he ordered, and they followed her hypnotically down a hallway to a place he couldn't see. Once they were gone, Gerard let the snake drop. He moved to follow Adelita, but Quentin called his name: "Gerard – stay."

"I need to ensure that she..."

"Gerard," Quentin interrupted. "She knows her own mind. She can make her own choices. She'll make the right ones." He realized then as he spoke how much he had come to like Adelita. She was a good friend, and a fantastic ally. She was, most likely, going to let her dark side fly right now... but maybe she deserved that. Maybe everyone was going to get what they deserved today.

"The rest of you," he continued, "I'm glad to hear you want to make this lab the best it can be. We are going to turn you into a subsidiary of the other New York City lab. Nicholas leads it, and he will be your overseer too. He will help you fix how you do things here. But you all have a lot of making up to do. You have a lot of patients here, right now, who need real *care. Ethical care. Get to it. And know that we're watching."*

One tiny person whose gender he couldn't guess spoke up. "Will Sheila stay here? Where is she?"

Quentin cast a quick glance in the direction of Sheila's office. "Sheila will not stay. That's all you need to know." But now that all that was done, Quentin needed to know how things were faring for Vivian, so he turned and started off down the appropriate hallway.

Chapter Twenty-Two

Sheila punched in the code to her office door and we entered. I closed the door behind me and leaned against it.

"So you know Zoe," Sheila began. "So then you know she orchestrates this. What is there to align? We all know her goal. It is ours as well."

I stood up straight and moved closer to Sheila. "There's no way she's doing this alone."

"Well no, of course not; we all do it together."

I shook my head. "Yeah, but most of the people out there are just scientists. They're not *orchestrators*. Zoe can't be everywhere at once. So who helps her execute her plan? Who gives the orders? You?"

Sheila laughed. "Oh no, not me. I may lead this lab, and order a few small projects, but it is far from a power position in Zoe's hierarchy. There are regional leaders above me, and they only have a bit more power."

I knew that much, at least. "They can time travel. That's a pretty big jump in power."

Sheila shrugged. "It is nothing compared to what Zoe can do."

I had guessed that too. "What *can* Zoe do?"

Sheila shook her head. "I don't know. More."

Fine. Maybe she didn't know. Maybe no one did. "So what is the hierarchy like? You, then regional leaders, then...?"

Sheila frowned. "If Zoe wished you to know this, wouldn't she tell you?"

I pressed my lips together. "If Zoe didn't wish me to know, why would she let me be here, working with you? On this critical project?" Sheila seemed to weigh the decision, her eyes darting from me to the floor and back. I caught her eyes on the next dart. "Sheila – tell me."

She was no human, so I was not going to pull facts from her so easily. But this she may have already been leaning toward telling me, so the extra push helped. "She does have help. A council. Six people, spread across time and space. They are nearly as powerful as she is, or so she told me."

"Who are they?" I pressed.

She shrugged. "I don't know. I do not know who they are or where they are. Most lab leaders don't even know as much as I told you."

That was an interesting question. "Why do you know that? Is it because of the Energy Components Project? Because you've been assigned something so high priority? Or... because you came up with the idea for something so valuable to Zoe's mission?"

Sheila sighed. "I did not invent this research. Zoe only needed me to understand why it had to be kept to the highest standards of confidentiality. Which is why I know her name at all."

"So it is something to do with the council, then," I prodded. "The project order comes from one of them?"

Sheila turned away from me, facing the desk to my left. "Vivian. It is confidential. I cannot tell you. Why does it concern you so?"

"Because I need to know who's doing this," I said, "who has the power to do it. Who's instrumental in Zoe's plan." And here it would be. "So I can stop them."

Sheila turned back toward me in a whip. "What did you say?"

"You heard me," I snarled.

Her eyes bulged and she stepped back toward the desk, bumping into it. She shook her head. "I don't understand."

I was done playing around. "Tell me who ordered the Energy Components Project."

She shook her head rapidly, panic seeming to overtake her. "I can't! I told you, I can't!" I rushed forward and slammed Sheila into the desk so hard her back cracked. She yelped in pain. Papers jostled and some fell to the floor.

"*Tell me,*" I urged.

Her eyes were huge and unblinking. "I can't!" she wailed, her voice pitching higher in desperation.

"Why not?" I sneered mockingly. "Will Zoe be mad?"

"Yes!" she cried out, her face pleading me. "Yes, she'll destroy me!"

"Well, then you have a choice," I said, tightening my hold on her collar, lifting her an inch off of the floor. She choked and gasped for air. "You can just tell me and risk whatever Zoe will do later, or I can force you to tell me and then kill you, and even if you are strong enough to block me, which I don't think you are, I'll kill you first and then ransack this place until I find what I want. In all of this paper, somewhere there's a record of it, isn't there? So either way I will find out. Only one way do you stand a chance of living."

Sheila sobbed again and her face sunk. "Oh God," she despaired. "Forgive me, Zoe. Forgive me; I have no choice."

I lowered her to the floor and released her. "You get it now."

She looked resigned as she turned to her desk. She moved to the right-hand side of it, which was gray just like the other sides, and concentrated on it. It flashed a blue light and when that dissipated, a new drawer was there. Sheila reached out, opened it, and pulled out a few pieces of paper. Tears continued to stream down her face as she flipped through them. Finally, she pulled out one, took a deep breath, and held it out to me.

I took it and began to read. It was some sort of directive, and as I read I quickly understood that this was the order for the experiment. I would know who'd ordered it from the signature at the bottom. My eyes skipped down, unable to wait. And when I read it, I understood why Sheila had been so afraid. This wasn't just a release of classified information. This was a timeline violation.

The signature at the bottom was mine.

Now I felt as though I was the one choking. I shook my head. "This is impossible. It's some sort of trick."

Sheila took a step to the side. "It isn't. It's authenticated from Zoe. She sent it to us from the future."

My blood was pounding through my body. It was impossible.

"Please don't tell her you know. You will see… in time… the experiment is necessary. It's important."

My blood reached a fever pitch and fury swelled inside me. "*It's a nightmare*," I snarled, and without conscious effort I pounced on her, pushing her against the desk and sinking my teeth into her neck. She struggled and tried to hit me with some sort of attack – I felt scratches and gashes tearing into my sides, but I didn't look to see what was happening and finished my meal. I felt her life pass into me and only then released, her dead body sinking to the floor.

I took a few steps back, and then my knees gave out and I sunk onto the floor myself.

It's impossible.

My mind latched onto that phrase and rolled it over and over again until I heard the doorknob to the office jostle. Reflexively, I folded the directive and tucked it into my bra, the only pocket I had.

I must have been a sight, because Quentin rushed over to me, kneeled next to me, and grabbed my arm. "Are you okay?" he asked, his voice tight. "You're hurt."

I bobbed my head. "I'm fine. It'll heal." How badly was I injured? I didn't know. I didn't care. I hadn't felt the urge to pull

Sheila's soul, so it couldn't be that bad. I became aware that papers from the desk had fallen all around me on the floor. Sheila's body was leaking dead blood and pus. It was becoming rank.

He stroked my hair and continued to survey me nervously. "She attacked you? So…"

"It was her." The lie rolled off my tongue easily. Too easily. "I pushed her and she confessed. She ordered it, with Zoe's knowledge and consent."

Quentin nodded, not checking me for lies because he didn't think I would lie. Because he trusted me. But he shouldn't have. I shouldn't trust me either.

"Let's get you home," he said, guiding me to stand. I let him. "We can tell the others when you're feeling better. Everything else went well. Most of the scientists want to stay and do things the right way. Adelita is handling the ones that felt differently. It's over."

I shook my head. "This part is over."

Quentin twisted his lips. "That counts for something."

I looked him in the eyes for the first time since he'd entered the room. He was so worried about me. I had to look completely shaken. Which I was. "It does count," I said, and mustered the best closed-lipped smile I could.

*　　*　　*　　*　　*

Despite my protestations, Quentin insisted I take the whole bed in the Sphere and rest. He didn't ask why I was so messed up. Maybe he assumed it was a spell she'd put on me. But she hadn't magically attacked me, not until the end. Maybe she thought Zoe wanted me whole.

I couldn't argue with him anyway. I was in no shape to do anything or talk to anyone. So, naturally, when Quentin went out to get me some food, Coretta came in.

She sat on the edge of the bed while I laid on top of the sheets, propped up by two pillows. She looked at me softly and took my hand. "I see your face, and the enormity of what you have experienced. But I cannot assume what it was. It could be several things. Will you tell me what transpired?"

I felt my eyes welling up. Could I tell this to even her?

Of course I could. She likely already knew. I fished out the paper and lamely held it out to her. She took it and read it.

For a long moment, she held the paper in her lap and looked down. Then, without a word, she lifted the paper and began tearing it into shreds. I stared at her, watching, not knowing how to respond. When she was finished, and the paper was small strips, she wadded them up into a ball and cupped it in her hands.

"You've told no one of this?" she asked. I shook my head. "What did you say?"

"That Sheila ordered it," I said, feeling a sucker punch of guilt, and horror at myself, to my gut. My head was swimming with words of hate, words of self-loathing. I didn't try to stop it.

Coretta nodded. "Good. Because you did not do this. Not yet. Vivian… your future is still yours to choose. Will you let a piece of paper tell you what to do? This paper is nothing. You can choose to do whatever is right for you when the moment comes. And you will take responsibility for what you do then. When you do it. When you choose it. Whether it is this or something else. But not now. You are free, and this paper does not change that." She leaned in toward me and her stare increased in urgency. "And I know that whatever you choose to do will be whatever is the best possible choice at that time."

It was hard to bear her irrepressible faith in me. "I'm glad you do. I don't."

Her eyes narrowed. "I do not care whether or not you believe it, because it is true. Now. Answer my question. Will you let a piece of paper tell you what to do? Tell you *who you are*?"

I stared at the ball of paper shards in her hands. Was it my future, written in my own hand? Did I really think anything could be changed? That I had the power to do that?

I didn't. Not really. But I also couldn't go down without trying.

I took the ball from her, cupping it in my own hands, focused on it, and set it on fire. The paper burned orange and yellow, the flame mostly contained within the perimeter of my palms, but flickering in short streams from between my fingers. After not quite a minute, it was ash, and the flame extinguished.

Coretta pulled her cigarette baggy from her pocket, opened it, and held it out. I took her meaning and poured the ashes into the bag. "I will dispose of this. And when Quentin comes back you will pull yourself together. There is more to be done, and you have choices to make. And... I know now that they are ones I have seen. So if you would, when you are able, it is time to return me to my time."

I stared blankly at her. She was going to leave me again. Could I bear that? Now of all moments?

Reading my face as always, she tutted at me. "You will see me again, my love. And you will witness all of the secrets I have had to keep from you." She chuckled lightly. "Now you will become the keeper of secrets. You will need to keep what you know from me, just as we will keep this paper from the others. There is no cause for them to judge you for an act you have not yet done, and may not do."

I swallowed hard. "I wish that I could see you again after all of this. Once everything is done and we both know everything."

Coretta pressed her lips together. "If we do, that will be a joy to me as well."

The Sphere door opened and Quentin walked through carrying a *jug* of blood. "Oh, hi Coretta. Did Vivian tell you..."

"About Sheila?" Coretta interrupted. "Yes. I am not surprised. The woman was wicked. She has met a fair end."

She was wicked... immoral, with horrific methods... maybe she had met the end she deserved.

But then, if that were true, what did I deserve?

I wanted to change the subject very much but the only thing I could think of was another subject I didn't love. "We will need to take Coretta home," I said. "It's time."

Chapter Twenty-Three

The Sphere was kind to us this time and landed us exactly where and when we'd taken Coretta. Geoffrey's body was still bleeding on the floor, but it was coagulating and cold now and very unappealing.

"Goodbye, Coretta," Quentin said, waving at her awkwardly. He didn't seem sure about the right way to bid her farewell. Were they friends? Did he think so? Did *she* think so?

"Goodbye, Quentin," Coretta replied. She put her hand on his left shoulder and leaned forward to air-kiss his right cheek, a gesture he understood and reciprocated, and then they did the same on the opposite cheek. That answered that – yes, she thought they were friends. Then she turned to face me.

"If you know what's happening here," I had to ask, "what are you really going to do to stop there from being more missing women and children?"

Coretta's eyes dimmed. "With this lab dismantled, I think the women and children of here and now are safe. There are many more elsewhere who are not. But I cannot save everyone. My role is here, helping the homeless and stricken as I long have. Saving others from the Society falls to you."

I looked at her, studying her face, her hair. "When will I see you again?"

She smirked. "I do not know how long it will be for you. But… I do not think it will be very long to wait."

I pressed my lips together. Every night was too long.

"Go now," she said, "before Francine comes looking for me." She took my shoulders in her hands and kissed my cheeks.

I didn't want to go. "How can I do this without you?"

"Vivian," Coretta said commandingly, "you can do anything without me. Now you get to find that out."

I felt myself losing control again so I grabbed her and held her close to me. She gave in and put her arms around me too. *Don't cry*, I thought. *Have some control over yourself.* I bit my lip, clamped down, and didn't cry.

When I released her, I stepped back. "Until next time, then." I couldn't say goodbye.

She smiled softly. "Yes. Next time."

I turned around and walked directly past Quentin into the Sphere, not stopping until I was well inside, past the bed and next to the mirror. I didn't turn back around until I heard the door close.

Quentin was looking at me sympathetically. "Are you gonna be okay?"

Probably not. "Yeah. Eventually."

*   *   *   *   *

That day I had a new dream, but this one wasn't a prophecy, or at least it didn't feel like one. I was standing in a room I'd never seen before – an office of sorts, but luxurious. The walls were papered in pomegranate red, with one window to my forward-left cloaked in equally-red drapes trimmed in gold lace. To the right of the window was an opal desk, marbled and shiny, and a matching chair with gold cushions that also matched the drapes.

On the desk was an old-fashioned quill and inkwell next to a small stack of paper. Something was written on the top-most sheet, and I moved closer to see it. Scrawled in elegant, swirling script was one phrase: *There is light in the darkness.*

The room suddenly turned pitch black, and there was no light to be seen. In that moment, a memory struck me from nowhere. A dream, one I'd forgotten, of a woman with a voice like silk and flesh like ebony who came to me the day after Coretta died. It had been her. She had been watching me all this time.

Zoe stepped out of the darkness like the moon emerging from behind some dark cloud. Her rich brown eyes twinkled, somehow, despite there being no light source, and her coarse, frizzy black curls seemed to sparkle. Sparkle like the sky of Dohain.

"I have been waiting for you," she said, her voice familiar from my dream. It was eerie to hear it again.

"So it would seem."

She folded her arms across her chest. She was wearing a gray shirt with denim overalls, like something out of the early 1990s. Not exactly what you'd expect from a world-traveling, time-traveling leader of a massive corrupt organization.

She had no reservations about looking in my eyes. She knew what I was. Would it be worth it to try to mind control her?

Zoe scoffed. "Don't bother."

I scowled. "You can read my mind too, then?"

"Yes. But I didn't – then, I only read your face."

I shook my head. Enough. "What do you want from me, Zoe?"

She grinned. "Oh, that isn't the right question at all. The question you should be asking is how I can help you."

My eyebrows went up of their own accord. "How *you* can help *me*?"

"Indeed. I told you to find me. Vivian. Work with me. Together, we could uncover a perfect immortality."

I laughed. "It's my fae power you want, then, is it? Well I hate to disappoint you, but I won't use it. So it's no good to ask."

Zoe's expression turned... hard to describe. Confident, but sad. "Oh Vivian. I see I've come too soon. You're not ready."

I shook my head. "I'll never be *ready* to help you."

Zoe now shook her own head. "Yet, I'll always be ready to help you. When you are ready to accept. Until then..."

*　　*　　*　　*　　*

When I woke up, I didn't tell anyone about my dream, either.

We had returned to 1943 to say a temporary goodbye to Adelita, Gerard, and Scott before heading back to my home.

"Are you going to be okay?" I asked Adelita.

She nodded. "It will take some getting used to. But I seem to have stabilized. It is not getting worse anymore."

I exhaled. "That's a relief."

Adelita's face suddenly fell. "A moment," she said, and briskly walked upstairs.

It was a surprising turn, and I worried that she was much more upset than she was letting on. Maybe we could find a pill to fix her. If they were going to do work like this, it could at least help rather than hurt.

"Has Coretta returned to her time?" Scott asked.

I nodded. "Sorry she didn't say goodbye."

"I understand," he continued. "Will I see her again?"

I nodded again. "I think so. Though when, where, or why, I don't know. Or who she'll be. What she'll know or remember. I don't know any of that."

Scott walked up to me and put out his hand. "Next time, we may find out together."

He seemed a little kinder, gentler than the guy I'd encountered in the kitchen over steak. I still didn't know if it was real or an act, but I could hope for real. I took his hand and pulled him in, putting my other arm around him. He acquiesced to the hug, and when I released he was smiling.

Scott turned to shake Quentin's hand as Adelita came back down the stairs, moving slowly. She was carrying Cori. When she got close to me, she held her out, and I took her.

"I know you will care for her," Adelita said, trying to keep the sorrow from her voice. "It is better that she not stay here in any case. It may be too dangerous, with all we do."

I stroked Cori's head. "She deserves a safe, loving home. I'll give her one. Don't worry about that."

Adelita bit her lip. "I do not worry," and she forced a smile.

I leaned in to her with my free arm – one-armed hugs were the order of the day, it seemed – and held her tight, Cori nestled between us. "I'll see you soon."

Gerard had just stepped back from a man-hug with Quentin – one of those back-patting, not-too-squeezy hugs. He moved to me as Adelita took his place. "Do be careful," Gerard said. "The future may not be safe either."

I grimaced. "I'm sure it's not. But I don't know how long I'll be there anyway. There are a lot more labs to take down. We have no idea how many."

Gerard nodded. "We will continue investigating here, in other cities. Perhaps by the time we meet again, we will have a better notion of what faces us."

Did I have to worry about them while I was gone?

Yes. I definitely did.

"You be careful too," I said, and Gerard gave me a soft hug.

I looked at Quentin, who was done with his goodbyes and waiting for me. "Ready?" he asked. I nodded, and we moved to the door. I turned back for just a second to wave again, and the others waved back.

When we closed the door behind us, it felt as though a chapter in my life was closing. I wasn't sure what that meant.

Who was I now?

"Maybe we should get another bottle before heading back?" Quentin suggested. We'd done a number on the jug. "It'll be a little easier here than by you."

"Do you mind getting it yourself?" I asked. "I'm…" I didn't know how to explain.

Quentin opened his mouth slightly but then closed it and slowly nodded. After a moment he said, "Of course. Take some time. I'll be back soon."

As he walked off, I went into the Sphere and shut the door behind me. I put Cori down and she ran to the bed, snuggling up in the blanket.

Our job was just beginning, so I knew we'd see all of them again, and probably soon. But I had to go back to my future, at least for a short while. If the Society existed across time, it didn't much matter where I waited for the next shoe to fall, and… the more time I spent around others, the more the truth settled in on me.

I was alone.

I had spent most of my life alone. I couldn't have counted the nights if I'd tried, but I was sure the scales weighed in that direction. But when I think about those nights of being alone, I was… physically alone. A quiet apartment, solo strolls through the park, nights out seeking a meal on my own. But I was never *really* alone, because I could always call on Coretta. Maybe not every hour of every night – time differences matter – but some hours of every night. Every night, if I needed her, I could just send her a thought and she would always reply.

But tonight, I had no one. I couldn't talk to Coretta – she wasn't here physically, and I couldn't send then-Coretta a mental message without risking who-knew-what. And I couldn't talk to anyone else, not about the reality of what was coming. I was alone, really alone, for the first time in centuries. For the first time since that night in 1520 that I met her.

I was a different person than I'd been then. I hoped I was, at least. But there were parts of me that were frozen in place from the night I was turned, some parts of my brain that were locked up tight… a read-only disc, if I let the parts of my brain that did change and adapt name it. And they were screaming at me now.

The proof is in writing now. It was bad enough to be nothing. Nothing can't hurt anyone. But you're worse than that. You're a monster.

I squeezed my eyes shut. "Shut up," I said out loud.

Your fate was always written. Your destiny written in blood.

I gripped the edges of the console. "Shut up," I murmured again.

After this, what you've done, you deserve everything bad that happens to you.

"SHUT UP!!" I screamed, slamming my fists on the console desk. The screen that usually passively offered Past and Future flickered, lines of static taking over instead.

It wasn't going to offer anything. My future wasn't something presented to me, not on a screen, not by birth, and not on a piece of paper. And Coretta wasn't going to be able to help me. I couldn't count on her to talk to, to stop my spiraling thoughts. I was going to have to do that myself.

My future is what I do, I thought, seizing control. *My future is what I choose to do, who I choose to be.*

But who was I? Who would I choose?

Thinking about it made me shake. Because nothing was straightforward or simple. I could choose to be kind… but could I? To Zoe, if I ever got the chance to stop her? What good is having a rule if you know you'll break it? The 'don't kill' strategy of superheroes like Batman or the Flash only works in fantasy. In real life, the people you let live could commit genocide. Real life is living like Cassian Andor – making hard choices, including killing.

But Cassian also chose not to kill, sometimes. And he chose sacrifice, too.

I didn't know if that was the role model I was supposed to look to. But role models were a sham anyway. Maybe I could be like Cassian.

I pressed my lips tight. Whatever I aimed for, in the end, I would be me. And I struggled to be okay with that. I would have to earn being okay with that.

I grabbed the sides of the console's screen. "Hey!" I exclaimed, talking to it, to myself, to both of us. "Get your shit together. We have work to do."

The screen fizzed for another moment, but finally flickered white, then black, then landed back on its usual screen. Past, Future. What was the difference?

Chapter Twenty-Four

I had been back in my apartment for just one day when I remembered that this wasn't going to work.

I wouldn't stay here for long. I would travel. I would work, a lot, maybe fight, get hurt, get killed. I wouldn't have the spare time I needed to do it right, the way she deserved. And I had a promise to keep. So I'd called Adelita by putting a message in her mind – older Adelita, the one who had, perhaps a year and a half earlier, come to my door with a note. I asked her to meet me at my apartment while Quentin was tidying up in the Sphere, and she did.

Cori recognized her immediately and ran to greet her. I was glad for that. Adelita sat at my small table near my door and picked her up.

She was definitely older… and not just a year older. Without my blood to sustain her, her body was beginning to catch up to where it was supposed to be. Her skin wrinkled and cracked; her hair seemed drier and more coarse; her joints seemed to creak as she moved. Yet I was relieved; she was not metal.

"So, we meet again," Adelita said. Her voice was rougher too. "I was not expecting to see you again."

"I wasn't expecting it either. Not to see… this you, anyway. But I need to ask a favor."

Adelita laughed. "Another one?"

I grinned. "Just one more. I… I have to go soon. I have a lot to do… much that you already know, I'm sure. But for me, it's my future, and it's a path I have to walk." Path, I was starting to sound like Coretta. "It wouldn't be fair to Cori to have to endure all that with me. She deserves a stable home and constant attention." I studied Adelita's reaction. "A safe, loving home," I added, quoting myself.

Adelita's eyes widened. "Are you asking me to care for her?"

I nodded. "I am. I know you loved her. Do you think…"

"Yes," Adelita interjected, her face lighting up as she looked down at Cori, who'd snuggled on her lap. "Yes, I would love to take her home, and I will give her everything she could need or want. But…" and her eyes turned dim at that, "I will not live much longer. I can feel myself slipping… and it is fine; I do not fear death. I would love to see my sister again. But Cori will outlive me. What comes of her then?"

I sighed. This was the harder ask. "I thought of that. I was wondering if… and I know, I know this is a lot, but… would you be willing to live another ten, fifteen years? I would pay for your living; you wouldn't have to worry about money, or food, or shelter. I know it'll delay you seeing your sister, and resting. But…" I let my sentence trail off and left it there.

Adelita had not looked up from Cori, scratching her behind her ear. "Ten to fifteen, you say?" She paused, and then finally did look up at me. "I can manage that." And she smiled, and I was relieved.

That taken care of, I couldn't avoid asking about a spoiler. "How are you? Your skin… is it… can you feel anything?"

Adelita looked at me curiously. "Then that's where you've come from. When I had only just transformed."

I nodded. "Yeah."

She studied me, her brown eyes tracing my features. "Yes… that was when I last saw Cori. I recall now. You may touch me if you wish. You'll see my skin remains hard. Yet… I can feel again."

I ran the tips of my fingers along the back of her hand. Solid. Like brick, still. "That's great news. I won't ask how that happened. I'm just glad it did."

Adelita nodded. "Me too."

She stood, and I retrieved the jar that had once held, and would now again hold, my blood. I bit open my wrist and let the blood pour into the jar until it was about a quarter full. That should do it. She cupped Cori in her left arm and took the jar in her right.

"Vivian," she began, her voice wistful.

"Don't," I interrupted. "Just don't."

"I was not going to tell you of your future. I was not going to warn you. I think you already understand what is coming for you. I only mean to say…" But then she paused, a long, thoughtful pause, and she shook her head. "Thank you for Cori."

"Thank you for caring for her." I hugged Adelita, who had no hands to hug me back with. "I don't know if I'll see you again. If I don't… thank you. For everything."

Adelita smirked, moving toward the door. "You don't know the half of it."

I laughed, and she laughed too, and then she was gone.

*   *   *   *   *

After Cori was safe with Adelita, there was nothing left to do. It was quiet. The silence was suffocating, so I went to put some music on.

I looked from my records to my tapes – what remained of that crappy medium anyway – to the CDs and finally the three varieties of iPod and iPhone. I was a veritable museum of music. I thought that I must still have my gramophone somewhere. I settled on a CD, Alice in Chains' Dirt, opening the case and popping out the disc.

"You did the right thing," Quentin said. He was sitting at the small round table near the door to my apartment, where Adelita had sat just before, and had been since completing his Sphere cleaning chores.

"Yeah, grunge is always the right thing," I agreed absentmindedly.

He laughed. "I meant giving Cori to Adelita."

"Oh," I said as I placed the disc in its tray, closed it, and pressed play. A few seconds and the music began to burst through the room. I returned to the table and sat across from Quentin.

He was in the chair I'd usually sit in, the one facing the door. My chair, pulled out as it was, blocked the door a bit. Down the hall, footsteps said someone was coming home.

But I wasn't sure I'd ever be home, really there, ever again.

"How long do you think we have?" I asked.

Quentin shrugged. "Time machine. How long do you want?"

I shook my head. "Dohain didn't happen by accident. We'll go where and when we're supposed to."

Quentin sucked his teeth, making a 'really-Vivian?' face I had seen on Coretta many times. "That's very fatalistic. Why don't we take control of it?" He leaned forward. "How long do you want?"

I sighed. "Forever. But… I know too much now. Zoe has six powerful allies who do her bidding, who execute her mission. We have to find them and pick that house of cards apart in the right places. The places that will make it all fall down."

Quentin nodded. "Okay. How do you want to start?"

I shook my head. "I don't know."

He smiled. "When do you want to start?"

I looked at the table. There was so much to consider and I had no idea where to begin. All I knew was I had to begin. There was too much at stake to wait.

I looked up at Quentin, who was still smiling at me. It was nice to be here, home – for now.

It was decided. "Tomorrow."

Epilogue

In her dream, there was a wall.

It was a dream, so naturally it was metaphorical. But to her eyes as she stood there, it was real.

Zoe was wearing denim overalls and a pink bow in her hair. It wasn't the best style for her - her shape was immeasurably more flattered by a snug tank top and long, silky skirt. But, if this was the outfit Zoe liked right now, it's what she would wear.

Zoe's deep brown eyes traced the wall, her soft lips pressed together in fury... but then they loosened, and she smiled. "How did I not know this? That you, a woman out of time, were the most powerful? This wall is... impressive."

Coretta choked back a laugh. "Oh, you think so? Yes, I do too. Yet, it was not placed by me."

Zoe walked up to her, slowly, her hips swaying with each step. "Vivian, then? This is not a fae power."

Coretta smirked. "No. Not Vivian. She wouldn't know how."

Now Zoe stood face-to-face with her. "Gerard. A mental ward?"

Coretta giggled, unable to hold the silliness of it all in. "A mental ward, yes. Gerard, no. Zoe, there is no need to persist. I will not tell you, and the wall ensures that you cannot make me. If you want to steal from me inside knowledge, of Vivian or anything else, you won't get it." And then Coretta pursed her lips and let her eyes turn dark - a move of intimidation that made Zoe's eyes widen. "The only inside knowledge I will give you, Zoe, is that you have the power to change your path at any time. Your past does not dictate your future. You can be a better woman, if you choose." She leaned in so that Zoe could feel her breath. "I hope you do."

Zoe tilted her head, just slightly, and leered at Coretta. "You think that because I need Vivian, I fear you? I don't. In the future, you won't have a word to say about what she does. Your hold on her will be lost. You know that it is already weakening, don't you? It's been slipping through your fingers for some time."

That made Coretta laugh, a full-bellied chuckle. "My hold on her? Oh Zoe. If that is what you think, you know nothing at all." Coretta smiled. "Vivian will do exactly what she wants without a peep from me. She always has." She stopped there; any more would say too much.

Zoe leaned in closer, so close their lips nearly touched. "I will find out who placed this wall."

Coretta grinned. "Yes. You will."

www.ingramcontent.com/pod-product-compliance
Lightning Source LLC
Chambersburg PA
CBHW051418170626
46809CB00006B/2217